Black City Skyline
and Darker Horizons

Black City Skyline
and Darker Horizons

Barry Lee Dejasu

Barry Lee Dejasu

Foreword by T.E.D. Klein

Hippocampus Press

New York

Published by Hippocampus Press
P.O. Box 641, New York, NY 10156.
www.hippocampuspress.com

Cover photo by Barry Lee Dejasu.
Cover design by Dan Sauer, dansauerdesign.com.
Hippocampus Press logo designed by Anastasia Damianakos.

First Edition
1 3 5 7 9 8 6 4 2

ISBN 978-1-61498-367-5 (paperback)
ISBN 978-1-61498-368-2 (ebook)

Contents

Foreword

Providence, as everyone knows—or at least as devotees of horror fiction know—will forever be associated with its native son and greatest booster, H. P. Lovecraft, who famously declared, "I am Providence, and Providence is myself." Today the place is identified with the Old Gent the way Stratford-upon-Avon is identified with the Bard. Indeed, to those of us who consider ourselves Lovecraftians, it's sometimes referred to, only half-jokingly, as the Holy City.

But the welcome news contained in Barry Lee Dejasu's *Black City Skyline*—and it may be the single piece of welcome news you'll find in these tales—is that Lovecraft isn't the only horror writer to call Providence home.

Of course, Dejasu's city is nothing like Lovecraft's, and the modern conurbation that forms the setting for many of these stories is far from quaint and anything but holy. Although you'll find mentions here of Weybosset Street, lamplit Benefit Street, and the tunnel under College Hill, his Providence is not one of gracious colonial mansions, cobbled streets, Poe-haunted churchyards, and "steep alley steps by vines conceal'd, where small-paned windows glow." Rather, the city and its environs, in these tales, are a place of highways, pizzerias, shopping centers, shabby apartments, and office cubicles next to the printer. The lockdown is on in some stories, and some characters show up in masks. The beautiful Industrial Trust Building—a beloved landmark that, in Lovecraft's day, dominated the skyline and symbolized the city's prosperity—is today, as in the book's title story, a haunted relic. Dejasu's visionary young men, tinkering with weird devices in quest of forbidden knowledge, are as intense and obsessed as those in Lovecraft, but they're a lot scuzzier. And I don't think Lovecraft ever wove plots around yellow-stained old mattresses and the things lurking inside them. (Dejasu's "Sleep Harvest" may give new urgency to the familiar warning about not reading horror tales at bedtime.)

There were undoubtedly more vestiges of Lovecraft's Providence still present when, in October of 1975, I attended the first World Fantasy Convention there—a fairly historic occasion in our little genre. I remember, in particular, a "young writers" panel on which Charles L. Grant boasted that he'd improved upon the old vampire myth, which, he explained, had been "done to death." He'd invented a new variation that, instead of feeding on blood, "fed on failure."

Now, the problem was that, relying on that sort of abstract notion, Charlie was being too clever by half. His stories never scared me.

I think Barry Lee Dejasu remembers the things that do scare us, and that ultimately they're pretty basic, pretty traditional, in fact downright primitive. True, his stories themselves are anything but primitive—they're subtle, highly crafted, and often quite demanding, which is a polite way of saying that some are difficult, with clipped, oblique dialogue, deliberately withheld information, and characters with mysterious motivations who know more than we do—but in the end the horror they deliver is decidedly tangible, as tangible as the hairy, many-legged things that go skittering in and out of these pages.

And he doesn't hesitate, on occasion, to conjure up real monsters. Sometimes, in fact, I suspect he enjoys describing entities expressly designed to outpace our imagination (the way Lovecraft did in his memorable tongue-in-cheek description of creatures "not altogether crows, nor moles, nor buzzards, nor ants, nor vampire bats, nor decomposed human beings," but some monstrous combination thereof). It's as if Dejasu has thrown out a challenge to some future special-effects team: *See if you can possibly come near to giving form to THIS!*

And it works. Though I happened to read most of these stories in a snowbound country house over a chilly winter weekend, I don't think it was entirely the cold that made me shudder. Just as A. E. Housman said that good poetry made his skin bristle when he was shaving, I have a private way of judging the effectiveness of a piece of fiction: I know it's good when, after reading the last line, I hear myself mutter "Wow!"—a small expression of joy repeatedly evoked by the stories in this book.

—T.E.D. KLEIN

Conventions are, indeed, all that shield us from the shivering void, though often they do so but poorly and desperately.

—ROBERT AICKMAN

The Night Belongs to Us

On the edge of town, beyond the trees and underbrush of Baker State Forest, I stand before the quarry where we used to play.

Overhead I hear a low croak and look up to see a solitary, black bird, a crow or maybe a raven, fleeing toward the south. It disappears over the trees, and I listen for other birds, but hear only a distant car horn.

Between the last of the trees stretches a squat barrier gate. I place my hands upon its grimy metal piping, upon which is mounted a NO TRESPASSING sign, vandalized with an indecipherable shape in mustard-yellow paint. An unnatural clearing stretches beyond this, and at its far end the grass gives way to piles of jagged boulders and half-excavated rock from an abandoned project. The cracked, grass-whiskered asphalt continues past the gate, disappearing into soil beyond the trees. Several feet ahead of the asphalt is a table-sized slab of granite that didn't used to be there.

Remember how you used to think there were vampires buried here, Beau? You were twelve and I had turned thirteen a couple of weeks before. We'd biked out here one evening to get away from the uneasy grownups and the annoying curfew that had just been instituted a couple of weeks prior and stopped at the entrance to the clearing. It was still a wide, flat field at that time, and a couple of earthmovers sat on its far edge.

I remember watching the grin on your face as you told me your vampire theory, and I narrowed my eyes and said you were full of it.

You said your father had spoken to Mrs. Cardoza, the councilwoman. She'd seen someone a few weeks before, while on her way back into town from a county meeting that had run late—someone who had gone missing. *And,* you'd said, *it was one of the* construction workers!

I got a chill at this. *I thought they all got trapped in a hole in the ground and died.*

They did. *Only a few of them survived. But then people started seeing them again at night! Vampires, I'm telling you, man!*

You're so full of it.

Oh, yeah? Well, why do you think they started the curfew?

It was a fair point. Since the accident, several people in town went missing, and within days of that, nobody was to be outside past sunset. Even so, I snorted at your theory. *Prove it! Maybe there's dead bodies, or maybe not. At least we'll know for sure, right?*

We grinned at each other before pedaling out onto the open soil. At the pebble-lined border we began to dismount our bikes when you gasped and pointed down at a curved, yellow shape that poked out of the gravel like a seashell.

Dismounting my bike, I crouched and brushed away rocks and soil, frowning as more of the shape appeared. I grabbed its flat edge and dislodged it with a grunt.

It was a construction helmet.

We looked at each other, eyes and mouths wide, and then back at the helmet.

Filthy though it was, it wasn't streaked with red or barnacled with decayed matter, nor was it even cracked or smashed.

When we heard the voice, we looked up to see a tall, dark-haired woman at the edge of the quarry. She was standing beneath a low tree, head cocked to her right above a brown dress, and I paled when I recognized her as one of the first people to go missing in town.

It's getting dark, she said.

I grabbed your arm as her hands lifted beside her head, then spread wide, her face splitting open down the middle, revealing the shadow behind it. Around her the trees began to shake. Several huge black shapes spilled out, long and wormlike. Their torpedo-shaped ends crashed upon the ground, and their bodies arched up, stretching higher than any person.

We turned and ran. You went for your bike as the smashing sounds grew louder behind us. *Leave it,* run! I shouted.

A siren *whooped,* and I saw a police cruiser skid to a halt at the quarry entrance, lights flashing, no doubt on curfew patrol. A woman jumped out, and I turned to you—then skidded to a halt when I realized you weren't there.

You were still running, half the distance back, probably having struggled with your bike before abandoning it. Behind you, the black things were loping leglessly forward. And all around them, at least a dozen running people had appeared, the woman from the forest among them.

They were silent but for the crunch of their feet and moved in one steady crowd with the black things. Several of people wore neon-green vests, but most of their heads were unrecognizable masses of writhing, oily-black anemones.

Then something grabbed my arm, and I screamed, glancing up to see the cop beside me, shouting. I screamed again as I felt something hit my foot—the helmet, tumbling and rolling around over the rocks.

I ran to the cruiser and dove through the open driver's-side door. As I squirmed into the passenger seat, I saw the cop approaching. I looked past her, and my eyes widened.

You'd gotten so close, but one of the black shapes was not ten feet behind you, stretching up, up, *up.*

Then the cop jumped into the car and gunned it even before she shut the door.

I screamed for her to wait for you, Beau, I really did. But as she tore the car around, I saw the obsidian tower behind you toppling forward, its end barreling straight down, and then I lost sight of you as the world spun around me.

The construction helmet now sits among the overgrown weeds at the edge of the gate.

I glance up. The sky has turned a murky lavender.

The police are probably making their rounds, but I'll wait a little longer. I've gotten in trouble for being out after dark before, and I'll probably do it again.

All that's left between us, Beau, is the night, and the memories it brings.

Across the quarry, the shadows between the trees thicken. A short shape steps into the fading light, and your pale face turns to me.

The night wears it well.

Penumbra

1

I'm sure you've heard the rumors about this place, my friend. His-torical buildings like this are full of secrets and shadows and dust. This old citadel has seen a lot from its vantage in the clouds over the past century, and now it stands as a testament to time and a destina-tion for journeys' ends.

Your company started out in Boston, yes? Well, it's been almost a year and a half now, but I'd like to welcome you formally to Provi-dence. I hope you're settled in by now, after some of the troubles you had last year, to say nothing of the statewide quarantine . . .

I'm sure your clientele didn't feel very enthused about in-office vis-its during that long year. But hey, you guys seem to be doing okay now. Sometimes moving on is the only thing we can do when the floor drops out from under us. Take it from me—all of us at Zoot Suit LLC had to do the same thing once, only a couple of weeks before we moved in below you guys.

Our marketing agency was still in its honeymoon phase, in a man-ner of speaking. I was one of the original billing admins, and although it had already been a few years, three directors had already come and gone, and Zoot Suit was still finding its sea legs. Even so, we'd gener-ated enough revenue to get us to the next step we'd been yearning for—a bigger office. And then, when your firm announced your final-ized deal to reopen this skyscraper, we had to grasp at that straw—and sure enough, we got it.

That fall, our days on Weybosset Street were numbered. We weren't about to miss our landlord—I'm sure you've seen his property

15

signs all over downtown—and were eagerly preparing for our move to Westminster.

We'd spent weeks getting office equipment, paper products, and more all squirreled away. Everybody had been given two big plastic storage bins to fill, with a strong insistence on pitching whatever wasn't needed, as well as a strict limit on the numbers of bins per person—between you and me, a few of the other managers have bad hoarding tendencies. Rooms and hallways had them stacking up in corners and along walls like oversized Jenga pieces.

In light of the move, however, there was a question floating around the office—to hold our traditional Halloween party, or to keep things minimal for the move?

The "office focus group," which was just the fancy name for the kids who were assigned to oversee day-to-day operations, was ready to nix the party altogether—but one of them, a girl named Staci, thought it might be a good opportunity to celebrate our move, as well as the October tradition.

The de facto leader of the group, a guy named Luke, was being a pain in the ass and insisting that there wouldn't be any party, in the interest of keeping the move light and cheap. The debate went on for a few days, but eventually they agreed to a compromise that Staci thought of, pending some assistance.

Brandt—I honestly can't recall if that was his first or last name—was an administrative assistant, and the office's resident horror geek. He had an acceptable, if limited, business-casual wardrobe, and never even went out of his way with costumes or makeup during the couple of parties he did make it to. He was a tall, awkward, heavy-set guy. Very sweaty, too—I remember being on many a winter smoke break like this one, where I'd see him coming from a hidden spot somewhere a few blocks away, and despite the bitter cold his whole forehead glistened with an oily sheen.

Brandt didn't really have any friends in the agency. He was always very polite, very quiet, and didn't hover around or stare at any of the women. But as much as he kept to himself, hardly anybody ever spoke to him, unless something work-related came up. I tried to make conversation with him every now and then, but his responses were always quick little mumbles and chuckles. I never saw anyone come by his desk to ask him how he was doing, or if he'd seen the latest superhero movie, or if he wanted anything from a group lunch order. There was the office . . . and then there was Brandt.

His desk's fiber-lined walls were covered with dozens of thumb-tacked photographs, drawings of symbols, reports of scientific discoveries, and quotations from different authors. Magnets of vintage horror movie posters were stuck to the front of its metal drawers. And along the top edge of the desk's back he had little clay or wood statuettes of castles and creatures, and worn action figures of Dracula, Frankenstein, and the Creature from the Black Lagoon.

One time I got him talking about a book he was carrying out to his lunch break. It was an old ratty paperback, some science fiction or horror thing from Lovecraft or one of those guys. I honestly forget what it was, but I remember how he acted when he talked about it—his animation over it was less of excitement and more of relief at being able to discuss something that meant so much to him. I didn't have much to contribute to the conversation—always been more of a non-fiction fan myself—but I was happy to give the kid a chance to talk about, well, something.

There were probably as many rumors flying around the office about him as there are here, about this building. But since these walls don't talk—at least, that's not one of the stories that I've heard—I doubt they hold a grudge over what people have to say about them. And I was never aware of Brandt holding a grudge, either—but I'm sure he knew exactly what thoughts lay behind the occasional side-eye thrown his way.

So the focus group approved of Staci's idea of approaching Brandt to do the decorations for the party. A few people witnessed him nearly jumping out of his skin when he got her email requesting his assistance. He looked back and forth along the row of desks on either side of his, and his big shoulders rose and fell with a quick, heavy breath, as he fairly pounded on the keys in reply.

Later that day he met with Staci and did a lot of listening as she threw some ideas his way. She told him to keep things "spooky and fun, but in good taste," so nothing gory or graphic. He could use one of the color printers, if he needed them, and could do things like hang rubber bats and spiders and ghost figures from the dropped ceiling tiles, and perhaps even put up statues and other props. What's more, the agency would refund him for any expenses, up to a point. He'd mulled this all over, then told her that he knew exactly what he would bring in, and that it would be precisely what she'd asked for—spooky and fun, but in good taste.

First thing the following Monday morning, I spotted Brandt passing by the break room, clutching a wrinkled, water-stained cardboard box in his hands.

He saw me and nodded, grinning eagerly, and I asked him if that was his lunch. He stopped and shrugged, snickering, then stammered something about decorations. This was the first I'd heard of the matter, and so I told him to be careful about putting stickers on the walls, because the paint stained easily. He made a very forced-sounding laugh and kept walking, and I made my way to my desk.

After I dropped off my stuff and logged into my computer, I headed to the break room for coffee. On the way, I peered past the rows of desks in the main floor space, where several printers and scanners were arranged around a central cooling unit, upon which sat something boxy and black that I didn't recognize. So I went over for a look.

My shoes scraped to a stop on the faded, navy-blue carpet before the hub, my brow lowering as I took in the object set upon the cooling unit until I was frowning as much as a doctor scrutinizing a patient with a hole in the cranium.

It looked like the repurposed head of an old-fashioned streetlamp, like the ones lining Benefit Street, down to the trapezoid of black-painted iron frames and glass faces. However, each face was festooned with masses of thin black tendrils, probably soldered-on metal decorations. Upon closer examination, the glass beneath wasn't the clear variety you see on those, either—it was the same dark shade of red like one of the lenses from an old-fashioned pair of 3D movie glasses. It was the ugliest lamp I'd ever seen, and the look on my face must have made that obvious, because after a moment I heard Brandt chuckle from nearby.

I turned to him, raising an eyebrow. "New emergency exit display?"

He snorted and shook his head. "Nope. Party decoration."

"Oh, okay." I nodded, then frowned. "Little early for that, no?"

He shrugged. "Figured it'd look good. Help set the mood. You can look at it if you want. I don't want everybody touching it, but . . . I trust you."

When he shrugged, I couldn't help smirking at his thinly veiled request. He looked like a proud kid at a science fair.

I'd figured it would have been heavy, but when I hefted the infant-sized object in my hands I was a little surprised at the muscles in my arms that were used. I tilted its apex toward my face, my gaze traveling along a heavy cable that snaked out from a hole in its top, the other end of which was connected to one of the power outlets.

I felt my brow lowering as I tilted it back, twisting its layered faces to make some sense of the tendriled chaos that crowded each scarlet glass panel. I held it up higher and could smell iron and age as my gaze followed some of the metal curls, which seemed to form patterns and shapes that were lost by my brain as quickly as they'd registered.

An opening on the bottom was made apparent by the only part of it that didn't match the rest—a soldered-on square of aluminum, scuffed and stained with age and storage. I nearly turned it upright again when my gaze caught sight of several streaks of yellow paint that formed a misshapen cross upon its surface. At first I thought it looked almost like a swastika, but as I looked more closely it reminded me more of a stick figure dancing, perhaps balancing on one leg with its arms stretched out, its head's movements illustrated with little dashes haloing its uneven shape.

I do need to make mention of something a bit odd, in hindsight, that comes to mind about that symbol. Down on South Water Street there's one of those "little free libraries." I guess the word "free" holds a lot of appeal, because I've never seen a book inside there. Its white metal is scuffed and stained and covered in graffiti. Well, in the past month or so it got its newest addition from some street-art entrepreneur, one of those big, unintelligible tags declaring God knows what. Point being, it looks a lot like that symbol on the lamp.

If I shrug any more, my shoulders are going to give my ears a massage. It's perfectly possible I'm just reading too much into it. With the creative license some graffiti has, sometimes a tag looks as much like a can of beans as it does someone's name. Maybe the symbol on that library box is completely unrelated to what was on the lamp—but I'll insist until the day I die that the two were damn near identical.

"Wanna see it in action?"

I blinked and looked up to see Brandt grinning. "Mind if I pay my respects to the caffeine gods first?"

After he enthusiastically permitted me my morning ritual, I went into the kitchen and stood over the coffee machine, watching it slowly gurgle and splutter into my mug. A tiny insect drifted before my eyes and I leaned back, flinching, to swat at it, making a mental note to tell the office manager to remind people to take home their food containers rather than leave them beside the dishwasher for nonexistent maids.

As I stepped out of the kitchen, I saw someone approaching and raised my mug in greeting, then started so quickly when I saw a big, glowing shape vanish into thin air beside me that I nearly spilled the hot liquid all over myself.

I peered around, my pulse surging into a quick tempo in my ears. Across from the kitchen, the nearest row of desks was empty. At the opposite end of the space, several managers' office doors were open to the gray ambiance of morning. Frowning, I looked back the other way, my vision registering a lingering afterimage, and I shrugged and began to walk back to the printer hub, then slowed to a stop again. "What . . . ?"

The unfinished question caught Brandt's attention. He was standing beside the printers, grinning as he turned to me, the entire right side of his body glowing a bright shade of scarlet. "Whaddya think?"

I didn't know quite what to think of the phosphorescent red cloud that filled the air, hovering over every desk and between every chair. Did I say "cloud"? It was more reminiscent of ink spilled in water, the colorful shapes twisting and unfurling in stark contrast to their surrounding transparencies. Patches and tendrils shimmered and flared, refracting—or, seemingly, producing—more of that strange red light. Shapes seemed to form and drift about in it, but they warped out of existence as quickly as they'd appeared. And in the middle of it all, the rippling blobs of scarlet glared, swelled, and emanated from between the tendril-choked faces of the lamp.

Brandt said something, and I blinked and turned to him. "Sorry, what?"

"You like it?"

"It's—it's something."

"It's nothing right now. Wait until Friday night, when—"

He fell silent and glanced around, then leaned quickly over the printers to unplug the cable from the outlet. The red shapes disappeared as Luke rounded the corner from the front entrance to the office, frowning as he looked back and forth from the lamp, to Brandt, back to the lamp, and then finally to me. "What's up?"

"Just getting ready for the party." Brandt all but puffed out his chest as he spoke.

Luke glanced at the lamp again, then nodded. "Oh."

As he walked away, Brandt's smile dropped a little, then returned when he met my gaze. "Red skies at morn, sailors be warned," I muttered, and made my way to my desk.

I spent the next hour getting caffeinated and aggravated as I caught up on the weekend's backlog of emails. Several managers and a couple of partners had started up a lengthy chain of messages expressing their questions and concerns over the forthcoming office move, and how it would affect everything from day-to-day operations to— you guessed it—billing, and if everybody should plan on working from home while the move occurred. Some wondered if there would be some way to stay working in the current office up until the weekend before the start of the next work week. There were many other contradictions and suggestions and complaints that inevitably come with an office move. I was tempted to delete every message that began with "RE:," but held my patience as I scrolled through them, although my sighs and under-breathed curses grew more pronounced with each one.

So it was that when I heard a couple of people murmuring and tutting to one another from their desks nearby that I finally decided to give my eyeballs a break and walked over, empty coffee mug ready for its first refill of the day. The two HR workers, Marina and Christine, glanced up at me timidly from their neighboring desks, and I stopped before them and shook my head. "Are we there yet?" I asked, and they both giggled.

"Almost," Christine said.

Marina grabbed a sheaf of blue-printed papers and waved them in the air. "Get the rest of your printing done on printers one, four, and seven, because those bad boys get disconnected and packed up tonight!"

"Keep Whine-One-One on speed dial," I said, thinking of all the complaints that were bound to come from tunnel-visioned staff throughout the office. "You may have to call a waaambulance."

After another laugh, Marina's eyebrows lifted, and she pointed at me with the sheaf. "But for this year's party, I don't have to send out a bunch of reminder emails about taking down decorations!"

2

The next morning I entered the break room to find Jeff, the office director, speaking in hushed tones with Connie Warrington, the building's manager. Connie introduced herself as if we'd not met previously at a half-dozen or so office events, and then casually demanded to know when I had left the previous evening. After making a joke about forgetting to clock out since Labor Day, I told her, making sure to mention that my dog was unable to fend for herself too late in the day. I didn't know if I was about to be asked for additional evening service, and I wasn't about to volunteer for it—which was why I was surprised by Jeff's explanation. "Someone left the front doors unlocked last night."

Connie shook her head sadly. "Joe Q. Anyone could've just moseyed right on in to your business."

My eyes widened behind my glasses. "Well, that's not good."

"No," they both said. Jeff went on to explain how there were still four people in the office when he'd left, whom he would of course be speaking to later, but that he already had a suspicion of the neglectful culprit.

Now, before you ask—no, it wasn't Brandt. He was, like me, a firm believer in the restrictions of an hourly schedule. Start on time, leave on time. I didn't even need to hear confirmation of his clocked hours from that day, which came to be known throughout the office later, to know that he was long gone before a pair of frosted-glass panels had left open to the whims of the city at night.

Such as it was, the answers to those questions did come about as the day went on, although other questions arose in their place like reproducing Hydra heads—questions that had left those final employees' heads itching.

The first began with a copy writer named Desmond, whom I overheard talking with Luke and Staci. I had gone to check with Jeff on an account when he raised a finger at me to wait outside his door while he finished up a phone call. Instead of watching the potted plant in his office corner grow, I listened in as Desmond explained how he'd grown curious about the lantern as the day had worn on and had at one point asked Brandt about it. Brandt had stated that it was something akin to a projector, but that its projections wouldn't be like anything they'd ever seen. This, of course, had piqued Desmond's curiosity, and he'd requested an audience of the device in action. Brandt, however, had told him that he'd have to wait until the night of the party for that, along with everybody else in the office.

I'm sure you can figure out what happened next.

Around eight that night, Desmond and Luke were in the thick of fast-tracking a project for one of our bigger clients. Luke was determined wrap it up a couple of days ahead of schedule, but Desmond began growing weary of burning the midnight oil when they heard the whirring of the cleaning crew's vacuums and carpet washers. They called it a night and began to head out, when their attention was mutually captured by the foreign black and red object that crowned the printer cooling unit. After some debate—and, I have no doubt, a few jokes on Brandt's behalf—Desmond decided to switch it on.

Neither of them was prepared for how bright it was, and they staggered back, shielding their eyes. Luke turned, his hip bumping the back of a neighboring office chair. Desmond, on the other hand, shielded his gaze from the glare, which was how he then saw a tree growing—and glowing—from the office floor before him.

"It was thin, and it was leafless, but it was definitely a tree," Desmond recounted. "Like one of those younger ones that get planted in sidewalks after roadwork gets done, really skinny and with all the branches pointing straight up."

"So what was it?" Staci asked.

Luke rolled his eyes and shook his head. "It was a prop for a haunted house."

"Oh, come *on!*" Desmond groaned, rolling his eyes. "You freaked out when you saw it!" He must have noticed me looking at them, because he turned to me, drawing the attention of the others as he raised his voice. "He totally did!" When Luke protested and tried to excuse himself from the conversation, I held my hands up as I turned around to wait for Jeff.

Thankfully, it was a short wait, and I stepped in as they started speculating on how the lantern worked. Luke was in the middle of saying something like, ". . . really did look like there were bugs crawling on it, though."

The next unanswered question came about late that afternoon, out on the front steps. I'd no sooner lit my cigarette when a short, potbellied man emerged from the front doors, his eyes and cheeks slackened with haggard exhaustion and frustration. I recognized him immediately as one of the two cleaning people, José. I could tell from the expression on his face and the bulging grocery tote bag in his hand that this would be the last time I saw him.

"You look like you missed the last TV at a Black Friday sale," I said. "What's going on, friend?"

He shook his head and spat out a string of Portuguese. I felt bad, not just because he was clearly upset, but because my Portuguese was limited to the basics of *thank you, hello, goodnight,* and *goodbye.* Most of what José had to say flew about five feet above my head as he prattled on.

At one point he said in English, "I think it was not real, you see?" before elaborating in his first language. He must have seen the glaze forming over my eyes, for he shook his head, looking frustrated. He raised his hands before his chest and pressed them together, curling his fingers inward and arching them out from their wrists, wriggling his fingers in and out as if he were playing a weird instrument, or miming a crab's moving legs. He looked hopefully at me, then shook his head again. "A—demon!"

I lowered my brow. "Demon?"

He pointed at the closed doors behind him and nodded quickly. "Yes!"

"You mean you saw a demon?"

"Yes."

I started to ask him more, but then he sighed. "He laugh at us, so we— We run away. We very scared!" He shrugged. "And now I got to go home!"

Before I could say anything, he turned and walked down the sidewalk.

I went inside, feeling bad. I didn't need to ask Jeff if Bianca, the other cleaning person, was still working there—although he'd later give me exactly that grim confirmation. At the time, however, I was more curious about the shadow over the previous night's events—and I knew one person who might know what lurked inside of it.

I didn't want to be too obvious with my inquiry, so I pretended I was walking by Brandt's desk when he looked up at me. He was wearing big black headphones, and seemed distracted with work, but as I approached he looked up quickly. I nodded, smiling nonchalantly, and to my satisfaction his hands reached up to tug his headphones off his ears as he muttered something like "morning," even though it was already 3:37. I carefully inquired about how his day had been going and wasn't surprised to hear him snort and shake his head.

"Starting to think I should've skipped decorations." Before I could ask why, he added, "Someone turned on the lantern last night and *left* it on all night."

I frowned and nodded. "Sounds like a fire hazard."

"Well, maybe . . ." He shrugged. "But that's beside the point."

"Which is . . . ?"

He narrowed his lips to speak, then turned away, chewing on his inner cheek for a moment. "It's *not* a toy. You don't leave something like that on overnight. Especially when it's not *yours!*"

"Whoa, hey!" I scoffed and raised my hands. "I left right at—"

"No, no, not you!" He mirrored my gesture and shook his head. "No, I just mean . . ." He sighed and looked around, and I also did a quick survey for any judgmental glances in his direction, but as expected, everybody was too busy doing their jobs to care about the loner in the corner. Even so, I knew he was disquieted over the potential scrutiny, and I suggested that he step outside with me for some "fresh air."

The sky between taller buildings is always a little darker than other parts of a city, no matter how clear a day it may be, but that late October afternoon seemed to be extra dark as we went outside. Even before I could take my favorite corner of the front entrance, Brandt moved out onto the same area of concrete where José had stood only a few hours before and asked, "Have you ever heard of Timothy Garrett?"

I lit my cigarette and shook my head. "Can't say that I have."

"He was a scientist in the nineteen-thirties. I honestly don't know much about him, but he did a lot of stuff with photography and visuals. Was involved with a lot of controversial scientists and religious groups and went missing at the beginning of World War II. Anyway, long story short, he was a relative of mine, my great-uncle.

"Now, my mom didn't really talk to her older sister, who died a few years ago. Her sister, my aunt—for all she was one, to me—owned what was left of Dr. Garrett's stuff. Hoarded it, I guess, probably wanted to sell it all or something. I don't know, because like I said, my mom never really spoke to her, even up through when she fell ill and died.

"*Any*way, my mom wound up inheriting my aunt's stuff, and then out of it all came . . ." He gestured past the glass doors.

"Hey, now." I raised my eyebrows and nodded, then took another drag. "So you think that was something he was working on?"

"I have *no idea*, but . . ." Brandt may have been hiding a smile from his face, but it was amusingly obvious in his voice. "But that lantern is definitely something scientifically inexplicable."

"Walks like a duck and quacks like a duck. But let me ask you—"

"Why'd I bring it in? Because *it's cool*, man! It—I don't know how it works, exactly. I've taken the top off before and looked inside. There's a socket like you get on any standard light bulb, but there's all these mirrors and prisms and stuff. I have *no* idea how it works, but—well, you saw what it does!"

"To an extent."

"Well, just wait until Friday. You'll see it in action."

3

Our business that week looked like an average fall season's worth, in the books. The only spike in numbers we saw were of the packing crates throughout the office.

Desks and filing cabinets were emptied with painstaking efficiency—as a rule of thumb, I usually keep my desk embellishments to a minimum, so my preparations for the move weren't very invasive or time-consuming. The limited printer selections, and with them, staff members' patience, began to disappear.

By Thursday night, select team members were given the choice to work from home to ride out the rest of the week while the office was transplanted into the skyscraper a couple of blocks away. I'd say about two-thirds of the staff did exactly that—which, in hindsight, was probably for the best.

Friday morning I walked past the security desk and stopped in the hallway facing the entrance—as well as the ruddy glow beyond the frosted glass doors. I swiped my office badge and went inside, squinting as a scarlet migraine met my gaze, then slowly opened my eyes to behold a field of shimmering, scarlet forms spread out before me.

Gnarled tree trunks sprouted up out of the worn leather armchairs in the waiting area, their branches crookedly stretching toward a mercifully unseen sky, thronged with masses of dangling, knotted vines. Low, jagged shrubs, lumpy stones, and clumps of grass and weeds littered the carpeting. I half expected to hear hoots, chatters, cries, and zipping of fauna to accompany the flora, but the only sound I could hear was the soft hum of a miniature refrigerator somewhere beneath a group of iridescent leaves that grew out of an otherwise flat wall.

"*Boogey-boogey-boogey!*" a theatrically hoarse voice shouted behind me. I blinked and looked for the figure of normalcy that came with it.

A dark, tall shape materialized out from between the downward-reaching arms of a shimmering tree—and I let out my breath when I saw it was Jeff. He chuckled and looked around. "Think this is too much up front here?"

"Only if any clients show up."

"Not today. They've all been informed about the move. This is only for us. I just figured this might be better placed in here for the party, is all."

I cringed when I realized he'd transferred the lantern to the top of the aesthetically pleasing but unmanned secretary's desk. "Did you tell Brandt?"

"Not yet, but I'm sure he'll be fine with it. Plus, I'm sure he has other decorations coming."

I didn't want to stir anything, so I remained silent as I walked to the gossamer forest.

I held my breath as I entered the throng of floating images. I was too bewildered to smirk at myself as I realized I was sidestepping a few of the shapes, even as my feet and arms passed through other projections. I don't know how on earth such tricks of science could be explained; but then, I wasn't in the right place to solve such a mystery, not as I passed beneath branches full of unfamiliar, circular leaves. My legs stepped through craggy rocks covered in glowing, swaying tendrils. And beyond the open doors of a nearby darkened conference room, I thought I saw a pair of long, thin, dark red objects dart up and back, scuttling out of view beyond the doorway.

I let out my breath as I emerged from the edge of the forest, then glanced around, relieved to be back in the beautiful, migraine-inducing glare of the overhead fluorescents. I shrugged off a shiver even as I saw a blood-red, ovular blob scuttling across the floor toward me. Without thinking, I lifted my foot and smashed it down on the thing, arthritic ankle protesting as the bottom of my wingtip shoe pounded against the carpeted floor.

Staggering back, I glanced around, my breath vanishing from my lungs as I watched the projection continue its progress across the floor, untouched and unfazed by my foot. I cringed as my eyes took in the rings of chitinous scales that ringed the entire expanse of its arthropodal form, reminding me of the nightmare-bugs of Australia, with which a friend of mine who lives there has an unpleasant fascination.

I needed coffee, and spent the rest of the morning reassembling my grip on reality around that mission.

As the day went on, I noticed that no paper jack-o'-lanterns clung to any of the walls, no plastic skeletons dangled from desk edges, and no inflatable witches or illuminated spooky trees loomed at waist height in corners and by doors. I didn't even see so much as a bundle of artificial spiderwebs or a single rubber bat. There was only, as ever, the lantern.

I stayed away from the front waiting area for the rest of the day— but that didn't make much of a difference. Brandt's choice in decoration made that a certainty.

Around ten that morning, Staci asked for my assistance in setting up a spreadsheet. When I showed her what to do, she giggled and said that she figured she'd known as much, but was having trouble concentrating back at her desk because of the throng of glowing, ropelike tendrils that drooped and occasionally twisted in the air above her desk. I figured it must have been part of the phantom forest that had sprouted up around the office, but minutes after Staci had returned to her desk she reappeared around the corner from mine to say that the floating distraction was gone.

At two I had a conference call with Tim, one of the contract supervisors. He was more amused than bewildered by what he dubbed a "tree lamprey" that had lowered into view for him as he'd carried his motorized scooter through the front. What he'd at first thought looked like a massive seed pod hanging from one of the tree branches had swayed, then wriggled, then seemed to unfold from itself, revealing a wide, tooth-ringed funnel of horror that snapped at a spectral insect which zipped by directly in front of him. He'd started and nearly kicked his scooter across the floor, then relaxed when he saw a bulge in the middle of the dangling thing split open, revealing a glistening, three-pointed pupil that twisted and swiveled about. It was, in his opinion, "an excellent field demo for Industrial Lights and Magic."

And around three, when I went to bring some envelopes to the mail room, I stopped before the doorway, where something of a cross between a spider and a crab, the size of a golden retriever, cornered Nicole, the operations clerk, at her desk. I tried to remind her it wasn't real, but she nervously pointed out that I was standing behind the thing as if giving it a wide berth. I snickered nervously as I realized I was trying to identify which side of its circular carapace was its front. Taking a deep breath, I stepped forward and passed right through it, and although Nicole's shoulders dropped a little, she kept staring at the doorway behind me as I approached, as well as when I left.

4

When I saw Brandt later, I frowned. I think I must have been subconsciously expecting him to finally don a costume this year but was a little surprised to find him exiting the breakroom wearing worn loafers, black jeans, and a worn sweater. His spirits didn't seem to fit in with the day, either: the corners of his mouth lifted in a flat, polite greeting, to which I responded with a Groucho Marx exercise of my eyebrows.

"Big day." I pointed my empty coffee mug at the nearest stack of storage crates. Mercifully, there hadn't been even a question that one of the very last items that would be disconnected for the move was the coffee machine.

"Yep." He scratched his chin with a hand that clutched a plastic-wrapped cheese stick. "How's your, uh . . ." I turned and frowned at a spectral expanse of lumpy rock that stretched from around the farthest cubicle corner, down the sloped surface of which a multitude of indeterminate shapes scuttled and crept. "Your projector, there?"

"Oh, it's fine. I'm sure you saw someone *moved* it."

I didn't say anything.

He shrugged. "But I *guess* it looks better up here."

"Maybe better lighting too, I guess?"

"The lighting doesn't really matter. It'll always be a little different, wherever it goes."

I cocked my head, and Brandt shrugged.

"Have you ever heard of a tesseract?"

"Outside of sci-fi movies, no."

"Er—" he cringed. "Sorry, never mind. You need your coffee."

A truer statement had never been made, but I could tell that his fascination—and his excitement about being able to share it—had been activated. I had an early feeling that he might not get a chance to tell this to anybody else, and although that ultimately proved correct, I didn't want to leave him hanging when he felt like he finally had somebody to share this with. "No, it's fine. Just lay low on the jargon if you can."

"So you know dimensions, right? A dot is a first-dimensional object, a line is a second, a third is . . ." He lifted his hands and gestured around. "Well, you know. *Us.*"

"All right."

"If you were a two-dimensional being—just a line drawing or something—and somehow got brought out into the third dimension, it'd blow your mind, right?"

I nodded. I had to congratulate myself on following him this far, considering the lack of caffeine in my system.

"But if you tried to show or even tell your other two-dimensional being friends about it, it would be kind of impossible for them to wrap their heads around it, right?"

"I can relate."

"Sorry, sorry. Basically, if you somehow held a prism over your two-dimensional world, everyone would be able to see its shadow, with all these weird lines that don't make sense." When I didn't say anything, he went on, "So imagine a fourth dimension—not time travel, I guess, but whatever you want to think of it as—that *we* can't perceive or conceptualize."

I smirked and shook my head. "Sorry, now you're starting to lose me."

"But that's just it—that's an appropriate, or even *the only,* reaction you can have to this, because even if you had an oil truck's worth of coffee IV'ed into your veins, you'd never be able to *truly* know how to imagine a fourth-dimensional object."

As I inclined my head back, frowning, I think Brandt could tell I was starting to understand. "So that . . . lantern is actually a tesseract?"

"No. No, but what you're *seeing* from it, for lack of a better way to put it, is the same as a two-dimensional being seeing the shadow of a three-dimensional prism."

My eyes widened slightly. "You mean—"

"I'm pretty sure that what my great-uncle was working on was a way to *see* the shadow of something that we *can't* see otherwise." He lifted an arm and pointed at the row of desks, where glowing red rocks peeked out from beyond the farthest one. He turned back to me, grinning like the proverbial cat that ate the canary, and lowered his voice. "That's not just a projector, you see. It's a *window*."

After a long moment I nodded and raised my coffee mug. "And *this* isn't a full dimension, it's an empty one." I left Brandt chuckling as I made my way into the kitchen.

5

I was happy to see absurd familiarity after that. Christine wore a massive inflatable fat suit with a ballerina tutu printed across its girth, her feet tripled in size in a pair of literal clown shoes. Luke was dressed in military garb, with a metal hook poking out of his left sleeve. Marina's face was painted in a Día de los Muertos manner, but she insisted she was dressed as a character from a Disney movie. And when I asked Desmond why his torso was housed in a giant plush carrot, he immediately dropped to the ground and pressed his arms and legs tightly together and said he was "healthy."

In the early afternoon Jeff and Connie went out to pick up booze, and Nicole called in an order for several pizzas. Marina went through every office and to every desk, reminding people that the printers would be disconnected at four o'clock sharp. And the last sets of unused storage crates were taken and used up, inciting a few arguments among several material-dependent employees.

Around four-thirty I went for a smoke and passed by one of the conference rooms near the front, in which all the costumed workers had gathered for a group photo. I had a good laugh at the full lineup of costumes and makeup, but my smile faded when I turned back to the red light spilling from the nearby corner that led to the front, in which a few floating shapes swayed, drifted, and crept in and out of view.

Projections, shadows—whatever they were, I pursed my lips as I walked toward them, picking up my stride, trying to remember to breathe as I kicked through rocks and thick-stemmed shrubs. Even so, I bumped into an armchair as I stepped around a waist-high thing that squirmed, contracted, and swelled with all the dexterity of a tongue, its surface covered in rippling, bulbous boils. I half crouched under a cloud of floating, wriggling, palm-sized grubs, and gasped as a bulbous shape materialized out of the ceiling overhead before drifting back into it, trailing a throng of swaying, segmented appendages.

Brandt's description of the nature of the lantern crept into my brain like a silverfish emerging from a crack in a wall. Although none of these things were real, or at least were in any way physically present, they were, in every sense, far too close for comfort—and if Brandt's implication held any merit, they were even closer than that.

Reaching the front doors, I pushed through with such a clumsy effort that my knuckles rapped the glass with a noisy *gong*. Stepping out, I pushed the door shut behind me, pausing to take a deep breath before turning to exit to the street, nearly running into the glowing red set of long, skeletal, taloned fingers that stuck out of the air directly before my face.

I staggered back with a grunt, forcing my half-raised hands back down to my sides as I sighed, more annoyed with myself than I was startled by the phantom appendage.

If a spider somehow developed hands, I think they'd look something like what stuck out of the doorframe at head height. Its multiple sets of thorny, doubled-knuckled digits flexed and twisted, each wicked, daggered end scraping and tapping over one another in total silence. Not wishing to meet its owner, I finally made my way outside.

I dragged on burning tobacco as I beheld the buildings set aglow by the sun's lengthening stride toward the solstice, watching a bus precariously circumnavigating the narrow, curved street and barely avoiding clipping every one of the tightly parked cars. The sheer tedium and precision involved was blissfully commonplace, a reality that was as intoxicating as the nicotine from my smoke.

As the embers of my cigarette crept closer to my fingers, I turned and glanced at the front of the building. Directly above the outdoor ashtray was one of the outdoor lights that clung to its wall like an oversized luminescent barnacle. A flurry of moths, their wings like dozens of fluttering flower petals, lighted and hovered along the plastic housing, inside of which their late brethren had collapsed into uneven piles of jumbled, burnt wings and upraised legs, like so many fallen Icaruses before them. My brow lowered as I stared at them, and I experienced a tightening sensation along my shoulder blades, which then erupted into a full-body shiver. After a moment I tossed my smoke and went back inside.

6

The evening and the shadows and the projections grew, and with them all, the excuse to partake of food and drink in celebration. At five o'clock sharp the party began.

The party itself wasn't much beyond what you'd expect. Laughter, bottles tipping up and down, mouths chomping down on slices of pizza, and endless exchanges of stories from trench and home alike, filled the room. I was surprised to spot Brandt among everyone, although his solitary presence stood out among their paired and grouped ranks as much as a sore thumb in a pile of good index fingers.

There was something else that was noteworthy about the party, in hindsight: everybody was gathered in the kitchen, which was on the opposite end of the office from the lantern and its projected alien meadow. It was understandable, to say the least, but it also made me feel bad for Brandt. Even so, he seemed to be enjoying himself.

My bladder began to swell under the labor of two ales, and I had to excuse myself. As I circumnavigated through the flora and fauna, I saw Luke coming from the front waiting area, looking white as a sheet before the specters' glow lent their ruddy complexion to his tense-looking features. We exchanged mystified shrugs as we passed each other, and I elbowed my way to relief.

I was on my way back to the party when I heard a low humming sound. I stopped and glanced around, feeling the skin on the back of my neck tightening. But as I moved past the front area and through the shimmering leaves, trunks, and creatures, I saw Marina crouched beside one of the printers and contemplated grabbing a third beer.

I almost succeeded in enjoying the rest of my evening when I saw

Desmond across the room as he flinched and shook his head. Somebody had brought in a small portable speaker, which was blasting retro-styled electronic music, so I couldn't hear him, but his wrinkled nose and working mouth said plenty. I sniffed at the air, then immediately cringed. I was about to ask who needed a new pair of underwear when Jeff exclaimed and backpedaled from one of the tables, looking down.

"Alcohol abuse!" Luke shouted playfully, but Jeff held his hand up.

A few heads turned and brows lowered, and I peered over a couple of shoulders to watch Jeff as he looked around and smiled to everyone, shaking his head. "Thought I saw a ghost!" A few people chuckled at this, but I could tell the humor in his voice was nonexistent.

I let the attention shift back to the party for a couple of minutes. Brandt, I saw, was making his way to the bathroom. I made a mental note to check in with him as I moved over to Jeff, who was standing idly beside the table, glancing down every few seconds or so.

"What's, uh—?"

"Bug," he said in a low voice. "Big bug."

I cleared my throat. "Are we talking about a roach, here, or—?"

"*No.*" He looked at me with all the intense secrecy of someone with an embarrassing tear in their pants. "It's like one of those *things* from Brandt's magic lamp."

I peered down and saw only the curved edge of the table, upon which sat a grease-stained paper plate, a crumpled napkin, and an empty beer bottle. "Under there?"

"Hasn't moved, so I don't want to cause any alarm," Jeff said out of the corner of his mouth.

"You won't. It's not—"

"*Eugh!*" Staci squealed from behind me, and I closed my eyes so nobody would see them rolling. I turned and found her looking down at the other side of the table—and beneath it, the oversized invertebrate causing all the fuss.

It was the same giant insect that I'd run into the day before, its red armor an invasive blot of twisted nature superimposed upon the face of industrial, civilized habitation. It seemed disquietingly aware of its audience because it began to creep out from between the metal feet of the table, glistening in the ruddy glow of the light.

Jeff and Staci backed away on either side of me. This in turn brought more attention to the phantom guest, inciting a few gasps and cursing inquiries.

I snickered, and a few people looked at me. I turned and looked for Brandt, who'd returned from the bathroom, frowning and searching from one face to another for an explanation for the disruption. The music continued to pulse and swell, but all conversations had fallen silent, and all gazes fixed beneath the table or on me.

"All right, people, look," I said, raising my hands, one of which clutched my third and final bottle for the night. "Not to make a speech, but—"

"Speech, *speech!*" Luke bellowed, and the music dropped from its retro beats and synthesized sounds to a low series of crackles and groans. A few others applauded, and I smirked and lowered my gaze, raising my hands.

"This'll be quick. I've been doing this for fifteen years, ten before I started here, and I've never worked with a crew as fun and as involving as all of you. That said, I'd like to thank the focus group for holding this—"

A round of applause led to Staci and Luke to bow. I glanced over at Brandt, who was looking down, his eyebrows raised in resignation, until I said my next piece.

"But—I'd like to extend *particular* thanks to our own Brandt, here, who—"

Beside me, Nicole gasped sharply, and I saw the giant bug began scuttling toward me. I laughed and lifted my leg, extending my arms in my best Broadway finale as I stomped my foot toward the floor—

—and down on the thing with a terrible, wet *crunch.*

I think everybody was too surprised to even make a peep, for the only sound I heard in my own silent horror was the crack and slurp of my foot lifting from the back of the thing, strings of ooze stretching and dribbling between the sole of my shoe and the crushed exoskeleton on the floor.

And then everybody found their voices.

My own disgusted groan was lost in the chaotic choir of cries, curses, groans, and gasps filled the air. Everyone staggered back and began moving toward the exit.

The thing on the floor wasn't moving, but I nonetheless moved back from it slowly, realizing with a sinking feeling in my gut that the red light of the lantern couldn't reach the closed-off room—that the crushed thing's ruddy coloration was, repulsively, *natural*.

I moved backwards, dragging the heel of my befouled shoe to maintain balance until I was out of the kitchen and in the hallway, where I stopped to grind the slime into the carpet. A wave of nausea crashed through me, and I choked back the spasm that I felt in my upper abdomen as I turned to find everyone had gathered at the far end of the hallway. Between them and me stood Brandt, who was so sweaty he looked as if he'd had a glass of water dumped on his head. Our gazes met, and his lips tightened as he read the questions in my eyes—and then we both started when someone screamed.

Several people ran out of view, and Brandt and I charged after them. They all rounded the corner into the front, then stopped, colliding into one another as the group backed up, staring at something in the red glare.

Running after them, Brandt shoved his way through the onlookers and out of view. I jogged uneasily to the back of the group, then stopped and mirrored their wide eyes and agape jaws as I beheld the object of their transfixion.

What was horrifying about the jungle of shimmering shapes that crowded the space of the waiting area wasn't the assortment of life-forms, nor was it the fact that some of them seemed to be *moving toward* the lantern, which I now saw lay on its side on the countertop. No, it was the obsidian triangle that had apparently materialized in the middle of it all, a nearly perfect arrowhead the size of a sofa that hovered in the air before the counter, its point aimed directly at the overturned lantern.

Then movement caught my eye, and I saw Brandt stepping toward the thing, ignoring a few urgent hisses of caution. He stopped before the triangle, peering back and forth along it, murmuring quietly. When somebody—I think Nicole—shouted for him to be careful, he twisted his head back and raised his voice. "It's okay!" he said with forced calm. "It's okay, it's—it's not real." When a few disbelieving warnings came up, he turned and raised his arms. "None of it is real! It's all just—"

"P-projections," I stammered, and a few people turned to me.

"Right!" Brandt pointed at me, grinning. "Just, uh . . ." He turned and peered back at the triangle, frowning. When someone asked him what this was all about, Brandt's reply was muffled by the confused, startled voices of the audience he'd finally managed to gather for himself—muffled by their voices, but also by the same crackling, groaning sounds that I'd heard back in kitchen, but which was much louder, now. He was talking about something that sounded like either "inside" or "dim side" when he turned and gestured at the triangle— and my eyes went wide as I watched his forearm seem to temporarily disappear into it, like it was less solid and more—

"Shadow," I breathed.

A couple of people turned to me, and Brandt pointed at me again, grinning. "See? *He* knows what's up! But here, look, I'm sorry if this freaked everyone out. I'm sorry, everyone."

"It . . ." Staci said in a tiny voice. "It's okay, it's just—"

"I know, it's weird." I could hear the slight quaver in his voice, and if I were close enough, I probably would have seen tears on his cheeks as he said, "I'll turn it off now."

He walked to the counter and grabbed the cable, glancing along its length to where it was connected to the wall beyond. He moved past the overturned lantern, passing through the conical shadow before re-appearing beyond it, aglow in the red wash. He stopped abruptly, look-ing around, then turned back to us, frowning. He murmured something, then peered around, his eyes going wide. "Guys?"

A cold rush poured down the sides of my neck and into my shoul-ders. "Turn it off," I said aloud, but I was so bewildered that it sound-ed like a matter-of-fact statement.

"Guys?" Brandt's voice was a shaky, muffled whimper. He began to

step forward, then stopped and looked down, one leg stretched out behind him. I thought I could see it caught beneath the edge of one of the chairs. Then he screamed, throwing his arms up in the air as something rose behind him.

It was as much of a blur to behold then as it is to recall now, but I remember thinking that it looked as if one of the alien shrubs had become animated, multitudes of thin, reed-like fronds swaying atop several large, branch-like objects that lifted and stretched out—and only as they grabbed Brandt's arms and torso and pulled him back did I realize that they were *limbs.*

His screams were terrible as he fell beneath—or was tugged down by—the appendages as they swung down and up, making dragging motions above his thrashing form. Big, jagged clubs on their ends seemed to spray jets of liquid on him as he bucked and howled. His wild limbs stretched up tented sheets of the glowing material that the thing continued to spray and spin layers and layers upon him, his hands clutching and tugging at the cord that stretched out tightly in the air above him as his screams began to grow more and more muffled—

Then the light vanished, and with it the shadow, the creatures, the plants, and Brandt.

All went silent and still in the waiting area, which was then only illuminated and occupied by the furniture and the remaining staff of Zoot Suit, LLC, in the twilight of its old location.

7

The week in between of working from home was nothing special for us, as far as our work went. Some clients were annoyed at being unable to get proper models and demos in person, and things grew a bit difficult for the design team when several people quit without notice.

That Wednesday came through the announcement that the rest of the office had been successfully moved into the new location, and by Friday we were given the all-clear to move into our new home at the recently opened Superman Building. And here we are.

The common belief around the office is that Brandt simply up and quit, following his dramatic departure at the party. Sure enough, there was a typed message to that effect waiting in his emptied desk—seems he'd been planning on quitting for some time and had even given early word to HR to prepare his paperwork. He was going to use the fall party for his announcement. It was a hell of an exit.

As for that bug, well—whatever it was, and whatever crack into hell it may have crawled out of, I'm glad I never laid eyes or shoes on anything like it again. I like to tell myself that it had gotten the cockroach-like reveal of being uncovered during the packing up of the old office, but of course I don't buy that theory for a second.

After the party had been so dramatically concluded, Jeff had spoken with a couple of police officers who'd shown up to take what were ultimately inconclusive statements about what probably sounded like a horror display that had been taken too far. As far as I know, nobody ever got interviewed or visited by the authorities again.

The lantern disappeared along with Brandt. I figure he must have come in over the weekend and nabbed it before the movers potentially trashed it. That night everybody, including myself, had gone straight home and left the thing on the counter, its plug convincingly severed off from the rest of the cable. The lantern didn't show up in any of the storage crates after the move, and I've not seen it since.

I suppose, though, that you should know about one thing which *did* turn up after the move. Desmond was puzzled to find something stuffed into one of the crates that contained his desk belongings—a small aluminum square, its edges jagged with flecks of broken solder, one side scratched and scored and caked with black, sootlike matter, and the other side painted with a yellow symbol. Everyone figures it must have been found by one of the movers and shoved into the first available storage crate. Where it came from, nobody seemed to know—although I swear to this day, I thought Luke went pale when he saw it.

Obviously, the whole incident left many questions unanswered—questions that I can see right now in the look on your face. I've been left with just as many of them roaming around in my mind, but ultimately I fall back on the old standby explanation of, "I don't know, I just work here."

Well, it's almost four-thirty. I should probably get back inside so I can wrap up and go home to my dog.

Oh—and thanks for the cigarette. I'll bum you one tomorrow.

The Place of Bones

When the conversations began to die around the campfire, I suggested that we tell ghost stories.

"And," said Kenta, a history sophomore, "I think *you* should tell the first one, Margaret."

I couldn't help but smile at the throaty approvals from around the fire. My reluctance from several days before, when Kenta had approached me in my office at the college library, was still present—but I was now also flattered that my penchant for local folklore was enough for them to invite an old hippie like me to join their ranks.

We'd met at dusk at the foot of a long trail that led from the dorms, then walked around the base of the nearest mountain, until we were nearly a mile into perfect isolation. I must have seemed like a senile old kook when I met Kenta's friends, including a girl he'd met in town who'd introduced herself as Sharon. I stammered a lot and had to excuse myself as they started the fire, chalking it up to a dizzy spell. I'd retreated along the path and stared into the woods for a few minutes, fighting back tears as memories came to me, memories that I'd not thought about for nearly seven decades, as overgrown and shadowed as the forest around me.

I stood and grabbed a log from the pile to shove into the fire. "I do have a story that I could tell, but I'm not sure everyone would appreciate it."

"Well, *I* know a good one," Sharon said.

I turned as flames leapt out to taste their fodder, and saw her round, pale face beaming in their orange glow. She'd earlier said she was a dropout, but that her love of the land had been more than enough of a reason to stay, even when her education had come to a grinding halt for reasons she hadn't divulged. I wondered how she felt to be among students who were successfully doing what she was not. Although she'd laughed at the occasional joke or tale of misadventure, she'd mainly kept to herself all evening—until now.

Sharon turned, the corners of her mouth twitching upward in a controlled grin. "Any of you ever hear of the Bone Witch?"

Jake and his girlfriend Sophia snickered at the name.

Kenta asked if Sharon was referring to a video game character, but she shrugged. "I wouldn't know." She glanced at me, and I shook my head. I was actually *very* familiar with this story, but I was curious to hear her take on it.

She grinned, throwing her long blond hair back over her shoulder, and I caught a glimpse of glistening metal—a pretty gold necklace, half-hidden by the top of her blouse.

"This is a ghost story, from a long time ago. There's supposed to be a strange figure that haunts the woods throughout this area, from Stamford on up through Manchester, and even some places out by Hoosick Falls. People have claimed to see a woman in the woods, watching them from between trees and in caves.

"There've been different versions of her over the years. Nobody really knows when or how it all started, but in short, people sometimes go missing in these woods. Sometimes individuals, sometimes entire groups."

"The Vermont Triangle."

Sharon turned to me, looking a little annoyed at the interruption. "Yeah."

"The what?" Kenta asked.

"Back in the mid-forties," I said, blinking hard at a sting in my eyes, "at least six people disappeared in this area. It's how the Vermont State Police got started."

"That's right," Sharon said.

"Oh, shit." Jake's eyes widened as he whispered, "The two hikers!" He turned to Sophia. "Those two hikers I was telling you about a couple weeks ago." The corners of her lips curled down.

Sharon grinned. "Told you it was a ghost story."

Everyone fell silent, and she continued.

"Every once in a while, hunters and hikers sometimes find little objects in the woods like this." She removed what looked like a pale, uneven star from her jacket pocket. She offered it to me, and I took it, frowning—then almost dropped it when I realized what it was.

Bones. Several small bones, perfectly clean and smooth, their middles bound together with dark string. I gingerly handed it back to Sharon, but she nodded past me, so I turned and passed it to Jake. Frowning, he offered it to Sophia, who shook her head in refusal. Curiosity piqued, Kenta stood up and reached around the fire to have his turn.

"Are these . . . human?" Kenta muttered, staring at the bone fetish in his hand.

"For the sake of the story, let's say they are. I wound up with it a couple of years ago, from a girl named Becky who was driving up from Massachusetts. We don't talk anymore, but knowing what happened to her, I've never wanted to get rid of it." She took the bone-star back from Kenta and stuck it in her pocket.

"It would've been a three-hour drive for her, but it took her almost five in the end, and not just because she ran into a ton of roadwork. Not long after she crossed the border, Becky had to pee really bad.

"So she's driving along, squirming in her seat. It's early evening, and it's late September, so it's getting darker earlier in the day. She's praying that she can find a rest stop somewhere, but there's just more and more highway, and she doesn't want to pull over and risk squatting in a shrub of poison oak. So she keeps going until she can't hold it any longer, and pulls into a shallow ditch and gets out of her car.

"Becky really doesn't want to do this, but it's gotten pretty dark by now, and she figures that she can just go out of sight from the highway and do her thing. She locks her car and goes behind some bushes, turns around and looks. She sees a car go by, and she can see the driver, clear as day. So she thinks, in turn, anyone could see her. She goes deeper into the woods and finds a little bundle of bones, like this one.

"It's weird, she thinks. Maybe it was from roadkill. But she can't worry about that right now. She's got to pee!

"She walks deeper, and then she trips on something and falls—and almost pees herself. She stands up, expecting it to be a root or a stick or something, but lo and behold, it's a bone, as long as my arm. Now she's getting a little weirded out.

"Becky decides to get it over with, and steps behind a bush. As she's going, though, she sees a big white rock nearby. It's hard to see in the light because it's almost nighttime now. She finishes up and moves a little closer to the rock. It's about as big as—like that tree stump, over there. Then, when she gets close enough, she sees it's more bones. I'm talking dozens of them, a whole pile of them. And there are no skulls or anything, either. She can't tell if— Well, she *hopes* they're not human. They're all perfectly clean, no gristle or gore on them."

She paused for a moment. In that split second, a pin could be heard dropping. But before she could continue, someone said, "Could . . . ?"

All heads turned.

Sophia, her eyes wide, asked in a low voice, "Could it have been hunters? Like, after they skinned game or—something?"

Sharon inclined her head, frowning. "That *would* make sense, I guess, but these were so carefully put together, not just randomly thrown on top of each other. It was done with such deliberate design that it looked like a cairn. You know those piles of rocks you some-times find in the woods? So, imagine a cairn—of *bones*.

"And as scared as she is, she can't stop looking at it. And then she sees there's *another* one nearby. And *another*. There's a whole bunch of them, at least half a dozen. She's in a *field* of these bone-cairns.

"And then she hears something and turns. Behind a couple of trees she thinks she sees something white. It's really tall and high, way bigger than the bone-cairns. But before Becky can get a good look, she hears something again. She turns . . . and—"

"*Shit!*" Kenta bolted to his feet, startling everyone. He was looking past me, down into the woods.

I twisted back for a peek but saw only the orange-gray of the sur-rounding trees and the shadows between them.

"*¡Mierda!*" Sophia snapped, then sighed heavily. "Don't do that!"

Sharon giggled. "Good one," she and Jake muttered at the same time, and they shared a laugh. Kenta raised a hand, frowning, still star-ing into the woods.

I mirrored the look on his face. "What are you——?"

"*Shhh,*" Kenta hissed. "I'm serious, guys!"

I stood and turned to look down the path, but it was a jagged tun-nel of nearly perfect darkness.

A branch snapped, and then came a stranger sound—a quick series of dry clicks, coming unmistakably from the path.

"You heard that," Kenta breathed, to no one in particular.

We all rose to our feet.

"What is it?" Sophia asked, her voice barely a whisper.

Another series of clicks came—from somewhere behind us. Eve-ryone spun around, crowding one another beside the fire. "Screw this!" Jake hissed, and pandemonium broke out.

Sharon panicked. "Let's get out of here!"

Scrambling to pull out a flashlight, I blurted, "Just stay close to the fire!"

"*Oh, Dios mio . . .*" Sophia murmured.

Trying to raise his voice over all others, Kenta said, "Hold on! Maybe it's——"

Something crashed loudly in the undergrowth behind us, and every-one screamed. Chaos erupted, feet shuffling and heads twisting to glimpse in every direction. There were curses and gasps, pointing fin-gers and harsh whispers. The woods were a silent, amused audience to our panic.

I tugged the flashlight out of my pocket so quickly it tore the fab-ric. As I clicked it on and pointed it unsteadily, its pale glow revealed a blur of trees—and caught a glimpse of something white that shrank back between their trunks. I fixed the beam on the spot again, eyes widening, but it was gone.

Another peal of clicks came from somewhere above, as if the forest were laughing at us.

Kenta grabbed my arm and I jumped. His mouth was working quickly, pronouncing unintelligible nonsense.

Then that dry tittering came from beside me, and I yelped and spun around.

My beam caught something on the ground, a clump of pale roots beneath a nearby shrub. It twitched, then rose from the ground and began to spread, blooming like a giant white flower.

Kenta pulled on my arm. I staggered back, the flashlight beam fixed on the white appendages as they closed in on themselves, snatching at the space I'd just vacated, far too many digits clutching at the empty air.

Another clicking laugh came from behind us, and we quickly huddled together.

Then came a piercing cry, and something rammed against my side, knocking the wind out of me. I staggered back, hearing a thump and more screaming, and turned to see Sophia had fallen, her red jacket puffing out with the impact. At first I thought she was kicking one of her legs back, but then I saw something wrapped around her ankle, something big and lumpy and pale, that began to drag her toward its owner's hiding place.

Shouting, Jake grabbed at Sophia's hands. I looked around for something, *anything*, and saw Kenta diving for the woodpile.

Sophia screamed again, her face a grimace of terror and tears. Reaching past Jake, I grabbed her forearms and began pulling.

Kenta stumbled back, swinging a log like a baseball bat. He roared as the log connected with the bony arm with a sharp *crack*, then swung it again and again. There was a blur of white as the hand released Sophia's leg, and she seemed to fly forward. She, Jake, and I crashed into one another, falling into a heap on the ground.

Shouting and cursing, we scrambled to our feet and regrouped. Sophia was hysterical, and Jake hugged her, cursing incessantly. Kenta's gaze was hopping from one spot in the woods to another, and Sharon—

I cursed and spun in a full circle, knowing what I'd find—or rather, what I wouldn't.

Sharon was gone.

"No!" I ran to the tree line, looking around, but couldn't see a sign of her.

Kenta glared back at me. "What?"

"She's gone!" I stamped my foot on the ground. "Sharon. She's gone. Dammit!"

"Someone mind telling me what the hell is going on?" Jake said.

Sophia muttered, "It's the Bone Witch!"

"No, no!" Jake said. "That—"

Then everyone started shouting over one another. "You saw that thing—those things!"

"Guys—"

"Those had to—"

"*¡La mierda fantasma me agarro! Me tenía de los—*"

"Shut up!"

"*It's real*, okay?" Kenta practically shrieked, and everyone fell silent. "The Bone Witch is *real*, and it took Sharon, and—"

"We need to go find her," I interrupted.

Jake and Sophia took turns looking from me to Kenta and back.

"No, no, and *no*," Kenta spat. "No way am I playing rescue ops with—whatever the hell those things are!"

"Sharon!" Sophia shouted, and I echoed her. We called out repeatedly, and a moment later Jake joined in.

"This is ridiculous," Kenta muttered.

Sophia spun to him. "What if she's hurt, or—"

"The hell . . ." Jake muttered.

"We don't know that," I said, and shouted for Sharon once again, straining my lungs.

"Whoa!"

"We can't just let her get—"

"Look Margaret, I'm sorry, but we—"

"Holy shit, help!" Jake screamed.

I turned in time to see him pitching forward, his arms swinging wildly, hands trying to grab anything they could as he hit the ground. He was quickly lifted by two sets of those horrible bone hands and shrieked until his voice cracked. We all lunged for him, but he was already out of reach, and we could only watch with dumb, horrified wonder as he was lifted into the trees, until his feet disappeared between the branches.

Sophia and Kenta found their voices, shouting and screaming after him. I shone my flashlight beam up in time to see Jake being tugged backward through the thick branches and clumps of dark brown leaves, toward something enormous and pale and far, *far* too high up to sanely comprehend.

And then Kenta howled, and I saw another massive bone-claw smash out through the forest and grab his upper body, yanking him backward. I charged after him, Sophia wailing beside me, and then something grasped me around my midsection and *squeezed.*

There was vertigo and a blur of branches and leaves around me, smacking my face and tearing at my hair. I shouted, kicking wildly as I was lifted higher and higher, the night sky rushing toward me. I thought I saw the terrible face of the moon up there, big, jagged, and white, and so terribly close as it opened its hungry maw to my approaching form—and then my head collided with a heavy branch, and everything went dark.

A blink of light and sound.

A glowing blur, something pressed against my cheek.

Screams in the darkness.

Movement as I'm lifted upright, and something hard ramming into my back.

Someone—I think it's Kenta—screeches like a wounded cat, louder and louder.

I murmur something, but I can hardly hear myself.

I can see little points of light all around me, and something big and white floating behind it all. Then my head dips forward, and all is dark again.

I was half-aware of the singing for some time before I became fully conscious. It was dissonant, warbling, foreign.

Blinking, I could only see darkness around me, punctuated with blurry, softer shadows that slowly increased into gentle glows. I was floating in the cosmos, surrounded by the inert ghosts of starlight and the song of distant spheres. Disoriented, I squinted at the nearest star, trying to concentrate on it until at least my vision returned.

The light swam in and out of focus, growing alternately wider and narrower, seeming to shift and twist, until it became a tiny flame. My jaw slowly opened as I realized it was a candle, set on the ground by my left foot.

I stared at it until my vision cleared, and saw that it rested upon a small, star-shaped bundle of twigs. No—*bones*.

I felt dull pain in my neck as I turned to look elsewhere—then groaned as it burst into brilliant fire, waking me fully up. I opened my eyes and realized that I was sitting upright, my head resting on my chest. From the hard, painfully lumpy surface pressed against my back, I gathered been left lying against a big rock. I slowly lifted my head up, gritting my teeth as I did.

I blinked hard and realized that I wasn't hearing singing—it was a series of sobs and ululating whimpers, the voice very familiar. As I listened, the whimpers stopped.

Jerking my leg away from the candle, I tried to sit up, but something hard pressed against my sore chest. I looked down and gasped as I saw that I was tied down to the rock not with rope, but with several layers of bones—thick ones, thin ones, curved and straight, all bound together with black thread. They held well, too: despite all my struggles, I was kept firmly in place against the rock.

There were many more of those wicked candles placed on the ground around me, I now saw. There were several big, pale shapes nearby, nearly as tall as people, and I remembered Sharon's story from before. I didn't have to look to know what I'd been bound to—or what was holding me. I could feel, could hear the shift and scrape of so many bones piled upon one another, pressing into my back, making my skin crawl.

Adrenaline surged, panicking me. It took everything I had to push that down and try to examine my surroundings calmly.

I was in a clearing, the encompassing trees forming a jagged circle beneath the night sky, from which the stars distantly regarded this horrifying place of bones.

The whimpering voice came again. I turned and looked for its source—and my eyes bulged.

Several yards away from me was a low, dome-shaped hut or hovel, the crooked black opening in its side facing me like a gaping, hungry mouth. I immediately recognized the lumpy, mottled surface that made up its wall, riddled with holes, as human skulls. Hundreds of them, neatly stacked one upon the other, some with jaws, most without, and more than a few of them far too small to have come from adults.

When the voice spoke again, I tore my gaze away from the hovel. Although my eyes had adjusted to the candlelit darkness, I could only make out a big, pale shape, with something low and dark resting against it. I squinted at it until I recognized the red jacket.

"Sophia!" I cried, but my voice came out in a harsh, dry croak. As I cleared my throat, she yelled something back to me. "Are you all right?"

"I-I think my leg is broken!"

"Hold still!" I instantly realized what a silly suggestion that was. "Where's Jake? Kenta?"

"I don't know, I don't *know*, I—" Sophia lowered her head, sobbing again.

I tried to pry my arms loose with all my strength, but it was useless. I looked around, setting my jaw—and then I heard a low, guttural moan from nearby. From the hovel.

I couldn't recognize the voice, but it was male, and from the sounds of it, he was in death's embrace.

I turned to Sophia, saw she was also looking at the hovel. I shook my head, hoping she could see me—but then she started shouting.

"Jake! *Jacob!*"

I tried to hush her, to calm her, but she was too far away and too scared. Laughter came from the hovel, and the blood froze in my veins.

It wasn't quite the high, nasal cackling that part of me expected. No, it was a deep, lyrical laugh that trailed off with an unmistakable tone of mockery.

Through the door of the hovel, I saw quick movement, just the barest change of shade in the blackness, then it was gone—

Something was hurled out at me. I yelped and tried to duck, but the bones held me in place, and I could only cringingly turn my head as something struck my shoulder and fell to the ground. I didn't dare look at it. Instead, I stared at the doorway as its thrower emerged, laughing. Sophia's hysterical shouts died out as the Bone Witch stepped into view, a pale, grinning specter—the girl who'd called herself Sharon.

She was naked but for her gold necklace. Somehow I was expecting her to be wearing jewelry made of bones. In fact, I was more surprised by this than I was to see her casually striding out of the hovel toward me, slowly shaking her head.

"Let them go," I pleaded.

"What, *these?*" She raised her hand, holding something red and glistening that had smeared blood on her arms and body. I swallowed my nausea and forced my gaze to meet hers. Her smile broadened. "Too late."

"They're kids! They don't deserve this!"

"They're young and strong."

"Jake?" Sophia said in a tiny voice. "Jake . . . oh my God . . ."

"No!" I shouted.

The Bone Witch's smile widened. Despite her young and pretty features, I could see something far older and incredibly ugly behind that horrible grin as she turned and slowly stepped toward Sophia. She dropped the red object, which landed on the ground with a revoltingly wet *splat.*

She started speaking as she got closer to Sophia, but I could only make out the words, ". . . *you,* child . . ." Sophia began to loose a drawn-out, warbling cry.

"Please!" I cried. "*Please* . . . you don't want to do this!"

"Oh? *Don't* I?" she called over her shoulder. "Haven't you heard the legends?"

My thoughts racing, I shouted, "Wait, my story!"

The Bone Witch stopped and turned to face me, her eyes skull-like pools of shadow as she frowned.

"I never got to tell *my* story!"

She stared at me for a long moment, then turned back, the grin returning to her face as she approached me. "How right you are," she said, crossing her long legs and lowering herself to the ground before me. "Please, tell it to me now." She spread her bloody arms, grinning. "I have all night."

I wasn't sure if I was ready for this—but then, it was all I could do.

"It's a ghost story," I started, looking down at the ground. "I don't remember it all, other than what I've heard and pieced together over the years. I was only five years old at the time." I looked up at the Bone Witch and saw the perplexed look on her face.

"There was a girl who went to college right near here. Her name was Patty. She was eighteen."

"No." I looked up to see a new look crossing the Bone Witch's features—exactly the one I expected, and so I continued.

"One day Patty went for a walk, and she never came back."

"No." She raised a hand to her forehead, and damn if it wasn't trembling.

"She never came back. Her family got so worried."

"Stop it!"

"Her ma, her pa, and her sister went through the rest of their lives wondering what happened to her."

The Bone Witch jumped to her feet with a snarl.

"Ma died in 1961. Heart attack. Pa was taken only a few years later from a stroke. And her sister—" My tongue went still in my mouth as I heard a familiar series of dry clicks and rattles from nearby.

One of the vacant bone-cairns appeared to be crumbling open, as if something were bursting out from inside it. Then I realized it was shifting.

Before my eyes, bones dropped, tumbled, and crawled noisily over one another, slowly forming a hodgepodge shape. For a moment it looked like a person bent forward on hands and knees, but then the head—such as it was—began to take shape, looking like no animal I'd ever seen.

Sophia began to shriek, and the Bone Witch turned to her, grinning.

The bones had formed something between a bull and a bear, and it slowly turned around, horrifyingly silent but for ripples of clicks, taps, and clatters.

I turned back to the Bone Witch and snarled, *"Leave her alone!"*

"Enough, you!" she snarled, and something shifted against my side. I heard a few bony clicks, and a point of tremendous pressure formed against the left side of my abdomen—then exploded into pain. I started screaming. One of the bones had twisted and rammed into my side like an improvised dagger.

I desperately squirmed against my terrible restraints as the pain worsened, screaming louder, wet warmth seeping into my shirt and pants as I bled. I couldn't fathom what was happening to me, how much blood I was losing—but then I heard a high, keening sound, and realized that I wasn't the only one screaming.

Sophia was.

"No!" I managed. Sophia's shrieks got louder and louder, until I was sure they'd spare the Bone Witch and her horrible creature the trouble of tearing her throat apart.

Trapped in a world of pain and horror, I screamed the only thing I could think of, the only thing I had left.

And then there was sudden, horrible silence.

I squeezed my eyes shut, knowing what was surely happening. I listened for the wet rips and gurgles of slaughter . . . but there was only more silence.

I heard the soft crunch of bare feet padding on dead grass and leaves, and opened my eyes in time to see the Bone Witch looming over me. *"What* did you say?"

I coughed, and damn if I couldn't taste the life bleeding out of me. "Her sister. *Your* sister. It's *me,* Patty."

We stared into each other's eyes for a long, silent moment.

"Midge?" she breathed.

Then the silence broke with a loud crash, and I saw the bone-creature collapsing. It didn't return to its previous cairn structure, however—all its pieces simply crumbled apart like a kid's popsicle stick model, landing in a haphazard mess all over the ground.

When I turned back, she knelt before me, eyes wide and frantic. There was a cacophony of clicks and what felt like the rush of air around me, and then the bones that held me fell apart, littering my legs and my hands and the ground beneath. I cried aloud as the one piercing my side twisted, then went still, firmly wedged inside me.

"Midge, oh no, *Midge!"* she said, dropping to her knees and bending forward. I turned away—somewhere I'd heard an injury is easier to handle if you don't look at it—but when she tore the bone out of my side, spheres of blackness swam into my vision that were so dense, I was sure that this was it. *"It's . . ."* I shook my head, but everything seemed so slow, so laborious, and more of those black spheres were crowding in around me now.

"Shhhh, shhh," she whispered, and her voice began to form low, strange words.

"Just—" I managed, but it sounded like two long, drawn-out syllables.

She continued to speak, and I sank into the dark, hearing a voice echoing, calling out one final plea.

"Just—let—her—go . . ."

I don't know when I came around. I wasn't sure if I was still alive. Hell, for all I knew, this was some kind of purgatory, a purgatory in which my long-lost sister was sitting naked with me in a field of candles and bones. And a fire—I saw a fire had been built nearby. It took me a moment to realize that I could feel its gentle heat seeping into my cold limbs.

She was speaking again, but all I could hear was a low, droning sound, punctuated with the occasional syllable or pause.

I blinked, and more light entered my vision. I spent a long time with my head turned to the side, staring at the horizon, and could just see the veil of stars beginning to lift at its edges. I could feel the familiar texture of earth against my back, and realized that I was lying down now, no longer resting against that damned bone-cairn. I tried to sit up, but pain exploded in my left side, sending fireworks through my senses.

"Midge, don't move," she said, a slight echoing lisp to her words.

"What the hell ... happened?" I asked, meaning something far bigger than the moments—or hours—that had just passed. I took a heavy breath, then winced and let loose a grunt as deep pain lanced through me again.

A hand pressed to my shoulder. "Don't move. You're bleeding bad. I was able to make it stop for now, but—"

I nodded weakly.

Then an image flashed through my mind, of a terrified girl's face. "Sophia!" I groaned.

"She's gone. I—I let her go. She had a bad limp, but she'll be fine."

I let out a heavy breath, then nodded weakly.

"Midge, I'm sorry I didn't recognize you."

"I got old." I snickered, intending to add, *and I see you didn't,* but pain shot up into my abdomen, and the rest of my breath escaped in a soft wheeze.

"Why did you come back?"

"You and those other people vanished back in the late nineteen-forties." I shrugged weakly. "When those two hikers disappeared last month, I had to wonder. But what—what the hell happened to you, Patty?" I had spent most of my life asking this question, to Ma and Pa, to the authorities, to God, to anybody who would or could give me any semblance of an answer. Even the concept of death had been easier to grasp than the possibilities raised by this question. Asking it now, however, seemed so minuscule, so fickle, so normal, that I might as well have been asking about a disastrous choice of a boyfriend.

She sat back, looked to the distance. "You wouldn't understand."

"Try me."

She looked away for a long moment, then took a shaky breath and said, "I don't know where to start."

"For one thing, can you put on some damn clothes?"

She re-emerged from the hovel moments later, her feet bare and her jacket discarded, but thankfully not the naked, bloodied horror she had been earlier. She sat down beside me and regarded the fire for a long time, her necklace glimmering in its flickering light. She'd been wearing that necklace in an old photo that my parents had kept hidden from me until I was almost as old as her.

"So?" I said.

She regarded the fire for a long time, then spoke.

She'd been hiking the Long Trail into these parts, where she'd found a wide, deep hole in the ground. She stared down into it for so long she'd lost track of time, until night had fallen. She wasn't scared, only curious, the whole time, even when a figure appeared nearby—a bald, naked, grinning man with glowing orange eyes and something like a giant black spider growing out of the middle of his chest. He'd had big ideas that had spoken to her soul and fed into her dreams of a better, healthier world—a world that he needed her help to create.

She said something about being "augmented by the black," and something about the power of *structure,* of the power that lurked in everything and how you only needed to pick something apart to tap into it.

I had trouble making sense out of the rest. It may have been my lost blood, or maybe she was speaking in such advanced terms and metaphors that I was growing confused, but I didn't stop her. I kept listening, certain that this was a story she'd never told anyone, and would probably never tell again.

When she was finished, the stars had begun their slow retreat behind the first hint of blue in the sky. "Midge, I'm so sorry." She was crying, I now saw, but no tears touched her cheeks or even her eyes. She shook her head and sniffed.

I closed my eyes, took a heavy breath, and nodded.

"I'm sorry," she repeated, pressing her hand into mine. I took it and squeezed, then snickered weakly.

"What?"

I twisted my mouth into a sour grin. "My story. I never finished it." I coughed harshly and turned to her. "You'll like it. It's a ghost story."

Patty's trembling lips twisted into a smile that I had only ever seen in old photographs, and I felt her hand squeeze mine harder. "Start it over. Please."

I coughed again. "This is a ghost story, from a long time ago . . ."

Sleep Harvest

Slow down." Ryan sat up in the passenger seat.

"What?"

"I said slow d—" He twisted to look out the window, then sighed as April applied the brakes. A quick glance in the rearview showed there was nobody behind them, no spectators walking the dimly lit sidewalks. Good.

"What?" April was cringing. "Did I miss one . . . ?"

"Almost a block back. Pull over."

She cursed and apologized as she pulled the van over. Ryan hopped out before she'd even removed the key.

He didn't bother rummaging in the back for the equipment. He made his way down the sidewalk, hiking his coat up around his shoulders against the cool November air, dry and clear except for the faint trace of weed. April called for him to hold up, but he kept walking.

He stopped near the corner of the block, where an alleyway separated an empty residence from a closed barbershop, and peered into the space. Empty beer bottles, some intact, some in various states of shatter, littered the space. A couple of feet in, an old yellow mattress rested up against the wall of the barbershop, stained and wrinkled from interminable days and nights in the elements. On the ground beyond its far end was an old spool of telephone wire.

"Where is it?" April asked behind him.

He nodded into the alley, reaching into his coat pocket. "Gimme a hand."

Listening to the muted squeak and snap of latex as they pulled on their gloves, he glanced around, but the holiday was keeping most people indoors, either stuffing their faces or hibernating. Good.

They reached in together, arms and breaths interlocking as they grabbed the edges of the mattress and tugged. Ryan frowned, baring his teeth. The sucker was heavy. He reached further in and pulled harder, satisfied as it began to move.

They dragged the mattress out until a few feet of it sat on the pavement between them, and then reached back in to grab the rest of it. As it came into the pale glow of a nearby streetlight, Ryan took one more cautious look. Nobody around. They just had to drag it to the van, bring it back, and take care of it, and then they could be as thankful as everyone else in—

Two teenage girls were standing on the porch of a nearby house, staring at them. At *him*.

For the two years he'd been working on this, he'd managed not to get arrested, as unofficially procuring discarded mattresses from the streets wasn't exactly legal. And although April had managed not to screw up so far, there was a first time for everything.

"Heavy," she grunted.

"Keep going." He didn't want to draw any more attention to them—and telling her that they were being watched would only make things worse.

"What are you doing?" one of the girls called over.

April dropped her end of the mattress and spun, wide-eyed.

"Oh, great," Ryan muttered, and raised his voice. "We're, uh—"

"City of Providence," April called, and he shot a glare at her as she began walking toward the girls on the porch, and he stayed behind, the mattress awkwardly balanced against his leg. "Discarded bedding pickup is scheduled for this week."

Ryan suppressed a smirk. *Not bad.*

The girl who'd spoken glanced at her friend, who shook her head and said something unintelligible. The first one said, "Like a service or something? For beds and stuff?"

"Yes," April said. "We're trying to beautify our city next year. That's—that's our motto."

Ryan caught another whiff of cannabis on the air, and now he saw a tiny orange glow being kept not too subtly behind the second girl's back.

"Think—uh . . ." the first girl said, ignoring her friend as she punched her arm, "Think we can give you one?"

Ryan blinked.

"Uh . . ." April turned back to him, and he nodded. "We're just finishing with this one, but if you want to get yours outside meanwhile—"

Ryan watched the girls go back inside, then muttered, "In the future, don't—*advertise* us like that."

"How is that a *bad* thing?"

"If there are more people living in that building, we don't want *all* of them bringing shit down to us and talking us up all over town."

"Sorry." April sighed and picked up her side of the mattress again.

"It's okay. Let's get this into the van."

They managed to drag it fully out of the alley and into the street when April yelped and dropped her end, flinging her hands up into the air.

"What?"

"Spider! It's *huge!*"

He cringed and shook his head. "Come *on*, are you . . . ?" He released the mattress, letting it flop back against the side of the alley again. The loose end drooped a bit, but it stayed put, and he walked around it, sighing heavily. He squinted at a dark spot on the mattress, leaned in—then snapped upright. *"Whoa!"*

A dark brown star clutched the side of the mattress, several inches below the edge that April had just been holding. The spider *was* big, its outstretched legs at least as wide as his palm. He'd grown up in an old, old house out in the countryside, and had had to deal with plenty of these critters. He stepped back and raised his foot, nudging the thing with his boot. It scuttled vertically until it reached the mattress's upturned edge. With one quick movement he smacked his hand at it, and it disappeared into the alley.

"Ugh, I *hate* those things."

"Well, it's gone, now. Wanna help?"

April was silent, and no doubt annoyed, as they threw the mattress into the van, then drove closer to the house in time to find the two girls carrying out parts of a disassembled bed.

As they worked, one of the girls explained that she was transferring back to a state college in her hometown and couldn't bring it with her. *First-world problems*, Ryan thought as they took the bed frame and the box spring. They'd have to dispose of those parts later, but for the sake of show—thanks to April's volunteer act—he loaded them into the back of the van as April went inside the house with the girls to retrieve the mattress, which turned out to be one of those fancier, memory-foam models that ended in "-pedic," and was still in good shape. No doubt, the girl's parents had spent a small fortune on it.

They carried the mattress over to the van, and April told the girls that they could handle it from there. One of the girls tried offering them a twenty-dollar bill, and although Ryan tried to protest, April graciously took it. The girls thanked them again and headed back inside.

"They were honestly embarrassed that we caught them smoking," April said as the front door closed. "I told them not to worry about it, but . . ." She held the bill up and giggled.

They went over to the back of the van and opened the door—then April gasped and jumped back.

"What now?"

April stared past the open door for a long moment before saying. "Sorry. Thought I saw something."

Ryan's lips tightened. "Another spider?"

"No." She sighed and opened the other door, muttering, "Never mind."

They picked up the heavy mattress with grunts and huffs, and half carried, half dragged it to the van and slowly shoved it in alongside the first one. As they did so, Ryan thought he saw something move inside, but he chalked it up to a trick of shadows and sighed. "I'm tired. Tell Sydney we'll be there soon."

They drove out of the city and along increasingly darkened, tree-lined roads. In daylight, several large, well-kept houses could be seen standing high on secluded hillsides. Ryan pulled up before a wide, ornate, metal gate. He reached out his window to punch in a code on a small electronic panel, and the black gates swung slowly inward.

As they traveled on the long, curving driveway, April thought she could see several silhouettes lurking in the darkness. As on previous occasions, when the headlights swept across them, the shadows melded into shrubs and patches of dead grass. She wondered if Ryan had ever seen them, but he never said anything

At the end of the road, a looming black monolith stood, a single yellow rectangle in its surface the only hint it was a house. A faint greenish-gray ambiance shone from somewhere behind it and grew brighter as the van followed the curved road around the side of the house until a wide, brightly lit garage appeared. Their cars waited off to the side, leaving ample room for unloading the night's procurement.

Sydney came out from the garage and watched the van come to a stop before her. "Pretty late job."

"It's only seven-thirty," April grumbled, pulling out a fresh pair of latex gloves from her jacket pocket.

"Let's get it over with, so we can *all* go home," Ryan said, opening his door and climbing out.

April exited and met Sydney's gaze, then gave a cursory nod, but the greeting was not returned. Sydney was also wearing gloves, she saw, but they were made of good-quality treated leather.

As Ryan pulled open one of the doors, he shouted, leaping back. "Jesus!" He staggered several feet away, shot a glance at them. "Rat!"

April cringed. First a spider, now a rat? Was tonight all about skeeving her out?

"*Where?*" Sydney snapped from behind.

"Right—" he pointed, then frowned.

April moved in a wide circle around him to look at the van from a safe proximity.

He shook his head, jaw agape, then crouched down and peered beneath the van. April ducked and squinted past him. The ambiance from the garage only shone a little of the way beneath. "Gone," he muttered unconvincingly, standing up. "Which one do you want first?"

Sydney gave him a long look. "Whichever one you didn't get from an alley."

Ryan and April reached in and hauled the thick, heavy mattress out and carried it into the garage, then let it flop down onto the concrete as Sydney began to remove her gloves.

April looked back at the van. The first mattress was a lumpy crescent moon resting against the van's interior. She stared at it for a moment before joining Ryan, who was removing equipment from the shelves and setting it all down on the table beside him, and Sydney closed the garage door behind them.

Ryan and April attached fist-sized jars full of amber-colored liquid to the bottoms of flat-ended devices that had once looked to her like garden hoses. Then they fetched red magic markers from jars on the shelves before them and turned to the mattress, before which Sydney stood, rolling up the sleeves of her dark red sweater. She'd also removed her shoes.

The two silently moved to either side of the mattress, uncapping their markers as Sydney gingerly stepped onto it, then closed her eyes and took a deep breath. She crept forward, keeping her balance atop the thick material. She reached its end, turned, walked back, then stopped and pointed straight down with both hands. "Heads."

April crouched and leaned in, estimated a roughly two-foot space along the mattress's surface, then looked up and saw Ryan doing the same. They nodded to each other, then drew red lines along the foam toward each other, meeting and overlapping where Sydney's weight formed a slope in the material. Although they worked very closely to her feet, they carefully avoided touching her.

Eyes still closed, Sydney crouched and got onto her knees, then shuffled backward until she was kneeling before the line. She leaned forward, her hands hovering over the mattress on the other side of the line before pressing into its surface. "Here." Her left hand patted one area, then she drew a circle on it with her fingertip. "Right here."

April traced her marker around that area, forming an uneven circle.

As she did so, Sydney patted another section of the mattress on its far side. "Here." Ryan followed suit with another circle.

Sydney's hands continued to glide over the head-end of the mattress. Her left hand paused. "Hm." April looked up in time to see Sydney's frown turn into a smirk, and she giggled. "Here."

April shook her head as she traced another, smaller circle in the indicated area, then drew an *S* inside it.

Both of Sydney's hands went back to the first, wider circle, and she leaned slowly in, looking almost as if she were going to sniff it. Her fingertips poked and rubbed over the fabric, and she indicated a few smaller areas, which April traced and marked accordingly, *A, N, N, C.* Then Sydney reached back over to Ryan's circle. *N, A, A.*

"Anxiety," Sydney muttered. "Fear. Anticipation." She nodded to herself. "Exams. And—here." Following her extended finger, Ryan traced a second line around the last one he'd drawn. "Relief." She opened her eyes and smiled. "She passed."

The red lines and lettered shapes were coming together to form a dense, intricate design along the end of the mattress, looking like an abstract topographical map.

Sydney stayed crouching, her narrowed eyes and upturned lips both curious and proud.

After a moment she stood and stepped off the mattress. "Go for it."

April and Ryan fetched the devices from the counter and returned to the marked-up mattress. April switched her own on, and a faint humming sound filled the air. Bending back down over the mattress, she pressed the device's flat nozzle onto one of the indicated shapes— an *N*—on its surface, pushed a button, and slowly began to move the device around the inside of the shape in small, circular motions. The light amber liquid swiftly darkened, as if ink had been spilled inside. She pulled the device away, drew an *X* with the marker over the spot on the mattress, then unscrewed the jar from the device and placed it back up on the counter. As she grabbed a new jar, Ryan came over with the fruits of his own labor, its contents a dark, clear green.

They set to work on a couple of other patches, and each came away with jars of dark blue.

Then they went back for more.

They worked at the indicated areas on the mattress for almost half an hour, producing seventeen extracts in total. Finished, Sydney washed her hands in an industrial sink in the corner of the garage. "Let's get on with the other one."

Ryan and April brought the first mattress back out of the garage and laid it against the side of the van. He'd bring it to a dealer in western Connecticut next week. He didn't know how extensively the mattresses were refurbished, nor did he particularly want to.

He pulled the latch on the back of the van, then hesitated, thinking of the rat from before, then tugged the door open quickly, stepping back. When nothing came scrabbling out, he let out a quick, shallow sigh.

He and April pulled on a new pair of gloves, grabbed the mattress, and hauled it into the garage.

"Yeesh, ugly one." Sydney carefully stepped out of the way as they carried it into the middle of the space, set it on its side, then let it flop onto the floor.

April gasped and pointed at it. "Ugh, not *again!*"

Ryan glared at her, then looked down, and his eyes widened as he saw another spider, identical to the one from earlier, was clutching the edge facing the garage doors. "The hell . . . ?"

"Whoa!" Sydney exclaimed.

"Do you have a towel or something?"

"A towel?"

"Yeah, something clean that won't interfere with your reading. I can smash it and—"

April sighed loudly. "Look, is there a spare jar or something?"

"Hold on, hold on . . ." Ryan moved forward and raised a leg to nudge the top of the mattress with his shoe. The spider scuttled forward, side to side, walking a dizzying path of uncertain direction before dropping out of view. He moved forward, ready to crush it into the concrete, then frowned.

"Where is it?" Sydney asked.

"It's—gone."

"*Where?*"

"I mean *it's gone.*"

"Is there a *hole* in the mattress or something?" April said in a small voice.

"Wait . . . hold on," Sydney said, moving closer. She reached out and tentatively felt along the side of the mattress. "No, no hole. None that I can *see,* anyway, and not big enough for the spider to crawl into. And something—" She fell silent, frowning.

Ryan watched her gaze fix on a point on the wall, her brow lowering, lips parted. She often did as much, but then her gaze dropped to the mattress, her jaw dropped open, and she snatched her hand back with a gasp. "Jesus!"

"What?" Ryan repeated.

"This . . . wow. There's—there's a *lot* on this one." She stood, staring at her hand.

"How much?" Ryan asked.

"Like, *a lot.*" Her gaze wandering over the stained, yellowed expanse beneath her. She crouched beside it and picked up a crumpled tag on its side, pulling it taut and squinting. "It's *saturated.*"

"Like the ones from that hospital?" April asked, still standing near the wall.

Sydney slowly rose to her feet. "More than those. *Significantly* so."

"Could it also be one from a hospital?" Ryan asked.

"Hospitals don't use queen-size mattresses," Sydney said. "At least, none that *I've* ever seen." She stared at the mattress for another minute or so, then looked up at Ryan. "Touch it."

Ryan frowned at her, and she raised her eyebrows in a silent urge. Taking a deep breath, he moved to the mattress, crouched, and pressed his fingertips against the material, which dimpled slowly in and swelled out again when he pulled his hand away. When nothing happened, he shrugged. "I don't—" Then he jumped to his feet. "*Jesus!*"

Worms, dark brown, glistening under the fluorescent lights, had appeared in the remnants of the dimple, and were squirming up out of a spot on the mattress.

"Wait." Sydney's voice was oddly calm.

Ryan couldn't do anything else as the brown, squirming lines fanned out like an ugly, unfurling flower, and then they began to separate from one another, leaving behind a bare patch of mattress at the center. It was then that Ryan recognized their movement: they were, in fact, *centipedes*. "Sydney, you're going to have to take care of those yourself, because I'm done with pest control for—"

"*Look!*" she hissed, and Ryan gasped.

One by one, they crawled and spread out until they spanned a good foot or so from each other . . . and then they vanished, one after another, atop the yellowed, stained fabric.

The room was silent as Sydney slowly, almost reverently crouched down beside the mattress again. "What *is* this?"

April shook her head as she uncapped her marker. "I don't get it."

"Me neither." Ryan pointed at the mattress. "*We* could see them."

Sydney, standing by one end of the mattress, her arms crossed over her chest, shook her head. "Normally, I don't *see* so much as *feel*. Like the one from the girls earlier, or the one from the crackhouse a few weeks ago—a *lot* of bliss was on that one, and a *lot* of pain. These are more like . . . *manifestations*."

April's eyes widened. "Like ghosts?" She'd come to accept a lot of impossible-sounding things as fact in real life, but even with all that, she was not quite convinced that there was any truth behind lingering spirits. "Ghost b-*bugs?*"

Ryan sighed. "We'll figure it out. Let's get this over with, shall we?"

April and Ryan positioned themselves beside the mattress. Sydney bit her lower lip as her gaze traveled over the mattress's stained but otherwise unimpressive surface, and then lifted one foot onto it and uncertainly slid it around. She moved forward and planted her other foot onto it and gasped softly. "Whoa. *Whoa*. This is—"

"Squishy?" April said, cringing.

"*Busy*. Wow. Um—right here. My right foot. Trace around my foot for now. Pretty dense, there."

April watched as Ryan crouched and traced an uneven outline around Sydney's bare foot. Sydney moved further into the mattress, then stopped, shaking her head. *"Whooh,"* she breathed. "Okay. Wow . . ." She bent down, held her hands out, and began to run them around over the material. April watched, waiting for some creepy-crawler to come popping out of nowhere again—but fortunately, nothing did.

Sydney snatched her hand back from the mattress and extended a finger, then twirled it in a wide circle over the vacated spot. "Here too."

April took care of it.

"And here!"

April shook her head as finding the head of the mattress grew increasingly difficult. At this rate, it seemed as if it might have been used on a floor by multiple people. Perhaps it *was* another crackhouse mattress.

Something small and dark drifted through the corner of April's gaze, as though Sydney had dropped or thrown something. She turned to it, then gasped and stood up. *"Fuck,* it's doing it again."

At first it looked like another wolf spider—but the longer she watched the fist-sized mass of dark brown, the more clearly she saw the fringe of writhing appendages clustered around its bulbous center. It was more jellyfish than arachnid, lifting and twisting about in the air with the slow, lazy motions that belonged under water. Her body gave a twitch, then a full tremble, as she watched the floating thing drift over the surface of the mattress—toward Sydney.

"Watch it!" Ryan snapped.

"Wait . . ." Sydney said, calmly stepping to the side of the thing's trajectory as it floated lazily past her, moving toward the opposite side of the mattress, where it disappeared.

"Will someone tell me what the *fuck* is going on?"

Biting her lower lip, Sydney crouched again. She pressed both hands down on the mattress, closed her eyes, and inhaled slowly.

"That mattress has seen a lot," April muttered. "More than we usually—"

"*Oh!*" Sydney gasped and spasmed, her torso wrenching upright, like she'd been sucker-punched.

"What is it?" April asked.

"Oh . . . God." Sydney's hands lifted beneath her agape jaw. "*Oh, God.*"

"*What?*" Ryan snarled.

"K-kids." She slowly turned her head, her gaze fixing on invisible points in the air around her. "Little kids. A bunch of them."

April and Ryan exchanged looks, and Ryan shrugged before saying, "What do you mean, like an orphanage? Immigrants? What?"

"No, they— *Ohhh!*" Sydney abruptly fell forward, dropping onto her hands.

April shuddered as Sydney spoke in a very low, very quiet voice, "*They're coming back.*"

Who? April tried to ask, but little more than a whistling breath escaped her lips.

"*Close your eyes, Wayne!*" Sydney said, her voice high and strange. "*Remember what I told you—they won't hurt us! They need us! We—*" She threw her head back and cried out, gasped, choked, fell silent, then dropped forward, burying her face into the mattress as she wailed, howled, whimpered, and sobbed.

"*Enough!*" April jumped forward and threw her arms around Sydney's midsection.

"Don't touch her!" Ryan shouted. "You'll—"

Sydney's head shot up, and she loosed a horrifyingly loud screech. "*He's here! He's* here!"

"Get help!" April shouted, and she could see Ryan rocking uncertainly on his feet. "*Go!*" she yelled over Sydney's cries, and Ryan finally disappeared.

Sydney began to thrash in April's arms. She bared her teeth and planted her foot into the mattress, tried lifting Sydney with all the strength she possessed—

—and then noticed movement around her. *All* around her.

An army of spiders scuttled out from hidden places on the mattress. Centipedes trailed up between them. Several rats skittered across April's shoes, squeaking and chattering. She kicked at them, and was horrified to hear their annoyed squeals, to *feel* the impact of her feet against them.

However and wherever they came and went, whatever they were— *these were real.*

More of those horrible jellyfish appeared, drifting about. A blurry cloud of pale, squirming, glistening grubs materialized and crowded the air beside her, producing soft, droning purrs. And then something else—something bigger—moved toward them.

April looked up, and though her jaw dropped wide open, her voice caught in her throat.

A naked man stood over them on the mattress. There was something big and dark hanging before his chest—no, set *in* his chest, growing out of it, a cluster of jagged, multi-jointed legs out of the most nightmarish arachnophobic terror, and his eyes glowed with the orange light of jack-o'-lanterns above his wide, toothy grin as he stepped forward, chuckling throatily as he leaned forward, reaching for Sydney.

"Go away!" April snarled, throwing a fist at his outstretched hand—

darkness and cool, musty air and the foul odors of piss and shit and something else, something earthy and old, all around the mattress on the floor

    beside the mattress, a huge hole in the floor, full of so much darkness

    small hands held each other, squeezing, shaking

    whispers, pondering, panic, despair, pain, pain, so much pain

    the singing began, two voices harmonizing

    PAIN, so much pain, screams and screams and screams

    one of the voices fell silent as blackness, shadows darker than shadows, begin to spill out of a small, upturned mouth

    a boy's feet twitch and begin rising, up, up, up, invisible hands pulling him into the air

    a girl thrashing and rolling about on the mattress, screaming and clawing at boils on her skin that rupture into bugs and spiders, a rat crawling out of her mouth another girl's hands grow long and black and thin and pointy, claws raking at the air

a boy shrieks as the wall before him ripples, bulges, then splits open like a suppurating wound

a girl watches the ground tremble and crack before her, swelling and rising jaggedly

and all the while, the man, the spider-chested man, touching their heads, their arms, their backs, grinning and laughing and laughing and laughing and—

A painful impact exploded against the side of April's head, and she saw Sydney's arm thrashing wildly about as she screeched like an animal.

April braced her feet beneath herself, threw all her weight up and back—and they pitched off the mattress and crashed painfully onto the cement floor, Sydney knocking the wind out of her.

Sydney's screams finally broke, dropping an octave and slowly devolving into a braying cry, which in turn warped into a series of whimpers.

April reached out and pulled her close. "*Shhhh, shhhh,* safe now. Easy. Breathe. *Shh.* I got—"

"*He's here,*" Sydney whimpered. "*He's* here . . ."

April shot a glance back across the mattress. The air was clear. The mattress was bare. The man was gone. Everything was gone.

"I-I can't work on that one," Sydney murmured, raising a glass to her lips in her shaking hands, which were once again safe inside their leather gloves. She wrinkled her nose at the acrid bite of the cognac, coughed briefly, shook her head. "It's—too much."

Ryan had returned to find April holding an unconscious Sydney on the floor of the garage. They'd carried her inside, but she'd regained consciousness on the way and, after a momentary panic, calmed down enough to let them lead her to one of the chairs in the darkened living room. A fire had been lit in the fireplace, and Sydney and April sat in the chairs facing it. Ryan stood beside Sydney's chair, his arms crossed over his chest.

"It's old," Sydney continued. "I didn't mention it before, but there was a tag on the side said something about 1983."

"It was sitting in an alley on the East Side," April offered. "But that could mean nothing. It might've come from anywhere."

"What the *hell* happened on it?" Ryan interrupted. "Seriously, Sydney, what *was* all that?"

"Oh, don't push her," a woman's voice said from across the room, and everyone looked up. "She's been through a lot tonight."

"There were kids," April said. "A *bunch* of them."

"You saw them?"

"When I grabbed Sydney, I guess I saw what she was seeing. Kids. They were being kept in a dark basement room somewhere." Her voice cracked as she said, "They were so *scared*. They were being tortured. And there was a man with—"

Sydney murmured something, and Ryan turned to her. "What?"

"Not tortured. They were being *auditioned*."

"Auditioned?" the fourth voice asked.

Ryan shook his head. "So what about all the bugs and things? What *were* all those?"

"Echoes," Sydney said. "Shadows. Imprints. Kind of like the extracts, but—different."

Ryan pursed his lips and sighed. He'd had enough excitement for one night. He didn't know what it all meant, and frankly he didn't want to. He looked at the far end of the room. "So what do you want to do with it? We barely got to map it."

"We won't extract from it."

"So it's garbage." Ryan's jaw tightened. "Two for the price of one. Great."

"Oh, don't you worry. I can assure you, you'll get your share."

"And the mattress?" April asked. "We can't let someone else use it." She glared at Ryan, as if daring him to contradict her.

The light from the fireplace was muted on the dark gray blouse that appeared, but it reflected off a gaudy necklace like a twinkling constellation. Despite the darkened interior of the house, she wore a pair of wide sunglasses, below which her thin lips lifted into a smile. "Oh no,

I'll hold onto it. As you know, I do have a penchant for . . . *fascinating* items."

Ryan and April went outside and walked back to the garage. Sydney stayed inside to rest a while longer.

April listened to the crunch of their feet on the gravel. The night air had gotten much colder, frosting the inside of her nose and throat as she breathed.

When they neared their cars, they stopped and stared at the closed garage door.

The mattress was still inside. They'd been told to leave it there, and that had been more than fine to April.

"I'm—not sure I can keep doing this," April said.

"I had a feeling."

"That obvious, huh?"

Ryan remained silent.

"It's kind of gross that we do what we do, as it is, but . . ." she shrugged. "I guess I never really thought about what we're dealing with until tonight."

"You *know* that that one was a fluke."

She turned and glanced at the dark property, where shapes continued to form and vanish in the darkness on its periphery. She huddled her jacket up around her shoulders. "*Was* it, though?"

When Ryan didn't reply, she walked over to her car and unlocked it.

"Good job back in there." She looked up to find him standing b his own car, facing her. "You kept your cool pretty well. Even after the spider."

She smirked, wished him a good night, and got in her car. She made her way down the driveway, past the gate, and out onto the road, already knowing that she wouldn't return.

What's Below Beneath

Welcome, folks, to another episode of *Peripheral Visions,* the show where *you* get to share your strange encounters of the unknown, the unseen, and everything in between. I'm your host, Jonathan Brown Menzies, and I'm currently reporting from a dog park on the East Side of Providence, Rhode Island.

Behind me you can see this very large metal wall of graffiti and rust. In fact, it's a lot more than a wall, but—well, I'll get more into that later. Oh, and, uh, you'll have to pardon my mask, and I apologize if you have any difficulty hearing me through it, so I'll try to keep my voice loud and clear.

As you've probably seen in my previous video, Rhode Island is currently in its third month of a "soft lockdown," following multiple reports of people coming down with a still-unidentified sickness in and around Providence this past spring. Hopefully the authorities will stop dragging their feet and clean this mess up soon, so we can all go outside and breathe like normal again.

So many of us have been stuck at home, facing the same walls and rooms and doors, day after day. It does a number on your mind, let me tell you—especially once you start paying attention to things that you normally take for granted.

That brings me to today's episode of *Peripheral Visions,* in which we'll take a glimpse into one of the oldest and strongest household sources of fear that most of us have faced at some point or another—basements.

Do basements creep you out? They're cool, damp, and dark, and sometimes crawling with bugs, spiders, and rodents. They are literally artificial caves built beneath your home—portals from the open, sunlit surface world to the secrets and shadows of the underground.

In today's submission, a casual laundry run led to a terrifying discovery directly beneath the narrator's feet.

This is . . .

"Why I Don't Go into Basements Anymore."

Since the Rhode Island lockdown started, everyday life has been flipped upside-down. Stores, restaurants, and schools are closed, or at best have severely restricted their hours—and sadly, with their sales and services plummeting, many businesses have been forced to close their doors forever.

Laid off from my own job, I'm living from one unemployment check to another. Money's been tight, and I'm struggling to keep ends meeting. But possibly my biggest struggle has been doing my laundry.

Although there's an open laundromat in my neighborhood, I don't feel comfortable spending tons of money to touch those machines that other people have been using. Who knows what kinds of germs might be crawling all over them— the mysterious disease included? For a while I tried to keep my clothes as clean and neat as possible, and hand-washed what I could in my bathroom sink— but I was only delaying the inevitable. After a few weeks I finally broke out my quarters and prepared to use the washer and dryer in the basement of my apartment building.

Like a lot of other buildings in my neighborhood, mine's a converted family home. I live on the first floor, and the basement door is at my back entrance, in the narrow hallway between my apartment and that of my neighbor, a girl I rarely saw even before the lockdown started.

I had to drag my overfull hamper into the hallway and awkwardly lug it downstairs. As I reached the bottom, I squinted back and forth along the concrete wall until I saw the light switch and flicked it up.

There was a single, naked bulb hanging from the wooden ceiling overhead. On the far side of the space, beside a set of rusty pipes stretching from ceiling to floor, stood the twin, pale shapes of the washer and dryer.

I hauled my hamper over to the machines and set it down, then threw in the first load. I started shoving in quarters when I heard a loud, sharp tap *that made me nearly jump out of my skin, and I dropped a few coins on the floor.*

I looked around, sure I'd see a rodent, but nothing moved.

After a moment I searched for the quarters I'd dropped. One was directly beside my shoe, and as I picked it up I spotted the other one lying under the edge of the washer. I tried to grab it, but my fingers accidentally pushed it deeper under the grimy metal.

Annoyed, I grabbed the top edges of the washer and pulled it away from the wall, grunting from the labor. I peeked over its rear edge, then cursed, still unable to see the coin, and gave it a few more tugs, until the hoses that connected to its back were stretched out in the air. I finally found the coin—as well as a wide, dark hole in the concrete directly beside it.

The hole was roughly two feet wide and perfectly round, the concrete edges smooth and going straight down, as if it were part of the floor's design. Although basements often have drains and other kinds of holes cut in them, I didn't understand why the washer was on top of this one—maybe it had a leak, and had been moved there?

I shrugged it off, then grabbed the fallen quarter and shoved it into the machine. I waited a bit, then got bored and went upstairs to play video games on my computer. I managed to do my laundry without any issue, other than shrinking my favorite pair of jeans a little. I didn't have a day job to take up my time, so I decided to come back with another load the next day.

Man, I feel this guy's pain on a spiritual level. When I first moved to Providence I had to catch a bus to a laundromat across town. Not only were the rides full of rather unsavory characters, the laundromat itself was grungy, and every quarter was worth its weight in—well, you know.

And now, with the lockdown? I don't blame him in the slightest for not wanting to go out. The outside world here is kind of scary right now, and nobody's properly prepared to deal with it.

For those of you from outside of Rhode Island, not much is known about the disease. It doesn't seem to have consistent symptoms, so it's difficult for the CDC and DOH to even confirm how many people have it. There are some weird, but thankfully unconfirmed, rumors going around about it, too, such as that some victims experienced strange, body-morphing growths and other physical affects.

Needless to say, I'd also want to keep my tasks as local as possible, creepy basement or not.

And as for the hole in the floor, that just sounds like a septic drain of some sort. My parents had one like that in their house's basement. But as to why the washer was on top of the one in this guy's basement, well . . . that *is* a little concerning—to say nothing of the noises coming from it.

The next morning I lugged my full hamper downstairs, stopping abruptly when I heard that strange sound again—a quick, sharp tap. *It reminded me of a snare drum, but deeper, hollower, and echoing. I stared warily at the hole as I slowly continued my forward shuffle.*

As I set my laundry down beside the washer and began to throw clothing inside, I thought it may have been a droplet of water landing into a puddle at the bottom of a well, or even rat clambering up an unseen pipe.

Then, as I was placing my change into the coin slot tray, I heard the sound again, and whatever was causing it. I straightened upright with a startled grunt as I realized it was coming from straight down inside the hole.

Whatever was causing the noise, I didn't want to hear it again. I stepped over to the washing machine and grabbed its top edges, then heaved with all my might, lifting and dropping its sides until it sat crookedly over the hole. For good measure I gave one of its sides a hard smack, and it thudded like a gong—but fortunately, there was no other sound.

I deposited my quarters and started up the wash cycle, then made my way back to the stairs, leaving the light on for my return. On my way up, I could've sworn I heard another, muffled tap.

Unexplained sounds get reported all the time. Somewhere in Connecticut a rumbling is sometimes heard coming from the ground, like an earthquake, but doesn't register on any seismic charts. For about a decade now, people have recorded the sounds of loud, trumpeting howls, hoots, and whistles echoing out of clear and unoccupied skies all around the world. I remember reading a report about distant drumming being heard in the woods in Maine a few months ago. The list goes on and on.

So I must admit that I'm a little weirded out by this guy's tapping sounds coming from a hole in the floor, especially here in the city. Although Providence doesn't have a subway, there's roadwork that seems perpetually unfinished here, especially on the East Side. Who knows what kinds of weird echoes that would make in the foundation of a nearby building? And to be fair, the subject never said anything about road work happening near his building, so it's perfectly possible that that's all that was. Regardless—it *is* a little creepy.

When I returned to put in the next load, I stopped short at the bottom of the stairs as if I'd run into an invisible wall. I sniffed at the air, flinching at the funky smell that I hadn't noticed earlier, a rich, sickly-sweet aroma. Even though I was wearing a mask, I had to wrap my arm around my face as I walked over to the washer . . . then came to a dead stop, my eyes widening.

The machine was crooked, its front turned almost fully sideways—revealing a foot-long crescent of the hole beneath its bottom edge like a grinning mouth. I told myself that the washer had probably shook and rocked around with its load, and wiggled off the hole, because I didn't want to consider any alternatives.

Holding my breath, I opened the door and took out my damp clothes, then used my hip to slam it shut. I opened the dryer and dropped everything inside. Then, turning the dials and letting out a heavy breath as it started, I gazed at the hole, staring intently at it for so long that I almost didn't notice something peeking up at me from behind the washer.

It was low to the floor and pale, its skin smooth and shiny. It inclined its elongated, eyeless head and seemed to stare at me. A hole opened in its tip, and something thin and dark shot out and whipped around in the air before snapping back into it, producing the same strange tap I'd been hearing.

I ran for the stairs and slammed the door shut. After a few panicked moments of pacing around my apartment, I called my landlady.

I can't say that I've encountered anything like what this poor guy says he saw in his basement, but I *have* had a few strange encounters of my own, and one of them comes to mind, the more that I think about it, as I read this story.

Actually, I don't even really remember much of what happened— only that once, when I was a kid, I wandered into some big, empty room somewhere. There were no lights, so only the ambiance behind me cast my shadow inside. Dust motes floated everywhere, and the walls were stained and filthy with trails of mucky water leaks. The ceiling sagged in places, and there were cracks in it. I kept hearing scraping noises, and some clicks and taps, and then there was this horribly loud—I don't know, *slurping* sound? I don't know how else to describe it. I don't even remember now how old I was, or where this room was, or why I was even there in the first place. I don't even remember running out—which now, in hindsight, is literally *all* I'd be doing if I were faced with that room now.

I just know that everything this guy is describing is giving me a *bad* case of déjà vu that's leading me back into that room.

Anyway . . .

My landlady, an older Portuguese woman, seemed confused by my report on the phone. She seemed to think it had been a cockroach, even though I tried to say that it was bigger, and more like an amphibian of some sort. In turn, she surmised that it must have been a big cockroach.

Annoyed, I asked if the girl across the hall, or any of the other residents, might have recently reported seeing anything. My landlady said that she hadn't heard anything—and what was more, that my neighbor from across the hall didn't live there anymore. This was news to me, as I hadn't seen or heard her move out; but apparently she'd fallen behind in her rent a few months ago and wasn't returning any of her messages. My landlady had sent her son to check in on her a couple of times, but she never answered. Eventually my landlady had gone over herself, only to find the apartment completely empty, as if nobody had been living there.

I didn't want to start going door to door with the other tenants about this, so I decided it might be simplest to take my landlady down and show her what I'd seen, and I begged her to come over.

She brought a big, heavy flashlight, like what police use. I was annoyed, sure that whatever I'd seen had retreated into the hole, and that I'd look like an idiot. I was almost relieved, however, that the smell was still very strong—if not stronger than before.

"Ai meu Deus!" my landlady exclaimed, and I could see her flinching above her mask.

I started to tell her that that was what I had smelled earlier when the tap filled the air, and I stopped a couple of feet from the stairs, staring at the washing ma-

chine and the hole beneath it—as my landlady walked past me toward it.

She pointed the flashlight down into the hole, shaking her head and muttering in Portuguese. I guardedly moved over, keeping as much distance between myself and the washer as possible. She shook her head again, looking up at me. I asked her what the hole was for, and to my confusion she said it was "new." When I asked what she meant, she said that in the fifteen years since she'd bought the building she'd never seen that hole, and didn't know how it had gotten there.

I grew nervous as she crouched down beside it, squinting. I told her to be careful, but she didn't say anything as she angled her head back and forth.

Then she looked up at me and said that there was an old, abandoned train tunnel under the city, part of which ran directly under our neighborhood. I knew what she was getting at, but before I could say anything the tap came again from behind us, and we both spun around to see the thing scuttling toward us.

It moved so quickly that it looked as if it had several sets of legs moving like insect appendages along its sides, its feet making flurries of quick slapping sounds on the floor as its long tongue shot out and retracted again—thwap!

We jumped back together, my landlady shouting "Ai Jesus!" over and over. I grabbed her wrist and tried to pull her to the stairs, but she didn't move. We watched as the thing moved past us, straight for the hole—and it scrambled over its edge and vanished.

My landlady ran back to the washer and grabbed its top edges, still shouting "Ai Jesus!" as she effortlessly heaved the washer fully back on top of the hole, despite her small size. She stood over it, panting, for a moment, then looked up at me with wide eyes.

I looked back and forth around the basement, then nervously up at the ceiling, expecting to find another of those critters clinging, upside-down, to one of the crossbeams like a massive spider, but there was nothing there.

My landlady pointed at the stairs and gestured for me to go first. When we got back up, she slammed the door shut behind us and drew the sign of a cross over her chest.

Just a quick reminder, folks—if you're enjoying this episode, be sure to hit the "Like" and "Subscribe" buttons below the video, so you'll be among the first to see the latest episodes of *Peripheral Visions,* in which I chronicle encounters with the unknown, the unseen, and everything in-between, as experienced by a viewer like *you!*

And of course, if you *do* have a story of something weird that you feel needs to be shared or investigated, shoot me an email in the link below!

I'd almost forgotten about my laundry until my landlady handed it to me in a plastic bag a few afternoons later. It was soggy and smelled funky, and I ended up taking it to the laundromat after all.

Later that week a contractor came by, and I heard him and my landlady speaking downstairs. There were no shouts of fear or sounds of feet running upstairs, and that afternoon the washer and dryer got taken out. The following week a couple of guys spent the better part of a day hauling equipment and supplies down and up the stairs as they plugged up the hole.

I never found out if it connected to the train tunnel that my landlady had mentioned. And despite numbers of searches on various sites about animals and cryptids, I have never identified that strange creature that we'd both witnessed.

Ultimately, the only thing that I know for sure is that I'm never setting foot in a basement again.

Well, if *that* didn't return me to my childhood days of being scared shitless in the basement at my family's house! I also live in a building with a washer and dryer in the basement, so let me tell you, right now, if I ever uncover a hole in the floor that I didn't know about . . . yeah, that'll be a giant *nope* on me ever doing laundry down there again.

Although I did my usual episode research for this story, I can't verify any of this happened—the subject wishes to remain anonymous, and would not verify any information about his location, nor anything about the missing girl from his building. And as to whatever the hell that thing from the hole was, I can't say for certain, without pictures, videos, or any other evidence. Sorry, dude—it's a great story, but I hope you understand that I don't fully buy it.

I should add one thing, however, and that is that I *was* able to verify one detail from this story—that train tunnel his landlady mentioned is not only very much real . . . it is what's hiding behind that graffiti-covered wall behind me.

As you can see, it's not a pretty sight. The ground before it is overgrown, flooded, and littered with garbage—but behind those metal walls is the entrance to a train tunnel, built in the 1930s and abandoned since the early '90s. It goes under College Hill, as much as a hundred feet underground, and stretches a full mile across the city, coming out on South Main. A matching wall on the other end sits beside a private parking lot. It's kind of sad, really, to know that this relic from the early industrial days of the twentieth century is sealed and buried and forgotten, directly below where people live and walk and sleep.

Sad, yes, but also kind of disturbing—for if something crawled into a basement from a hole connected to this tunnel beneath it, who's to say the tunnel itself isn't connected to deeper, darker places, crawling with all sorts of secrets, even further below?

Today is a relatively sunny day in Providence. There are some clouds overhead, a few vapor trails crisscrossing against the blue, and a couple of planes passing by. Birds are flitting about in the trees, and cars hiss and drone by on the street nearby. Any other year, this would be a day to comfortably step outside and breathe the open, fresh air of the sunlit world—but with the mystery disease on the loose and the subsequent lockdown, we have no choice but to stay home in buildings that, upon retrospect, might not be as safe from the unknown as we think.

If you enjoyed this episode, hit the "Like" and "Subscribe" buttons below, so you can tune in on my next story of the unknown, the unseen, and everything in between. I'm your host, Jonathan Brown Menzies, and this has been a tale of *Peripheral Visions*.

"Hello? Is Someone There?"

I don't know if I can convince you that any of this happened, any more than I have been able to convince myself. But after being followed out of my bathroom earlier, I've been stuck on my couch, makeshift weapons within arm's reach, staring at the kitchen doorway, awaiting your reply or *its* appearance—whichever comes first.

I remember my first instance of intently staring at an open doorway in my apartment. It had been in my early days with Louise, back when our relationship and the world had made sense. After watching a horror movie, I'd scared her by feigning terror at my open bedroom door, my eyes wide and my jaw agape—but after I revealed it as a joke, she'd told me that she didn't find it funny because of some of her own uneasy encounters.

Lately, I can sympathize.

We were in the middle of remotely watching a movie from our respective apartments when Louise had her first sighting of the night.

I'd gotten my first pair of glasses earlier that day and was in the middle of pushing them up the bridge of my nose when movement in the corner of my eye drew my attention to my phone, which I'd set up on a small tripod next to my bed. On its small screen Louise was frowning, looking somewhere out of view.

"You all right?" I asked.

A pale blur filled the screen, then stopped and materialized into the creases and joints of her hand. It lowered, and Louise sat upright in her bed, peering at something out of sight.

"Is it your nocturnal visitor?"

The only part of her that moved toward me was the corner of her mouth. *"Shhhh!"* I curled my lips inward, waiting patiently as she surveyed her room. After a long moment she took a slow breath. "Sorry."

I knew from previous instances that I should respectfully allow her to tell me about her encounters only if she was comfortable doing so—that she'd just as soon forget about the half-glimpsed shadow she'd spotted creeping about nearby. I didn't push for an explanation of what had led to her latest wide-eyed glance into the camera, and as usual, she didn't provide any.

We paused the movie and rewound it a bit, then took several minutes to bring our dinner dishes to our respective sinks. After we'd re-situated ourselves, we made sure we were at the same time on the movie, counted down, then hit play.

We'd perfected a system of remotely shared viewings over the past month and had successfully gone through three entire television shows and a film festival's worth of movies. And despite her certainty that her Massachusetts basement apartment was haunted, she was always the one who insisted we watch horror cinema.

I smirked as the movie resumed. It was a hokey, found-footage flick that obligatorily claimed to be tapes retrieved from a missing group of people—in this case, surveyors exploring an old mine in Pennsylvania. It was a complete work of fiction, although the acting and atmosphere were sufficiently immersive.

As the characters whispered, argued, and shrieked their way deeper into the gullet of the earth and began to go missing between convenient shots, I occasionally peered at Louise out of the corner of my eye. She sat with her face close to her phone, her cheek resting on her fist. Once or twice we made eye contact, and although we exchanged smiles, I could tell she was putting on her best game face while she kept her back turned to the kinetic unknown behind her.

She snorted as one of the characters—a tall, goateed young man— called out into a cavernous space, where a moment before, the camera had picked up something pallid and gaunt ducking out of view.

I turned to find her shaking her head. "These people . . . I can't."

"Want to stop the movie?"

"No, we have like twenty minutes left. I just can't get over how *stupid* they are. Even if this was real, listen to them." She puckered her lips and rocked her head back and forth. "'Oh, hey, I just saw someone—*clearly saw someone*—walking around this abandoned place! Let me go *ask them* if they're there!'"

"To be fair, how would *you* react in a—"

She rolled her eyes. "People don't do that in real life, hon. Only in horror movies—and these people are too dumb to realize they're doing it in their so-called *true story*."

"Fair point. It *is* pretty ridiculous when you think—"

A notification came onto my phone with a soft electronic trill. "One sec," I said, reaching for the small orange pill bottle on my nightstand.

"How are your migraines doing?"

I shrugged. "I've woken up nauseous in the middle of the night a few times, and I'm still rushing to the bathroom every couple of hours, but . . . I *think* the meds are working."

"Well, that's a start, right?"

I shrugged again, downing the pill. "I did have the beginning of one earlier, but I suppose my glasses might've exacerbated it. Nothing like a good lightshow to ruin—"

I fell silent as she twisted her body so quickly that I could hear the soft *pop* of her back. She stared at an unseen point for a long moment, then slowly turned back to me and smiled, shaking her head. "Sorry. Thought I saw something."

"So I gathered."

We enjoyed a good laugh over the movie's ridiculous conclusion, straight from the *Blair Witch Project* playbook of off-camera shrieking as the camera fell to the ground, and then agreed that the next movie we saw needed to be of reasonable quality.

"But how'll we know if it's quality?" I countered.

"There are all sorts of good rating sites."

I scoffed. "Yeah, because trusting the opinions of strangers on the Internet is always the best way to go."

"It does when it comes to health concerns."

I opened my mouth to protest, then forced it shut. It was a conversation I didn't want to revisit. Following a week-long series of strange illnesses that had struck several people in downtown Providence almost two months ago, Rhode Island's leaders became alarmed at the possibility of being the epicenter of some new and terrible outbreak. Soon the whole tiny state was put under a "soft lockdown," to monitor and quarantine all incoming and outgoing people, until the unknown disease could be contained and identified. No new cases have since been reported, but the air outdoors is still thick with unease.

Louise and I had only been together for a few weeks when the lockdown began. And even though she was thirty miles away, we didn't want to take any stupid risks. We did everything remotely, cooking the same meals in parallel kitchens, reading books "next to each other" in our respective beds, even taking simultaneous showers across the state line, with only electronic screens between us. But no amount of face-to-face time or words of affirmation and affection quite matched the real thing. And now, in our second month of being so close yet so taxingly far, we were growing restless.

"Well," I offered, "I do know of one movie with decent ratings."

"Let's do it."

As we got the film queued up, I saw her peering over her shoulder again.

I awoke the next morning and sighed when I saw the screen on the phone was black. We liked sleeping with our video chats up and running, so we could wake up to each other's slumbering faces. However, all I saw was a blinking notification of a text message. I groggily reached over and picked up the phone, frowning as I thumbed through to her message, sent at 3:37 A.M.

Sorry. It came back and I hid under my covers until it was gone, and we got disconnected.

"Sweetie," I said, the sounds of the toilet flushing behind me as I carried the phone into my kitchen. *"What happened?"*

Louise's face was a pale spectre floating against a field of muddy black on the screen. "Nothing."

I tightened my lips. "So you didn't see anything early this morning."

"No, I mean . . ." She looked away. "I *did*, but—it's normal. I'm used to it by now."

I moved into my living room and sat down on the sofa's armrest. "Sure don't *sound* like you're used to it."

"Yeah, but I mean, I'm getting used to what to do when—when it happens."

"It's clearly giving you anxiety. And *that* gives *me* anxiety."

"Way to be empathetic."

"Oh, come on. You know what I mean. I'm a little scared for you."

"Don't be. It's harmless. It just likes to . . . say hi sometimes."

I peered at the time on the top of my phone's screen and sighed inwardly, knowing I'd need to get ready for work soon. Even with the lockdown, my medical scheduling wasn't particularly thrilled with me working from home, since I was one of the few employees who lived in the same city as the office. "How did it 'say hi' this time?"

She inclined her head, her mouth working silently for a moment. "So you may have noticed I'm always facing you with my back to the room, like this." Her slender hand drifted into the screen and hooked a thumb over her half-visible shoulder. "My bed's positioned in such a way that I have to go past my dresser and bookshelf and sort of crawl into it. Because over *there*"—she pointed at the shadows surrounding her—"is a random metal pole that I guess is for support for the rest of the building. Sometimes there's something standing there."

"What does it . . . do?"

"Nothing. It just stands there and stares at me."

"What does it look like?"

"Can't tell. I've only seen it out of the corner of my eye. But it's thin and really . . . I don't know. I swear, one time I saw one of its arms lift up, like it was reaching for me or pointing at me."

I wanted to ask her how she knew it was staring at her, since she'd not gotten a good look at it, but I didn't want her to think that I wasn't taking her seriously.

"Anyway," she continued, "at least I don't have to look at it while I'm in bed. Only when I have to get up and go to the bathroom in the middle of the night. Or sometimes during the day when I'm working."

She was lucky enough to have a full-time remote job, but on days like this, when her attention was more concentrated on her surroundings, I'm sure she wished she had an office in which to hide away from her watcher in the dark.

"What do you think it is?" I asked. "Or who?"

She shrugged. "The ghost of some former tenant or something? I don't know. This isn't a very old building, probably built in the fifties."

"How often do you see it during the day?"

"Only a couple of times when I happened to be facing the pole. But I've—*felt* it. Like, you know when someone is nearby, while you're at your desk at work, zoning out in front of your computer? You hear something, like air pressure changing or clothes shifting, and you get that urge to look to the side, and someone's waiting for you there? I get that feeling sometimes. And of course, whenever I look, I don't see anything."

"I'm sorry." It was all I could think to say.

"Not your fault. Unless you *sent* him."

I shrugged. "Hey, *some*one's got to keep you company."

Louise extended her middle finger, and I blew a kiss at the screen.

That evening, after I took a shower, we made arrangements to chat online, but the moment I tried to call her up, the app notified me that she didn't answer. Frowning, I called her up again, and it once again hung up on me. I shot her a quick text to see if she needed some more time, thinking she was perhaps in the bathroom, but then my eyes widened when she replied, *Can't talk he's here.*

I lowered the phone and glanced around my bedroom, but there was no fourth wall to break in my helpless inquiry. Blinking rapidly, I thumbed in, *What's he doing? Can you turn on lights?*

A moment later she replied, *He's standing by my bed. He moved, Evan. HE MOVED.*

I cursed aloud and glanced around again, but when the posters and photographs on my walls offered no suggestions, I looked down again and saw a second message.

He's moving across the room. I'm standing at the far side, by the stairs.

"Go upstairs, dummy," I muttered, thumbing in a more polite version of the same urge.

A moment later I let out a breath I hadn't realized I'd been holding as she added, *He's gone. Can I call you?*

A moment later she was positioning herself in her bed, grunting softly and tucking a stray lock of hair behind her ear. "Sorry about that." She gave a quick glance over her shoulder before turning back to the screen, a strained smile on her face.

"So he . . . left?"

She nodded.

"How? Did he just vanish, or—?"

"He sort of backed up to the pole and . . . disappeared behind it, I guess? I don't know. It was weird."

I found myself thinking of vintage cartoon parodies of Frank Sinatra, in which he'd duck into view from behind streetlamps and mailbox poles. I shook my head. "That was kind of scary."

She rolled her eyes. "Why, *I'm* sorry, Evan! Did that make you feel uncomfortable?"

I suppressed the urge to roll my own eyes in response. I licked my lips and said carefully, "I didn't have a clue of what was happening. I hope you realize I *did* feel a little scared, myself."

"Well, just be grateful *you* don't have to deal with—" Her eyes narrowed, and she glanced away. "*Ooh* . . . okay, hold on." She began to move.

"Is he back?"

"No, bathroom," she grunted, heaving herself up and out of view. There was a blur of gray as her bedsheets and pillowcases shifted in and out of view. "Be right back!"

"All right!" I don't think she heard me.

My own stomach made a small, strained sound, but it wasn't a prompt to go to the bathroom—it was hunger. The trendy diet that Louise and I had started a few weeks before was still taking its toll on my system, as my carb-deprived body protested in naturally passive-aggressive ways.

I puffed out my cheeks and peered at the screen in time to see the bedsheets rushing closer, filling the view as the camera fell onto the mattress and rolled over. The tripod had likely toppled under the shifting foam from Louise's abrupt departure, and the view was now disorientingly sideways, the camera pointing at the foot of her bed. I could see the far edge of her bookshelf, full of paperbacks and hard-covers, and the space beyond, where the walls and ceiling disappeared into shadows and dust. Amid the shapeless dark, something black and narrow stood—the mysterious metal pole that was the haven of so much disquiet. I squinted, adjusting my glasses and grabbing my phone to get a better look at it, and as I did, the shadows seemed to shift and warp around it, likely in the glare of my room's reflected light, and I briefly imagined a figure thin enough to hide behind the pole, annoyed at being sighted. Curious, I raised my finger to the top of the screen and pulled down the settings bar. I dragged the dial for the screen brightness over a bit, and the glow intensified. Closing the bar, I peered into Louise's room again. The shadows surrounding the pole were muddier now, pixelated and even more difficult to dis-cern. One of them seemed to move, but as I stared at it, the shape warped back, bleeding and merging into its surroundings. I dropped the settings bar again and dragged the brightness to its full, glaring ca-pacity, then closed the bar and revealed two big, black eyes of anti-light peering out at me. I cursed loudly, smacking my hand against the phone and knocking it over on my bed.

"Optical illusion," I gasped, licking my dry lips. Tensing, I picked up my phone, but all that I could see was the pole again. I let out a long, heavy breath, and was relieved when I heard a rustling sound as Louise returned.

She softly cursed as she picked up her phone, which produced a series of loud scrapes, clicks, and pops. She turned it back on herself as she lay down and set it onto her bed, then immediately frowned at me. "What's wrong?"

"I'm hungry."

I had to order takeout for dinner—my nearly-empty fridge left me no choice. While I waited, Louise started preparing a makeshift fried rice dish.

"Do you feel safe ordering in?" From the vantage of the counter where she'd set her phone, I could only see her hand holding a wooden spoon at the stovetop.

"What do you mean?"

"Aren't you worried about . . . whatever the sickness is, literally getting *handed* over to you?"

I shrugged, although I knew she probably couldn't see it. "I figure restaurants have to be taking more health and safety measures than all the jackasses walking around outside like nothing happened. And I have some medical wipes. I'll just wipe down the container when it gets here."

"I don't know," she said, cursing as a bunch of rice spilled out of her frying pan and onto the stove. "I heard the disease is pretty wild. Nobody seems to know anything about it."

"Oh, come on, *someone's* got to know." I thought of the news bits I'd heard, from hair and teeth falling out to full-on physical disfigurements. There was even a rumor that some guy had melted like pizza cheese, but that was obviously an imaginative stretch. "At any rate, I'm not too worried about it. I just wear a bandana on my face whenever I have to go outside."

After a few minutes, I felt my bladder swelling inside my abdomen, and I excusedmyself, looking for somewhere to leave my phone.

"Want to call me back?"

"Nah, I'll be quick."

I set it down on my kitchen table, resting it vertically against the side of my coffee machine. Shuffling into the bathroom, I pulled the door shut behind me and did my business quickly, listening as Louise said something in the kitchen. I washed my hands and exited.

"What?" I called, but she didn't answer. I noticed, then, that the background hiss and crackle of her stove had fallen silent. "Well, *someone* gets to eat before someone else." I picked up the phone and frowned when I saw Louise's face staring back out from the screen. "What's wrong?"

She blinked slowly. "Did you come out of the bathroom, then go back in?"

"No. Why?"

She shook her head. "Nothing."

I tightened my jaw. "*Some*thing."

She bit her lower lip. "I thought I saw . . ."

"Your friend?"

"No. Not here. I thought I saw a shadow moving across the table. *Your* table."

I felt twin, cold fingertips travel up the sides of my neck. My lips tried to form a word, but no sound came out.

"Just a minute ago," she continued. "I asked you if you forgot something, but you didn't say anything, and then I heard the bathroom door open, and—here you are."

"Thanks," I muttered, glancing around at the doorway to the living room, then at the closed office door behind me.

"For what?"

"For giving *me* something to be paranoid about."

"*Paranoid?* Look, *you* don't live in a haunted basement. *I* do. I'm just telling you I saw something. Are your shades open?"

Annoyed, I glanced at the windows, where shafts of the day's remaining sunlight spilled between the Venetian blinds. "Yeah."

"So maybe it was a bird flying by or something. I don't know. I just know I thought I saw a shadow."

"Probably a bird. Yeah."

On a bathroom trip that night, I glanced over my shoulder at every darkened space behind me. Of course, nothing crept into the murky half-light, no figures ducked out of view, and no hands reached, finger by finger, around corners.

When I got into the bathroom and saw the shower curtain twitch and sway with what of course was the air pressure of the closing door, I sighed and walked swiftly up to it. I grabbed the fabric, black and printed with yellow squares in the shapes of city buildings at night, and tugged it open before me. No crouching menace pounced upon its surprised prey, and no creature twisted and glared over its shoulder at me. The only movement was the black shape that darted under the plastic liner bunched up on the far side of the tub and sent me pinwheeling back with a grunt.

My left hip smashed into something, and I spun, my arm smacking higher up against the corner edge of the cabinet. I groped with for the door handle behind me as I stared at the half-open shower curtain, but nothing else moved.

I cursed aloud, my mind racing.

Had it been a rodent? Perhaps a nightmarishly large bug of some sort? My first impression had been that of a coal-dark foot lifting out of view, but I knew that was impossible, even as memories of the skinny shape in Louise's basement crept across my thoughts.

"Enough," I muttered aloud. Glancing around, I grabbed a large, mostly full container of laundry detergent and held it out before me like a thick, short shield. If it was big, I would hit it. If it was small, I would smash it. And if it wasn't there at all . . . then I had nothing to worry about.

My bare feet lightly padded on the floor as I crept closer to the bunched-up curtain. I bit my lower lip, my hand trembling, the bottle jiggling. I stopped about a foot away, eyeballing the curtain, debating whether it could see me approaching through the dark fabric, then lifted my arm and swung the bottle's flat, wide bottom squarely at the lower end of the curtain, crushing fabric and plastic alike with a satisfying *thud.*

I jumped back, staring down at the hem of the curtain, waiting for the culprit to drop—or step—into plain sight. When no such thing happened, I rammed the front side of the bottle against the curtain, but still nothing emerged.

Forcing a few breaths into my tightened lungs, I finally reached up and grabbed the curtain and pulled it toward myself, then gave it a little shake before peering behind as much of the fabric as I could see before finally surrendering to my own embarrassment.

The next evening, after logging off from work, I glanced at my phone and sighed. I knew the inevitable conversation was best handled sooner rather than later, but I needed a chance to gather my thoughts before I told Louise.

I carried a couple of plastic snack wrappers into the kitchen, glancing at the closed office door as I threw them out, and watched a shadow moving beneath its bottom edge.

My gaze darted back to the lower edge of the door, where the white-painted plywood crowned the scuffed metal sill. The "office"—my vacant second bedroom—had been converted into a makeshift storage space, as well as a clumsy alternative for my sister or friends visiting from out of town from having to sleep on the couch. Boxes of books and magazines, printouts and receipts for my family's tax returns, and a massive plastic bin full of winter clothing crowded the floor space between my desk and overfull bookshelves. It was difficult enough for me to get around in there when embarking upon the nigh-impossible task of looking for, well, *anything*—and would be even more difficult for something to creep through.

Even so, I grabbed the nearest object I could—a frying pan on the stove, its surface and edges still caked with dried gristle—and cringed as the metal scraped and thunked noisily on the burner. I approached the door, lifting the pan beside my head, trying to visualize the best way to swing it at the intruder while using the door as a sort of shield. I reached for the handle and pushed the door in, swinging the pan like a misshapen hatchet—and cut only into the air.

I shot a glance to the right, eyeing the jagged passage between myself, a few piled boxes, and the far wall. I edged in along the space, keeping the pan raised, and spun to the left, where the only thin black shape that faced me was the row of crowded ladder-style bookshelves.

I shook my head and lowered the frying pan. I took a deep breath of the stuffy, stale air as I looked down over my chaotic collection. Recycled cardboard boxes still bore the names of online companies and different brands of liquor and wine, but with markered-on words to indicate their contents. Beside a three-high stack of boxes labeled *ART BOOKS—SELL, TAXES 2019,* and *RAM. CAM.—ALL,* the closet stood slightly ajar, a patch of inky black retreating deeper into its shadows the moment I looked up.

"Fuck," I breathed, lifting the frying pan again and moving toward the space. I stopped and switched the pan to my other hand, twisting and reaching back behind myself and groping at the wall until I found the overhead light switch. I flicked it on, a dull yellow glow settling upon everything except for the black crevasse. I reached up for the handle, channeling all the energy into my pan-wielding arm as I could prepare for a hard swing, and tugged the door open.

"So I have a theory." Louise licked her lips. "I don't think it's a ghost."

"All right," I said, peering at my bedroom doorway.

"Ghosts are stuck in one place, right?"

I shrugged, staring. "Uh, sure?"

"Evan, come on."

"Sorry, sorry," I turned back to the phone and let out a heavy breath. "Go on."

"I was watching some videos and documentaries about this earlier. Ghosts are generally situated to one place—where they died. But this guy—he travels. He's been in my basement, and now he's in *your*—" I must have been making a face because she snapped, "Will you listen to me? *He's there,* okay? You're seeing him, too, Evan."

I sighed. "I've seen *something.* But I don't think it's your shadow man."

"Okay, so what *is* it?"

"I don't know!" I barked. "I just know that the only thing that jumped out of my closet and scared the shit out of me was a goddamn coathanger." My thigh still ached with pain from the frying pan, which

I'd accidentally swung down upon it. "For all I know, it's my glasses, or my meds, or hell, even this diet!" I snorted, thinking back on my optometrist warning me about early illusions the glasses may give me during their maiden voyage. "It's a perfect trifecta of variables, sweetie."

"I like how quick you are to dismiss all this. Shows how much you believe *me*."

"I believe *you're* seeing something, over there. I'm just saying, I'm not. Besides, you're in Westport, and I'm in Providence. Ghosts don't travel over the Inter—"

"It's not a ghost," she hissed. "So who knows *how* it travels?"

"Look, I . . ." I sighed, closing my eyes. "I thought I saw something, the other day, when your camera fell over." I told her about the pole and the weird, thin shadow beyond it. "I'm not sure what it was, but I highly doubt—"

"But why didn't you tell me?"

"I didn't want to freak you out."

"Oh, yeah? Well, guess what? I *am* freaked out. This whole time I've been so concerned I've been going crazy, seeing things, whatever—and now *this*? *You've* seen it too, *and* now it's running around in *your* place?"

"It isn't running—"

"Wait!" Her eyes widened, and she inclined her head back, glancing around. For a moment I thought she could see it again, but then she nodded slightly. "That's it."

"What's it?"

"You saw it, here . . . and now you're seeing it *there*."

"I don't—"

"It travels by sight! That's it! It— Like, I don't know, it rides through people's perception, somehow? You saw it, so it was able to go from my place to yours!"

I bit my lower lip, trying to think of ways to avoid unintentionally downplaying her hypothesis while also trying to steer her from venturing too far down her own conceptual rabbit-hole.

"This actually makes perfect sense, now that I think about it," she continued. "People report seeing weird stuff all the time. Shadow people, the Hat Man, Slenderman—"

"Slenderman's an Internet myth," I quickly interjected. "You can track the exact website and author, and even the date and time, that it was created."

"Okay, fine, but *think about it,* Evan. All the same reports, the same kind of spooky shit, all from people who don't know each other. It's almost like—" She fell silent, her eyes seeming to grow even wider as she looked straight at me. "Aliens," she muttered matter-of-factly.

I couldn't stop myself from rolling my eyes even if I tried. "Seriously?"

"No, no, I'm not saying it *is* aliens, I'm just saying—what if this *explains* what people *think* of as aliens? Notice how they're always figures with two eyes, a mouth, two legs, two arms? What are the *odds* of all that? There's literally the infinite universe out there, where there's an endless variety of possible physiologies ... and the things that come down and visit this little pebble just so happen to be bilateral in form, like *us?"* She shrugged, her eyes widening.

I pursed my lips, waiting for her rant to end.

"Whatever these things *really* are, they're here, they're among us, they're observing us, and they're *spreading."*

I took a heavy breath. "Sweetie, I think you're—"

"What? *Crazy?"*

I rolled my eyes. "Oh, come *on*, I didn't—"

"Well, maybe I *am* crazy! Maybe I *am* seeing things, but that *doesn't* explain what you've *been* seeing!"

"I didn't see a shadow man," I said in as calm a voice as I could muster.

"Oh, but you *did. And* you *lied* to me about it!"

"But I didn't! Why would I lie about that?"

"Oh, I don't know! Why don't you tell me?"

"What are you getting at, huh? What can I *possibly* be hiding over here? Think I have another girl over here or something?"

Louise's eyes widened, and her voice lowered to a quiet mutter.

"Well, I don't know. If you've been lying to me about what you've *seen with your own eyes,* how do I know you're even telling the truth about *that?*"

My lips curled with a grim smirk. "Yes, Louise. You caught me. I have another girlfriend here, and we've been making you think your shadow man is now running around over—"

The video chat abruptly ended, and I snarled in frustration at the phone. I sighed angrily, then looked up in time to see a black outline disappearing around the corner of the kitchen doorway.

Any other time I would have escaped to a neighborhood bar after the evening I'd had, but with the quarantine, many public-facing businesses had become highly restrictive on their maximum capacities and hours, or even closed until further notice. My old dive, its walls, ceilings, and countertops festooned with nautical-themed memorabilia, was one of the latter—but even if they were open, I wouldn't have felt comfortable venturing out into the potentially contaminated air.

Such as it was, I spent the rest of the night with a bottle of cheap whiskey within reach, the TV in the living room loudly running sitcoms on autoplay, and every light on in every room.

I hadn't slept with all the lights on since I was perhaps seven and growing up in Massachusetts. A neighborhood friend from kindergarten had told me stories about a boogeyman in his home who wandered the house at night, opening doors and cabinets, and even once woke him by laughing in the dark at the foot of his bed. I hadn't wanted the boogeyman to come after me, so I'd done the only thing I could, and became very well stocked with flashlights and night lights.

I tried texting Louise a couple of times to apologize, but she was done talking for the night—and longer, as I soon found out. I ran through a mental list of different friends I could reach out to about this, including the one from my kindergarten days, but I didn't want to deal with the many likely questions, criticisms, and dismissals. I even debated calling my parents—but with less than four hours to midnight, they were likely already in bed. And besides, what would I even tell—?

My gaze darted from the television to the kitchen doorway to its left, and I suppressed a shiver.

I didn't see anything, that time . . . but I'd be lying if I said I wasn't waiting for whatever lurked around the corner to peer out at me, or to retreat into shadow if I were to approach.

I looked down at the box of pizza sitting on my coffee table, then up at the kitchen doorway again. I had consumed nearly half of it in my stress, but I didn't want to leave it out all night, which meant—

"I'm not even going to start!" I declared, sitting forward and grabbing the sides of the box. I carried it into the kitchen, my bare feet falling loudly upon the dirty carpet and dusty floorboards. I walked into the kitchen and straight to the refrigerator, which I opened and closed without an audience. I peered into the bathroom and, for good measure, walked in and whipped the curtain open, revealing only the shallow tub and the uneven tiles on the wall. As I passed the open office door, I glanced in at the piles of boxes and papers, clearly visible under the light. I re-entered the living room, smirking triumphantly as I glanced into my bedroom, then grunted loudly, backing up against the wall, my shoulders and head thumping painfully against picture frames as the very end of a long, thin shadow slithered beneath my bed.

Look, Louise, I'm sorry about what I said earlier. I don't want to text this all to you. I'd rather talk about it face-to-face. I'm not seeing anyone else. Even if I actually wanted to—HOW could I? I'm in the middle of a locked-down city, where everyone's practically afraid of radioactive mutation. I couldn't see anyone else if I tried—and I'm NOT trying, because I don't want to do that, because I'm happy to be with YOU. Okay?—9:03 P.M.

I understand that you're angry. I'll leave you be. Please message me when you're ready to talk again. Okay?—10:28 P.M.

Goodnight, Louise.—10:59 P.M.

I know you have trouble sleeping. Maybe you're reading this, maybe not. I'm having trouble sleeping, myself. I'm scaring myself half to death over here. Can we please talk? I could use the distraction.—11:14 P.M.

That sounded shitty. I'm sorry. I don't consider you a distraction. Please, let's talk.—11:21 P.M.

What tactics do you use on nights like this? I'm currently camping on the sofa with all the lights on and—11:58 P.M.

Sorry, final message for the night. I'm fine, banged my knee pretty bad. Since I still haven't heard from you, I guess I'll just wait for you to reply. I miss you.—1:42 A.M.

Good morning. I guess you're still mad. Please let me know when you're ready to talk.—5:36 A.M.

Thank Christ it's sunny. How are you doing, there? I'm getting worried about you.—8:20 A.M.

Louise?—10:14 A.M.

I started to type out another message, intended as a joke from our movie-watching experiences, but I doubted Louise was in the mood for humor at that point, so I deleted it.

I tried calling her several times, but I kept reaching her voicemail. I don't know what's happened to her. It's quite possible that she's also holed up in a household trench, prepared for a showdown against the shadows. Or maybe she's still mad at me.

I must have sounded like a lunatic with all my texts to her, but if I ever get the chance to talk to her again, I'll explain how I was, alas, *quite* scared, and felt that she was probably the only person who could understand, who truly *knew*, what I was going through—who'd also seen the otherwise unseen visitor.

I was certain I'd get a noise complaint for the sheer volume of my television that night, but mercifully I'd gotten none. Then again, it's only a matter of time before an isolated evening incident turned into an ongoing nuisance—for I certainly don't expect tonight is going to be any different.

After it had crept under my bed, I'd vetoed its game and closed the bedroom door—not that I expected such a measure to stop it from reemerging somewhere else, but I at least wouldn't have to keep a constant eye on the open door, through which it might sweep out and loom over me.

It had reappeared a few more times through the night. Once I found it ducking behind the open—and now closed—office door. Later I witnessed its spindly legs disappearing behind the open shower curtain. I'd held my bladder as long as possible after that, but when it got to be too much I'd carried a bright electric camping lantern into the room with me and set it on the edge of the tub, directly in front of the curtain. I'd slowly walked backward out of the bathroom, making sure it knew I was watching for it, only to spot it moving behind the refrigerator beside me. I'd slammed into the garbage can and did an awkward spin on my bare feet before the middle of my right knee precisely met the corner of the kitchen doorframe and made me nearly fall face down on the spot. I'd hobbled over to the couch and collapsed on it in agony and have hardly moved since.

I'm worried about the fact that my knee is only an angry red, although extremely sensitive to touch, rather than a swollen, yellow-black mess. I'm tempted to go to the hospital, but I can't imagine the crowds that may be waiting in the ER, full of people who were certain that their every pain, blemish, or other ailment is a symptom of the strange disease, which even then could indeed be lurking inside any one of them.

Then I thought of reaching out to you, to fill you in on all the things happening here. I don't expect you'll be able to do much from over there, if you even believe a word of what I've said. But here we are.

I have on the table in front of me a couple of frying pans, cans of soup and beans, a can opener, and a half-consumed case of bottled water. Five flashlights of varying size, the electric lantern, my laptop, and my phone charger complete my survival kit. I haven't figured out what I'm going to do when my bowels get the best of me, but for the time being I'm going the way of Howard Hughes with the empty water bottles.

I'm keeping the camera very much facing me here, with the retreating sun at my back and the rest of the room ahead of me, because— well, I don't want you to see the living room. I don't want you to see the kitchen doorway. During these fleeting daylight hours, it's the one spot in which it can hide. And when it finally emerges to achieve its purpose, whatever that may be ... I'll be ready.

But this isn't just for my own protection. What if Louise was right? What if it *does* travel by the eye? If *you* see it, it could wind up in *your* bedroom, in *your* living room, in *your* bathroom. Maybe it'll follow you around outside, hiding behind trees, beneath cars, and between buildings. Maybe it'll lurk directly behind you, mirroring your every movement.

Although—I hate thinking like this, but—what if Louise's other, even more worrisome theory is correct? If it *is* a visitor, some kind of big-eyed alien being from the shadows of the cosmos . . . who's to say it's the only one of its kind? What if this is only one instance of a larger invasion at work, around the—?

I need to go.

It's back.

The Archive's Wife

H ow's Oz the Great and Terrible?"
Caitlin threw a glare back at her brother, who was shrugging out of his coat by the door. His lips tightened and he muttered, "Sorry."

She turned to the window and crossed her arms over her chest. "Not funny, Josh."

"I said I'm sorry. But seriously, how's—how is he?"

She lowered her head, and her mouth parted in a huge yawn, as if her lungs had abruptly remembered their purpose.

Josh frowned, and his thick eyebrows lifted. "And how are—?"

"Can you just tell me what was so important already?"

He'd insisted, over text messages, that what he had to tell her was best done face-to-face, and since Caitlin had the rest of the week off, she'd asked him to come over.

"Right." She watched him walk across the room and drape his coat over the back of her couch, which he circled and dropped into with a soft grunt. "I think I might've found someone who can . . . do something about him."

She spun on her heel. *"What?"*

"Yeah. I called up a friend of mine, asked if she knew of anyone who might . . . know a thing or two about this stuff."

Caitlin's eyes widened. "What did you tell—?"

"Nothing, nothing. I mean, I told her that there was a . . . kind of strange thing going on at someone's house, but—"

"Who even *is* this friend of yours?"

"Nobody you know."

She'd feared as much. Since they were both little, her brother's tastes in friends had been questionable at best.

105

"But anyway, I told April that someone I knew—I didn't say it was you, don't worry—was dealing with kind of a . . . *situation* at their place, and that they were looking for the best way to deal with it, and so would she know someone who could help."

"Great, so I'm getting a visit from the Ghost Hunters?"

He sighed and rolled his eyes. "*No,* Cait. Like I said, I didn't tell her it was you. Anyway, she used to work with some folks who are into weird stuff, so I figured she might know who to talk to, and . . ." The hopeful grin that had crept onto his face died when he saw the look on hers. "*What?*"

"Really, Josh? 'Folks who are into weird stuff'?"

"All right, look. I have *no* idea what Ben was up to, and sounds like you don't, either. I don't know exactly what this person does or what they might have in mind. I'd have to ask April to even get their info. But honestly—do you have any better ideas?"

Her jaw tightened, and her eyes began to sting.

"I don't know," I went on, "if there's anything that can be done for him any more than you do. And not for nothing, but I'm trying to help *you* out here. So either—"

"Can you please . . ." Her voice cracked on the next syllable, and she closed her eyes, feeling the moisture building behind her eyelids. "Please, just . . ."

"I'm sorry. I didn't mean to—"

She shook her head, lips tightening, and waved an unsteady hand before her. He sighed. "I'm sorry, Cait. Let me know, okay?"

Her eyes still closed, she nodded quickly. She turned back to the window as the first tears began to spill onto her cheeks. She waited for him to leave, and when the door clicked shut she opened her mouth to release a shaky whimper, and all the other sounds that followed.

After a dinner of wine and scraps of reheated lo mein, she fetched the pillows and sheets from the messy pile atop her bed. She saw the sweat stains on the pillow and sighed. She hadn't changed the sheets—hadn't even slept in the bed—in almost a month. She glanced warily at the closet door beside her dresser, biting her lower lip.

Oh, just get it over with.

She twisted the handle and pulled it open, the stale air of dust and neglect meeting her nostrils. She pushed on a small plastic dome near the top of the door, and pale light illuminated the space. Snatching up a stack of bedsheets and pillowcases, she stepped back from the open door—then paused, inclining her head.

A few seconds of silence, then it came again—a quiet double-syllable.

No. She'd not heard her name. She'd made that mistake before. Her therapist had called it "associative mourning."

Then it repeated, and she threw the sheets on the bed as she all but ran out of the room.

Her feet began to drag as she walked down the hallway and stopped before the guest room door, which had remained closed for the better part of two months. She managed to lift her hand halfway to the doorknob when the murmurs beyond reached her ears.

Holding her breath, she twisted the knob and pushed the door open, and the sounds grew louder. She reached inside, her unsteady fingertips groping along the wall until she found a switch.

The overhead light had always been too bright, filling the room with harsh luminescence. She and Ben had opted for a bedside lamp, but on those rare occasions that she entered the room she used the overhead—not that she had much choice, and not that it really mattered anyway. Half of the room was in perpetual shadow, the very air devouring any ambient light at the far end. The head of the bed was a murky shape in the gloom, and beside it, where the bedside lamp may have still stood, the darkness was almost solid.

What was left of Ben hadn't changed since she'd last laid her tearful gaze upon him. He frowned out from the shadow, his features gray under some secret illumination. Beneath his furrowed brow his eyes were joined pits of the same ink-black gloom that surrounded him, his gaze unreadable, and under an aquiline nose and slackened cheeks his mouth was as dark as the rest of the shadow, an amorphous oval that shifted and worked with a deep, raspy voice that seemed to come from the very air around her.

"The infinite similitude of time is a void concept." His voice was a monotonous drone coming from a distant shore. Swallowing hard, Caitlin took a deep breath. "Within, as without, the creed dictates infantile paths along which creep—"

"You called?"

As always, Ben fell silent, his lips going still. She waited knowingly, and then he resumed. ". . . unilateral consciousness's perceptions of progress, a garden not unlike that described by—"

"Josh gave me info from someone who might be able to"—help, she wanted to say. "Someone who might be able to do something about . . ."

Her eyes felt as if they were swelling, and she turned her gaze to a nearby painting as he resumed speaking, something about accurate writings. Then she switched off the lights and left, pulling the door shut behind her.

To: jpdunce@ . . .
Re: Archiving #7

Hi, it's me again. I suppose you should know, the results of your little experiment are not going to be around for much longer. Whatever you two were doing has failed—and now it's going to go away, forever.

I've gotten good word that

Caitlin took a heavy breath, glanced at her empty wine glass, then sat back on the sofa, her fingertips lightly tapping the keys on Ben's laptop.

What, exactly, was the "good word" she'd gotten? What did she even expect would, or could, be done about the shadow in the guest room? Would anything she wrote even break "jpdunce's" silence, after all this time and so many messages that she'd fired off into the void of the Internet?

She'd found several messages to this person in the sent messages folder of Ben's personal email account. Each bore the word "Archiving," with sequential numbers, in the subject line. The bodies of the messages read like the nonsense perpetually being muttered in the guest bedroom—lengthy, verbose strings of descriptions about distances, spaces, passages, shapes, and journeys.

She stared at the open email screen, then minimized it. Her own face stared back from a photo that Ben had captured of her, her head half-turned, wide lips parted mid-laugh, eyes peering over her glasses with a combination of amusement and adoration. Beside her the TV was on, and although it was blurry, she could still remember the episode of Parks and Recreation that had been playing. She'd always found her image in the photograph to be unflattering, but Ben had loved it.

Her gaze traveled over the various icons and folders on the screen. She'd already perused all the files and pictures on his computer. No scandalous surprises awaited her—only more of the same confounding data and notes with which he'd filled several journals and folders in his office. He had lists of websites and books about various geographical locations and history. There were saved articles and ebooks about occult practices and pseudoscience. A folder was dedicated to a seemingly random assortment of photographs, of construction sites, stone walls, forests, wells, and maps.

Whatever the hell he had been archiving, he had been deep into it. But after the first couple of weeks since ... whatever happened, she had reluctantly abandoned all prospects of making any sense out of it all.

Caitlin snapped the laptop shut and stuffed it into the midst of the unread magazines beneath the coffee table. She twisted and fluffed the pillows, then pulled the quilt off the back of the couch and threw it over her legs. Switching off the nearby lamp, she curled into a fetal position and closed her eyes. But sleep, as usual lately, was a long way off.

The next morning she washed her hands of the feeling of Ben's face that had lingered upon them from a dream.

His face had been speaking between her outstretched fingers and thumbs, his skin a healthy if pale shade. He'd been recounting one of his favorite stories of their early days—of going to a used bookstore in Providence, and how excited he'd been to find a vintage Tarot deck featuring Jungian archetypes. She'd felt his cheeks tighten in a grin, had awoken with a smile on her face that subsequently caved under the weight of tears.

She picked up her phone and saw a text from her brother waiting for her, sent in one of the ungodly hours past midnight. *Any thoughts?*

She realized she was still running water from the sink—a recent habit. She twisted the handle, and as the water thinned into a leaky drip, she began to hear the droning murmur from the other side of the wall.

The voice fused with Ben's face from the dream, and she abruptly remembered him saying, *Remember that?*

"Remember . . ." she muttered, her gaze traveling, following an invisible trajectory, and then she left the bathroom and stood before the closed guest room door.

Forcing one of her balled fists to unclench, she seized the door handle and pushed it open. "*. . . except in the case of the southern windows, through which can be glimpsed the passages to what some have dubbed the Great Plains of Dimside. It is there—*"

"Hey." She felt the corners of her mouth tugging downward. Ben fell silent, and she swallowed hard and quickly added, "Remember that time we went to that Chinese restaurant downtown, next to the Dean Hotel?" Her eyes were kissed by gentle stings as she added, "I forget the name. But we got those spicy udon noodles, and I almost burnt my tongue out?" The corners of her mouth twitched in a confused state between a smile and a frown.

After a moment Ben resumed.

She clenched her teeth and blinked, her eyes feeling like they were swelling. "And the drinks we got weren't helping. You got a—I think it was their equivalent of a Moscow Mule? And my drink, I didn't even think about it." She snickered, beginning to cry. "It had so much sugar that it made my mouth feel it was literally on fire." She wiped her fingertips across both cheeks. "Do you remember that, Ben? *Do* you?"

His face remained still and silent, and then: "*Acknowledgment of the residents therein is advisable only in the presence of a common ground upon which . . .*"

She placed a hand over her eyes and let loose a breathy whimper, then gasped it back in.

Jesus Christ, just message Josh.

Her shoulders quaked with a sob and she lowered her hand, blinking rapidly to let the rest of her tears loose. If Ben was watching, he no longer cared—or no longer knew how—to respond to seeing her like this. Once he would have approached her, arms lifting, his voice gently saying *Hey . . . hey-hey-hey, it's—*

She froze, her eyes fixed upon the darkest part of the shadow to the left of Ben's face. Had something moved?

Had he shaken his head, or even raised a previously unseen hand? "Ben?" She stepped closer.

The only part of him that moved now was his mouth as he resumed speaking. She stepped within arm's reach, then inclined her head. When his cheekbones and forehead flexed and shifted in the unknown light, she narrowed her eyes, staring into the blackness that surrounded him, and gasped as something moved, a faint flutter of shadow against the solid black. She staggered back, blinking quickly, then forced herself to lean in again.

She'd never gotten this close to the shadow, had been afraid to touch it—if it could even *be* touched. What would she feel if she were to reach past him? Cold air? A breeze? Something damp and squirming? The wall? She wasn't about to find out, but if she could somehow *look past him . . .*

She knew there was no point in bringing a flashlight over: she'd tried shining one into the shadow dozens of times before, only for the beam to be inevitably swallowed by the too-solid darkness.

Leaning in until his face was mere inches beside her own, she fixed her gaze on a point in the amorphous darkness and waited—but not for long. The shadows shifted again, blossoming with motion, reminding her of aquatic movements, and all at once the shape vanished.

She let out a breath she'd not realized she'd been holding as she straightened, and the motion came again.

With a wordless exclamation she leaned forward again and glared into the dark, her eyes narrowing. She traced the receding motion, waited—and was rewarded with a new, rippling shape. It was too quick to get more than a fleeting glimpse, but her eyes registered several long, thin tendrils, their circumferences lined with narrow bands. She was reminded of swaying ropes, of swimming fish, of eels, of snakes . . .

She pulled back and straightened, suppressing a shudder, then walked back into the living room. Snatching up her phone, she texted Josh.

She was in such a daze when the woman with sunglasses introduced herself that she had already forgotten her name. The woman said that an associate of hers would normally be the go-to person to investigate a situation such as this, but since they were unavailable, she'd come herself.

Unsure of what would be proper etiquette to welcome the strange, sharply dressed woman standing at the front door, Caitlin uselessly fluttered a hand behind her.

"Show me."

Caitlin stepped aside as the stranger walked by, not bothering to remove her huge, round sunglasses as she entered the condo. She led her into the guest room but stayed by the door as the woman approached the shadow with slow, deliberate steps.

"Fascinating," she said in a voice so low it was practically a breath, and when Ben fell silent, she hummed faintly.

Caitlin crossed her arms over her chest and glared at a pair of canvases on the wall that unevenly portrayed the two ends of a bridge at sunset.

The woman's reaction was *exactly* what she'd been dreading when she'd messaged Josh the day before—all the clinical, impersonal poking and prodding of a curious scientist.

"How long has he been like this?"

Clenching her jaw, Caitlin muttered, "Since the first week of August."

"And how—"

"I don't know, miss. I came home from work one day, and there he was. I've tried for months to make sense of what happened, including simply trying to talk to him. I don't even know if that's really him or not! So, if I had *some* clue, *any* really, I—"

"Mrs. Burdick." The woman still had her back turned to her, one gray-sleeved arm raised, a pale, slender index finger extended on her jewelry-laden hand. "I only wanted to ask how *you've* been holding up?" In the silence that followed, she lowered her hand. "But please continue."

Caitlin turned her gaze back on the paintings. "I thought I smelled something burning, but I didn't see any smoke or anything, and the smoke detectors weren't going off. I knew Ben was home, because his car was outside, so I started calling for him, and then I came in here and—" Her voice cracked, and she looked down at the carpet. There was a small indent in the hardwood floor beyond its edge, where a vase had fallen and broken.

Taking a heavy breath, she explained everything else that she'd found. The emails, the notes and pictures, and the ever silent "jpdunce."

A soft shuffling sound arose, and the woman's feet appeared. Caitlin looked up at her, eyebrows twitching in a concealed frown as she saw her face peering back from twin reflections on the woman's black lenses. "What have you tried to say to him?"

"Memories. Things we did together. Places we'd been."

The woman nodded slowly, blond locks rising and falling over her shoulders. "Perhaps . . . that isn't what he wants to talk about."

"What do you mean?"

The woman walked back to the shadow, crossing her arms and inclining her head. She listened to Ben's droning words for a moment, then asked, "Where is the nearest access point?"

As Ben fell silent, Caitlin pursed her lips and turned away, her eyes stinging.

"Forty-one point eight-two-four-five degrees north," Ben muttered, and Caitlin spun around. *"Seventy-one point four-one-one-two west."*

The woman turned to peer through her shades back at Caitlin, her thin lips parting into a toothy, canary-eating grin.

Caitlin realized her jaw was hanging loose as she said, "What the *hell* was that?"

The woman turned back to Ben. "Is it currently open?"

"A window can only be closed against the elements enough to—"

"What is he talking about?" Caitlin snapped. "What are *you* talking about? What *is* all this?"

The woman held up a hand while she listened to the rest of the statement. Ben fell silent for a long moment, then began to speak again, seemingly changing the subject. The woman turned and walked to the back of the room. Although Caitlin couldn't see her eyes, she could tell she was pondering something.

"What's going on?"

"I don't think he was archiving anything, or even researching an archive. I think he *is* the archive."

"What—what do you mean?"

"I think he's been . . . *augmented*, if you will, into a database, of sorts. An interactive almanac."

"Become a—?" Caitlin shook her head, frowning.

"He speaks English—his native tongue, I assume, yes? I think that whatever kind of knowledge he was seeking, he found it." She turned back to the shadow. "In a manner of speaking, he *is* it."

"No. No! You're saying he became—*that?* As in *that's* what he *is* now? Like, he's not . . ." She couldn't say it.

The woman's lips tightened, and Caitlin closed her eyes and looked away as she began to cry. She felt a cool hand slip into hers, and it gently squeezed.

The woman was saying something. Caitlin shook her head. "What?"

"I asked if I could take a closer look at him."

"Yes. Sure."

"Thank you." The woman released her hand and moved back to the muttering shadow, her hands half-raised by her sides, as if tiptoeing into a church. She elevated her left hand toward her head, the smooth metal of her bracelet a twinkling star against the void as she removed her shades. She hummed faintly, her other hand lifting toward the shadow—then she gasped and stepped back, both hands dropping to her sides.

"What's wrong?" Caitlin's eyes widened.

"I . . ." The woman cleared her throat. "I think I saw something significant." She turned, her expression unreadable under her slightly crooked sunglasses. "Do you have a long, narrow object that I could use? A broom, for instance?"

Caitlin's mouth worked as she shook her head, then she turned and made her way into the kitchen. She pulled open the pantry door and snatched up the first narrow, vertical object she could reach, then returned to the guest room.

The woman was standing by the door, staring at the shadow. Caitlin offered her the—mop, she now saw—and the woman's head looked down at it. "Oh."

"Sorry, did you literally mean a broom?"

"This will do." Her thin fingers wrapped around the white plastic, and she moved slowly back to the other end of the room, rotating the mop until its rubber handle pointed out like a javelin. Stopping several feet from the edge of the shadow, she moved her arm slowly forward, until the end of the handle began to sink into the murk. Caitlin wasn't surprised to see the mop handle's length disappearing into the shadows—

Thud.

The woman's arm stopped, then slowly pulled back, and moved forward again.

Once again a dull impact as the handle rammed into something solid—followed by a metallic clatter.

"That's a good sign," the woman murmured.

"What is?"

The woman poked the mop handle into the darkness a few more times, then stepped back, turning, and raising it upright. Its dull gray rubber looked no different than usual, though neither of them made a move to touch it.

"Whatever the actual nature of this is, it's not solid. It's literally light and shadow. A projection. I've seen something similar to this before, but—"

Caitlin stopped listening as she turned to the back of the room and stared at Ben's face.

Remember our first date, Ben? We went to that bao place downtown. It was early February, I think. Almost four years ago now . . . God. It was so cold that day. My teeth were literally chattering.

And then when we got inside, you were so confused about the bao. I think you said something like, "I thought you said we were going for dumplings!"

We got some good stuff. You were crazy about that curry pork one, and the red bean dessert ones.

I remember the way you were looking at me. It was cute. I was trying to keep in mind that we didn't really know each other, but it was hard not to return that look.

Kissing you outside, in the cold, was—okay, it was awkward, I won't lie. I think you weren't sure if I was trying to open my mouth or something. I remember feeling your tongue, but I didn't use any. We talked about that later. "Saving bases," you called it. Remember?

Remember that?

Do you remember any of it, Ben?

Do you even remember me?

When he didn't say anything, her face crumpled into a sob. "Do you remember *anything* other than whatever the hell you're going on about, Ben?"

Two days following her visit, the woman had called Caitlin with news that she had found a possible lead for Ben's removal. Then she'd called again that morning with unmistakable pride in her voice.

Ben resumed his latest catalog. ". . . *ideal conditions of these cordyceps are high moisture and cooler temperatures, but this can vary, depending upon the age of the substrate . . .*"

Caitlin turned away, sobbing. She took a shaky breath, then muttered, "They're taking you away, Ben. That lady said she figured out a way, and tomorrow they're going to take—" A sound between a grunt and a click emerged from her throat, and her jaw snapped shut, her lips squirming.

As the droning resumed behind her, she squeezed her eyes shut and sniffed back tears. "I don't know how to do this, Ben. I don't know what to do. Do—do you have any advice for that?" Her eyes flew open, and she spun back to him. "How do I move on, huh?" she shouted. *"How?"*

He said nothing.

"No answer for that? *Nothing?* How fucking useful!" Silence.

Her jaw trembling, she took a slow, even breath, then asked in a low voice, "What does Caitlin Burdick do when her husband, Ben, has been—uh—*augmented* into—into an—*archive?*"

When the silence began again, she didn't wait to hear what he had to say. She pressed her palms to her ears and fled the room.

She opened the door and was startled to see a balding, middle-aged man standing before it. She didn't recognize his ruddy, tired-looking face, but the dark, wraparound sunglasses were indication enough of why he was here.

"Is she coming?" she said.

When the man didn't say anything, she looked down and saw he was holding a large cardboard box.

Setting her jaw, she stepped back and watched him move past her, his baggy trousers making soft brushing sounds as he entered.

"You'll have to forgive him," the woman said as she appeared at the door. "Being social isn't one of his responsibilities. Or strong points."

Caitlin shook her head. "Go ahead."

The woman's lips tightened, then she led the man into the hallway. Caitlin closed the door and followed.

When they reached the guest room, the woman pointed inside, and the man entered. She watched him for a moment, then turned to Caitlin. "It's up to you if you want to witness this or not. I'll understand fully if—"

"I'll . . ." Caitlin flapped a hand toward the open doorway. "I don't know."

"That's perfectly fair," the woman said, and entered the room. A moment later a scraping sound came from inside, followed by a muffled thump.

Caitlin balled her fists at her sides, chewing on her lower lip, then took a step toward the door.

There came a metallic rattle, followed by the woman's voice. "There, try the front corner first."

She remembered Ben laboring under the bathroom sink once, when they'd first moved in—how he'd insisted on taking apart the clogged pipes himself.

"Good," the woman said. "Now rotate it about forty-five degrees and . . . perfect."

"Jesus Christ," Caitlin muttered, squeezing her eyes shut, feeling tears slide down her cheeks.

"Are you doing okay out there?" the woman asked.

"Mm-hmm," she lied.

"Now just take the—"

Caitlin.

Her eyes fluttered open.

Caitlin.

"What?" She raised her voice and called, *"Ben?"*

"Pardon?" the woman asked.

"Did—did he just say my . . . ?"

"We're almost done," the woman said, and then in a much softer voice, *"Fascinating."*

Caitlin darted through the doorway, then stopped a few feet in.

The woman was standing near the back of the room, and the man was crouching before her, the cardboard box behind him, its flaps open. His arms were above his head, but lowering, and between them something smooth and clear sparkled in the—

Caitlin's eyes widened.

She could see the back of the room. The bed, the lamp—everything was perfectly, beautifully visible in the overhead light. "What the—?"

"It was as I suspected," the woman said, watching the man crouching beside her. "All light and shadow. Just like putting a shade on a lamp."

The man reached down past his bent knee, then slowly rose and turned—and Caitlin's eyes grew even wider when she saw the domed glass and highly polished cherry wood of a vintage bell jar—and the black, mercurial cloud that it contained.

"Is—is he . . . ?" She raised a trembling hand toward the bell jar but was unable to flex her fingers enough to point.

The woman walked before her and stopped. "Yes."

She swallowed hard, watching the man slowly lower the bell jar into the cardboard box with graceful care. She shot a glance at the back of the room. "And . . . ?"

"The air and surfaces are perfectly clean."

Caitlin let out a long, heavy breath, her gaze fixing on a dark shape at the head of the bed before turning back to the woman, who was holding out her hand. In it was a long, rectangular sheet of paper.

"It's the least I can do," she said in a low voice. "The very least."

Taking the sheet, Caitlin was unable to make sense of the string of zeroes at one end.

She looked up at the woman, at her twin reflections in her shades. Beneath them, the woman's lips tightened. "My deepest condolences, Mrs. Burdick."

They may have spoken further, or they may have remained silent: Caitlin would never remember for sure. She would only remember seeing the man lifting the box and carrying it out, the woman following him. She saw them both to the door, then returned to the bright, silent room.

She walked to the bed, staring down at the shape left on it before gingerly picking up the folded fabric. She hadn't seen Ben's Pearl Jam shirt all this time. Beneath it was a folded pair of jeans. As she picked them up, a belt slid off and clattered noisily on the floorboards. She bent and reached for it; then her hand paused and reached into the shadow beneath the nightstand.

She turned and sat on the edge of the bed, lifting her hand to her face. She slowly turned the smooth metal ring around between her fingers, then pressed it to her chest and closed her eyes.

He Walks This Road at Night

*I*n the southeastern corner of Massachusetts a cluster of townships make up the 556-square-mile area known as Bristol County. A drive along Route 44 from Rhode Island brings one through the towns of Seekonk, Baker, Rehoboth, Taunton, and Raynham—but what most may not realize is the unique area through which the highway cuts.

Where the towns of Seekonk, Baker, and Rehoboth meet is a stretch of Route 44 that locals have dubbed "Three-Corner Road." The very structure of this road is significant, for it is a breach into the structure of the land itself, where the interconnected borders of the towns should otherwise so neatly meet.

The breach of a border allows the dwellers from one land to spill out into another—and so it is rumored that on Three-Corner Road there is a breach between worlds, between the present and the past, and the living and the dead—and on occasion the spirits of the deceased sometimes wander into our humble land.

There have been numerous spirits spotted along Three-Corner Road in Rehoboth. The Village Cemetery has seen a gaunt man in a Victorian outfit standing over one of the graves, sobbing and laughing hysterically, and accosting and even chasing unknowing visitors away before mysteriously disappearing.

In this same cemetery, the disembodied voice of a child can be heard giggling from between the stones, always evading a curious witness's scrutiny.

And further along, only a hundred yards into the woods, stands Anawan Rock, which saw the surrender of Pocasset war chief Anawan to the British army, marking the end of the battle between the indigenous people of New England and the invading colonialists. To this day, sounds of chanting and war cries can be heard from the very air surrounding the megalithic stone. Fires can be seen burning on and around the rock, only to disappear when sought out, and conversely, sometimes the smell of campfires can be traced without any visible source.

However, perhaps the strangest occurrences of Three-Corner Road can be found on the mile-long stretch that cuts through the southernmost corner of Baker . . .

—James Richardson, *The Ghosts of Bristol County*
(Swamp Oak Press, 1991)

Jim climbed out of his truck and gazed at the legend-haunted highway. A large, dark blue sedan that had trailed him from East Providence continued past him, traveling up the road's gentle crest, reappearing a quarter of a mile away, following the thin gray band that parted the trees that had begun to turn yellow and red with the end of the summer. It was, as far as sunsets were concerned, nothing spectacular, nor was the location worth any particular view. But for Jim the location was everything to behold.

In the video, which he'd viewed at least seven or eight times that morning, a forest-green station wagon traveled along this very road. Through its windows the outline of its driver could barely be seen inclining his head, peering back curiously at whoever was shooting the video.

Jim turned and glanced back along the road. Based on the video, Jim stood approximately at the same vantage as the filmmaker, who'd then turned the camera back around, to the west. It was about ten yards away that a man had stood facing the road, wearing a red flannel shirt and blue dungarees.

"*Oh my God,*" a voice had whispered. "*There he is!*"

Whether or not the man had heard this, his left hand had balled into a fist at his side. His arm extended outward slowly, then swung back in, bouncing off his hip, and then he'd turned to stare directly at the camera and whoever held it. He had a round, pale face, wreathed by a thick beard and curly hair, both a deep ginger in color. His beard then opened around a toothy grin, and he'd begun laughing . . . but instead of the roaring guffaws one would expect, especially given the roar and crackle of the wind against the microphone that confirmed the ambient sounds of the area, the man's laughs were completely silent.

Then the camera had swung down, revealing a blur of black and brown as the filmmaker staggered back, making a disorienting bounce and sway as they ran. Then the ground grew still again as the camera was raised and pointed back again—but when the shot moved back to its original angle, the man was no longer there, the roadside empty but for a gray car that had appeared in the distance.

Jim shook his head, frowning. Although he stood alone, he couldn't help but crack a grin.

Come on, his former agent Betsy had said earlier in the week. *You have* to admit it's a bit spooky.

That it is, he'd conceded. *But I don't understand how it's relevant to me.*

It's your biggest selling point all over again. We had this exact same conversation *once, remember? I knew that people would eat your book up as soon as I read that second chapter. And now they can do it all over again!*

It's not the same, though. People don't get scared reading books anymore. That's what the Internet is for.

That's the thing—people always want more. *We can make a whole new marketing campaign around your book,* because *of that video. Have you seen how many views it's been getting?*

She'd gone on to tell him how videos and pictures of reported paranormal activity were high-traffic trends online. She'd said something about "creepypastas," whatever that meant. *And besides,* she'd added, *those kids wouldn't have* known *about him if it weren't for* your book! *The Highway Phantom is in the public zeitgeist because of* you, *Jim!*

Zeitgeist doesn't earn royalties, he'd said, and although he thanked her for thinking of him and promised he'd give her proposal some thought, he'd settled into another quiet night in front of the TV, the same as the majority of his evenings for over three decades since the publication of *The Ghosts of Bristol County.*

He'd enjoyed his share of author appearances and a few decent checks. In the early days of the Internet, he'd at first been elated to see a rise in its dwindling sales as interest in the strange sights—and sightings—of southeastern New England increased, but the resurgence was ultimately short-lived. By the turn of the Millennium sales had plunged, the publisher had folded, and nobody wanted to reprint old books about regional folklore. He'd been forced to get a second job, and his writing days were long behind him.

And yet . . .

Jim let out a long, heavy sigh.

"Looking for the Highway Phantom?"

He spun, frowning, to find the shouted inquiry belonged to a short, long-haired young woman standing beside a fern-green bicycle about six yards behind him.

"Oh— Uh, yeah. Yes, in fact!"

She walked her bike toward him, grinning, a pair of dying sunsets glowing upon her glasses. "I shot a video of him last month, right around here."

Jim inclined his head, frowning. "Wait a minute. Did you upload the video online?"

The woman's grin widened. "Already up to fourteen hundred likes and counting."

"That was you?"

"Creepy, huh?"

"Oh, yes!" Jim clenched his jaw at the over-emphatic tone of his voice, so he added, "Very strange."

"I saw him again last week." She pointed across the road. "Over on Perkins Road. But I didn't get a video. He was too quick."

"What, um, what happened?"

"I was out for the night when I saw him. He was heading for the highway. I took out my phone to film him, but by then he was already gone."

"That's—" Jim glanced back along the road, then shook his head. "That's unfortunate. And a bit strange, too."

"How so?"

"Oh, only that the—the reports have always only had him sighted here, on Three-Corner Road." When the woman cocked her head, he shrugged. "I actually wrote a book about regional folklore. I wrote about him pretty extensively."

"Nice!" She beamed. "What's it called?"

"I'm afraid it's long out of print, but it was called *The Ghosts of Bristol County*."

"*Holy crap!*" Her eyes practically popped out of her head and her mouth formed a small black O before she whispered, "*You're* James Richardson!"

Jim couldn't hide his own grin as he said, "In the flesh. Well, what's left of it, anyway."

She barked a guttural laugh, then shook her head, her long, dark brown hair swaying in a thick mane around her small shoulders. Grinning wider, Jim held out his hand to her. She had a firm, cool grip as she shook it. "Gemma."

"Nice to meet you."

"I *loved* that book, growing up. My brother used to read it to me when I was little. Scared the hell out of me."

He snickered at this. "Older brothers are good for that."

"So what brings you out here?"

"Oh, uh . . . research, actually."

"Writing a new book?"

If only. "No, uh, well, keep this under your hat, but my agent is actually pushing for a reprint of *Ghosts*. New edition. New material."

"This is—" She shook her head, grinning. "This is amazing! I never would've— God! It's *you!* You're here! This is amazing!" She fell silent, her eyes widening, and held one hand up, fingers outstretched as if making sure Jim himself was no ghost. "Wait, do you want to see where I saw him last week?"

"I think that would be fantastic, although . . ." Jim turned and frowned at the retreating daylight. "Perhaps you'd want to wait for a slightly brighter day."

"No way! He only comes out at night. That's when I saw him! It's only right down the road."

"Well, as long as I'm not keeping you up past your bedtime."

Gemma snorted at this. "Please. Want to follow me there?"

Jim smiled and hooked a thumb over his shoulder. "I can give you a ride."

He turned and began leading her to his car. Although Gemma continued to voice her excitement at meeting him, he wasn't listening. Seeing the hopeful glee in her face, he felt a deep, sour feeling in the back of his throat—for how could he disappoint her now? How could he take away from her excitement?

How could he tell her that, despite all his research and the references that he'd carefully curated for the rest of the book, he'd made up the entire story of the Highway Phantom?

The Highway Phantom, as he's been dubbed, is generally described as a tall, skinny man, wearing a red plaid shirt and denim coveralls, his head and face surrounded by thick, curly, ginger hair. He walks this road at night, hopeful thumb extended, but most people drive by, not wishing to welcome a stranger into their vehicles.

Once in a while some well-intentioned good Samaritan will slow down for the hitchhiker, only to get the surprise of a lifetime . . .

"Right about . . ." Gemma pointed. "There."

Jim slowed and pulled over, and Gemma eagerly climbed out. Exiting the vehicle with a grunt, he watched her snake around the front of the truck and point to a small yew, choked to only a few browning sprigs by the invading strands of a creeping vine.

"So I was headed back on my bike, and it was getting dark," Gemma said. "I saw a man walking over there, and I thought he looked familiar, so I slowed down, and then I noticed he was wearing blue coveralls and a red shirt. I was facing the opposite way from him, and he was walking back to the highway, so I didn't get a look at his face, but I recognized him. I knew it was him. So I pulled over, took out my phone, and by the time I looked up to see where he'd headed, he was gone."

Jim nodded slowly. "Think he may have run into the woods?"

"I would've seen him." Gemma turned to him and pointed at the trees beside them. "And before you say it—no, I don't think I was being punked."

Jim chewed his inner cheek. He didn't want to break the news to her, now more than ever, that a prank had to be exactly what this was. Instead, he offered, "I wonder what he was doing over here, and not back on the highway?"

"Ah!" Gemma grinned and raised a finger. "I have a theory on that. What if he's always been on this road, too, but nobody's noticed him?"

Jim shrugged, his thick eyebrows rising and falling. "Perhaps. I supp—"

"And—and," Gemma's grin widened as she wiggled her finger in the air, "he's only showing up now because more people are looking for him!" She raised her hands to either side of her head and fanned them out. "Like, we're opening our minds, our perceptions, so we're finally noticing things that were under our noses the whole time."

Jim smiled broadly. "I think that sounds like a solid theory."

"Thanks!" She snickered. "Well, I shouldn't keep you. There's a town curfew, anyway."

"Oh, is there? Have hardly been to Baker in recent years."

"Yeah, it's new, it's—" She looked away, her mouth twisting slightly, and she shook her head. "It's weird, I don't know."

"Well, now, would . . ." He cleared his throat. "At the risk of sounding like a creepy old man, would you like to stay in touch about this?"

Gemma grinned at this. "Wow, sure! Hang on." She rummaged in her bag, then removed a heavily creased business card. "It's old, but my number is still . . ."

Jim took the card from her outstretched hand and glanced at it with a chuckle. Under her name it said Dog Walker. He looked up to find her staring past him, eyes wide, and he twisted around.

A man stood not ten yards away from them. His features were difficult to discern, but the blue coveralls and red flannel of his clothes practically glowed in the twilight, as did the ginger curls of his hair and beard.

"It's him," Gemma whispered.

Jim's jaw worked uselessly, then went still.

The man continued to stand there, staring straight at them.

"Oh my God, he's looking at us."

When the memory of the video came to mind, and what was surely Gemma's voice saying almost exactly the same thing, Jim let out his breath, the corners of his lips curling up. He glanced back to find her staring at the man, her features furrowed. Turning back to the man, he grinned and raised his voice. "Very nicely done!"

Not to be dissuaded by an unconvinced audience, the man continued to stare at them.

"What are you doing?" Gemma hissed.

"I'm sold!" He smirked and looked at her. "Well done. Both of you. Really, I'm flattered." Gemma glared at him as he added, "But more importantly, I appreciate—"

Gemma looked past him again and gasped, pointing.

"—I appreciate it, really. I'm touched. Do you know how long—?"

"He's gone!"

"What?" Jim twisted, wincing at the arthritic protest in his left hip, his eyes moving immediately to the woods beside the vacant road. Indeed, the man had done a good job of making himself scarce.

Jim raised his hands and clapped, beaming. "Wonderful!" When he looked back at Gemma, she was glaring at him, her jaw agape. "No, please—don't be disappointed. This was great. And I'm touched that someone would go to the trouble to—"

"You don't believe it." Gemma's voice was tiny, almost childlike. "You don't even believe what you just saw."

He snickered and shrugged. "I believe you both worked very hard to give me a good scare."

Her eyes narrowing, jaw trembling, she whispered, "Fuck you."

"Oh, come now, Gemma—"

She walked back to the car and tugged the tailgate open.

"Gemma, I'm sorry! I'm just trying to—"

He broke off with a sigh as she dragged her bike out of the bed of his truck, then winced as she slammed the hatch shut.

She moved her bike onto the road, climbed on, and began to pedal back into town.

Jim sighed again, then returned to his truck.

There have been numerous occasions in which people have pulled over for him, waiting for many long seconds or even a couple of minutes before finally looking back for their would-be passenger, only to realize that the road beside them is empty but for the watchful trees. Although strange, this is perhaps a blessing of an outcome for these drivers, compared to what occurred one night in the late 1960s.

While on his way home, a man in a pickup truck spotted a red-headed hitch-hiker walking along the darkened road. He gave the horn a couple of taps and pulled over beside him, and the man came to the door and let himself in.

"Where we headed, friend?" the driver asked as the man closed the door, and he began to drive.

The man sat still in the seat, his eyes fixed on the road ahead of them, and didn't say a word.

Frowning, the driver asked, "I'm heading for Taunton. Are you in Reho-both?"

Still the man said nothing, didn't even move.

The driver shook his head and pulled over again. "Look, fellow, it's late, I'm tired, and I left my crystal ball at home. Either tell me where you're headed or get out."

This finally got the attention of the passenger, who then turned to face the driv-er. Staring at him, his pale, bearded face split into an ear-to-ear grin, and his shoulders began to quake as a deep, throaty chuckle filled the air. The chuckle gave way to laughter, and the laughter soon became hysterical cackles.

The driver tensed, backing up in his seat, instantly regretting his choice of words—not because the man didn't exit the vehicle—but rather, he did.

Before the driver's very eyes, the man became translucent, fading and fading from view, until the driver saw only his own scared reflection staring back at him from the passenger seat window.

Needless to say, the rest of the driver's trip home was far shorter than usual that night.

There goes a sale.

Jim immediately despised the thought that intruded onto his mind, and he smacked his hand on the steering wheel as he turned back onto the highway.

Realistically, he knew that any possible sales of the reprint would be complementary at best nowadays. But that wasn't what was bother-ing him—he kept seeing Gemma's hurt, spiteful glare.

A blur of blue and red emerged from the roadside and into his headlights, arms and legs pumping as the determined actor charged out before him.

Jim cursed loudly as he slammed on the brakes, the truck seeming to twist violently around him—and then came the horrifyingly loud *thump* of impact. Then the world squealed to a halt, and Jim was thrown back in his seat.

He'd hit him.

The man's face and raised hands had flown straight at the windshield.

He'd *seen* the man's open mouth with finality.

Jim shook his head, then scrambled to undo his seatbelt, limbs almost thrashing about with the surges of adrenaline in them. Several disorienting glances through the windows revealed that his truck was precariously angled across the middle of the highway. He opened his door and climbed out.

As he stepped around the front of the truck, his gaze snapped down to the broken man on the ground. Although his mouth was opened wide to shout, to scream, the only sound that escaped was a low, cracking groan.

He crouched over the man, reaching out to grab his shoulder, to shake him, to ask him if—

Not moving.

His eyes traveled over the twisted, tangled jumble of limbs, the neck that was twisted impossibly backward, so the man's face was planted directly into the ground.

He's not moving.

The same guttural whimper escaped Jim's lips, growing louder and louder, until it culminated in a tremendous cry that seared his lungs.

Rising, he managed to shove a shaking hand into his pants pocket to remove his phone. He flipped it open, jabbing a finger at three keys, then pressed it to his ear. Before the responder could finish talking, he blurted, "S-someone— I hit someone! It—" He turned and glanced around at the trees, the road stretching east to west. "Uh— Route Forty-Four, Reho— No, Baker! I'm in Baker, on Forty-Four, and . . . I'm by my truck, yes, I— What? He— Hurry, send help, he's—"

He glanced back at his truck, then down—and stared.

Although the responder kept speaking, kept asking questions, Jim was barely able to pay attention as he turned on legs made of granite. From somewhere nearby a horn blared, and a dark grey car sped around his crooked truck.

"He's . . ."

His voice warbled desperate attempts at words, seeming to come from a great distance away as he stared at the ground before his truck, unoccupied by body, blood, and anything else.

"He's . . . gone."

The final story worth noting in the history of the Highway Phantom sightings is perhaps the most bone-chilling of them all.

One night in the early '80s, a woman was driving to Rhode Island. The sun was a retreating orange glow ahead of her, and the road was empty, so the woman was driving a few miles above the speed limit—an infraction at best on any other occasion, but that night . . . it would cost her the limits of her sanity.

Near the border of Seekonk and Baker, a blur of blue and red appeared mere feet from the woman's high beams. She was so scared that she couldn't even scream—she applied the brakes and twisted the wheel, and although she knew it was too late, what happened was not what her horrified mind was expecting.

Although she didn't hear an impact, she knew she'd hit somebody as her car skidded to a halt. Jolting herself upright, she twisted and glanced back in her rearview, sure she would see the outline of a body in the red light behind her car. Unable to see anything, she quickly exited her car and ran out, shouting to see if the man was okay . . .

. . . only to see that the ground behind her car was completely empty, as were the ditches on either side of the road. Nobody stood nearby, in pain or otherwise. Nobody called for help. She was completely alone.

Puzzled, shaken, and breathless, the woman turned and got back in her car. She began to drive again, trying to think that perhaps she'd hit a bird or some other animal that had escaped into the woods. After all, there was no way a man could have survived—

Before her very eyes, the blur of blue and red appeared again, this time further ahead of her—and she saw, without a doubt, it was a man.

Once again she was too late to apply the brakes, and once again she seemed to hit him—but once again there wasn't a sound, nor any sign of impact. Regardless, she braked hard and peered around. Although she opened her door, she didn't exit her car this time. Her mind had begun to piece together the strange situation, but logic and belief waged a war for acceptance or denial of whatever had just happened again.

No longer wanting to play this strange game of nerves, she put the pedal to the metal and began to speed off down the road.

As if sensing her newfound determination, the fates conspired to give her a final scare that night, and they delivered in full.

Nearly half a mile down the road from the second incident, the man appeared before her again, but no longer on the road before her. Instead, he was now directly in front of her windshield.

Inexplicable by any sense of scientific logic, the man abruptly materialized on the hood of her car, kneeling forward on his bent legs, hands and face pressed to the glass of her windshield. So great was her horror that she cranked the steering wheel back and forth, trying to shake him off her car as he laughed hysterically at her through the glass, the whites of his eyes visible as his open, braying mouth sent chilling hoots and barks of his unearthly hysteria into her senses.

In a final, terrified, desperate attempt to lose the laughing wraith, the woman stomped on her brakes, and before her eyes the man flew backward into the air, cackling the whole way—and the last thing she saw before the car's momentum caused her to hit her forehead upon the steering wheel was the man's airborne form disappearing into the nighted highway's air . . .

"Clean," the officer said, lowering the device from Jim's mouth.

He knew that he'd have no issue proving that he'd not been under any influence after the two Baker PD vehicles had shown up—but he could only imagine how skeptical they were of the kook who'd claimed to have hit a man who had apparently gotten up and run away.

Jim turned and glanced up at the darkening sky, sighing heavily. As there was no body nor any vehicular debris on the road, the police had had Jim move his truck off to the shoulder to keep traffic clear. But at the rate this ordeal had been going, he'd spend all night on the road, which would be hell to navigate with his weakening vision.

The sergeant, a dark-skinned woman with hard eyes, rose from the far side of Jim's truck. She stepped around it, her mouth twisted into a tight knot on the side of her face. She hooked a thumb over her shoulder, at the woods. "And he came from this way?"

"Yes," Jim said, for the third time that evening. "He came running out, straight for the road, and directly in front of my truck. I barely had time to react."

"How fast were you going, do you recall?"

He'd already told the deputy the same thing twice, but he forced himself to remain patient as he repeated it for her.

She shook her head, looking distracted. "And you're sure you hit him?"

"I felt it. It was—the worst sound I've ever heard."

"I'm sure, but I don't see anything on the hood. No blood, no dents."

"R-right, but . . ."

"'But' indeed." She shrugged.

The police's radios squawked. The deputy answered his, walking back toward his cruiser.

"Are . . . ?" Jim let out a shaky sigh. "Are you going to arrest me?"

"No reason to, as of now, but we'll be in touch if we—"

Her radio squawked again, and she answered it this time. After a moment, a garbled response came through. "It's starting to get dark, Mr. Richardson. You should head on home. We'll reach out if we need you."

"Thank you, Sergeant."

He watched her walk back to her cruiser, his mind lost amidst a flurry of questions and half-formed answers that dissolved and dissipated before they even came close to making sense.

An approaching car slowed down, then sped up and passed them, its path unobstructed by the living or the dead.

Back in Swansea, Jim settled into his armchair, a glass filled to the halfway point with rye on the scuffed and wobbly coffee table. Beside it sat Gemma's business card.

A prank.

It had to be a prank, either between Gemma and her friends or being done *on* her and him. What other explanation could there be? He highly doubted Betsy would have gone to such a length on his behalf—*The Ghosts of Bristol County* was never a cash cow worth milking, much less nowadays.

I made the whole thing up!

He'd not sensationalized some urban legend, nor embellished a transplanted tale from some other location, and he certainly hadn't plagiarized something from another writer. It was such a simple idea—a phantom hitchhiker in southeastern Massachusetts! Excellent fodder for the imagination, nothing more.

Right?

He leaned forward in his chair before tutting aloud and dropping back with a grunt.

No.

He had no reason to think any more about this. It would be pointless.

Yet a moment later his curiosity lent enough fuel to his overworked limbs to rise and carry him to the rear vestibule of his house.

After his ex-wife had moved out a decade before, it had turned into something of a storage room. Overcrowded and dusty, and with enough sightings of yellowjackets beyond the glass of the perpetually sealed window at its far end for him to suspect a nest was tucked into an unseen corner, he rarely visited the vestibule anymore. Conversely, the preserved layout had a sole benefit: he knew exactly what was in the clutter.

He dragged aside several sagging cardboard boxes, full of books and winter clothes and *National Geographic* magazines. Behind them stood a stack of plastic storage bins, which he carried out, gritting his teeth and wheezing pathetically in his privacy, to his living room.

He shook his head and tightened his jaw as he glanced at the top one, which had a piece of paper taped atop it, reading *WALLS* in thick marker. The follow-up to *The Ghosts of Bristol County* had delivered a devastating blow to his writing energy, as its disappointing sales had come only months before Swamp Oak Press had declared bankruptcy, and he'd never been able to sell the title for a reprint. *The Walls of Southern New England* had ultimately been the final nail in his writing career's coffin.

The next one read *LAKES,* and although the tales of settlements around various New England lakes had provided plenty of information for the last of his 1980s titles, it was a subject he'd never had much interest in returning to ever since.

And on the bottom, the last bin read *GHOSTS.*

Jim set this one beside the coffee table and sat down in his chair. He smiled as he removed the lid and started removing notepads, yellowed newspaper clippings, and sheets of paper with handwritten notes. Everything from old headlines to tourist attractions had been useful fodder for his research, and as his gaze roamed over them he felt the excitement of thirty years prior siphoning into his spirits.

He'd rummaged halfway through the bin when he discovered a creased notebook upon which he'd written *Occurrences.* Its first page was dated September 7, 1989. As he flipped through the notes on strange phenomena from throughout New England, he remembered many an afternoon that he'd spent in various libraries. Although the notebook was dedicated to the subject, he'd only filled less than half of its now stiff and yellowed pages.

As his gaze wandered over various colors and grades of pen and pencil, scrawled in sentences and sometimes paragraphs, his search became more and more focused.

Marlboro, MA? (CONFIRM), read one. *Funhouse in burnt-down park, couple explored, something held woman's hand*

Another read *Westport, RI (CONFIRM HOUSE #) 2 families moved out in 2 yrs??*

On and on he read, line to line, page to page. Some of the stories had made it into his book, while many others had not.

Moodus, CT, noises from underground?

Burnt Hill, Heath, MA—Standing stones & shadow figures

Rehoboth, MA—Village Cemetery, Three-Corner Road—Old man & kid laughter

Disappearance—Rt. 44, 1968

Jim straightened up and re-read this last one, then quickly scanned the rest of the page and those following, frowning.

He'd written nothing else on the subject.

He quickly dug through the rest of the contents of the bin, but none of the other notes or notes had any relation to the 1968 disappearance.

Thinking for a moment, he glanced up and around.

A few minutes later he was in his old study, booting up his computer. A clunker from the mid-nineties, it took a while to start, but its lack of speed and efficiency perfectly suited his own lack of technical savvy.

An initial online search resulted in a flood of websites and articles about everything from amber alerts to runaway Alzheimer's patients. He added the words *Rehoboth* and *hitchhiker,* but the only related content that appeared were a few mentions of the Highway Phantom, quoted directly from his book. That brought a smile to his face, which quickly faded when the other results included re-posted links to Gemma's video.

He was on the verge of abandoning the search, the thought process, and the entire insufferable day's worth of trouble when one last link caught his eye, and he guardedly opened it.

A website, *Unknown New England,* had a whole page on disappearances dating back to the seventeenth century. He noticed that the missing-persons rate had dropped significantly over each decade, as industries, public records, and communications improved and expanded, with most reports involving circumstances that implied crimes and misdemeanors.

After slogging through a series of noteworthy disappearances in Boston, from children back in the 1980s up through young men in the early 2000s, Jim finally spotted an article that caught his eye.

On August 3, 1968, a car had broken down on Route 44, in Seekonk. The driver, Joseph Dunbar, had been stuck in a nighttime rain as he'd returned from a second-shift job. Several eyewitnesses had confirmed his appearance at a roadside diner, where he'd called for service. He'd stayed for a cup of coffee, left to return to his car . . . and was never seen again.

Jim vaguely recalled hearing of the disappearance. He'd been in his teens and had been aware of many reports from local radio and newspapers for a few weeks before the incident had faded into obscurity. Regardless, he grinned slowly and shook his head.

So there *had* been some kernel of truth behind his ghost story after all. It had been planted in the soil of his mind, long ago, and had only finally sprouted when he'd been strapped for time to complete an extra tale for his book.

And if a codger like him could have figured this much out, who was to say that someone else, someone more resourceful and inquisitive and imaginative, couldn't have done the same?

Grabbing Gemma's card, he walked into the kitchen and picked up the phone. He dialed and waited.

After a few rings, there came a brief series of crackles and warbling sounds, then Gemma's voice said, "Hello?"

"Hi, Gemma, this is—"

"Oh, Mister— I mean, Jim. Hey, look, I'm sorry about earlier. I shouldn't've blown up on you like that."

"And I'm sorry, too. But that's why I'm calling."

The next morning, Jim drove to Baker.

Although no kamikaze fool came barreling out in front of him this time, Jim's arthritic knuckles protested his tight grip on the wheel as he turned onto Perkins Road.

Through thick, unruly woods he drove, peering at crumbling stone walls that stretched through the forest corridors. He paused at an intersection and peered down the left fork, where the unmarked road took a sharp turn around a boulder and disappeared beyond a couple of dead, fallen trees. To the right, the road stretched past a clearing, from which several gravestones peeked crookedly. And ahead, the road continued toward a break in the treeline.

At the edge of the woods stood a lone ranch house, its windows boarded up tightly. Peering at it, Jim saw the windows were clean of the telltale chars of fire damage that would have justified the uneven planks hammered up on the frames, between which black triangles peered out at him. He rolled his shoulders to relieve a tightening sensation that snaked up between them and proceeded into the town square.

In the "business district," a family was walking before a squat post office, the two adolescents arguing playfully and smacking at each other as the mother shouted at them. Across from a closed diner, a row of brick buildings housed a bank, a laundromat, a general store, and the coffee shop that Gemma had suggested.

He pulled into a vacant spot on a meterless sidewalk. His old marble notebook tucked under his arm, he walked up to the café's door and peered through the scuffed glass. A couple of men who were probably his own age but appeared far older sat at the counter, and a bored-looking waitress carried a half-empty coffee pot as she walked through the kitchen's swinging door.

"Hey," a voice said behind him, and he turned to discover Gemma smiling behind him.

They went inside and took a seat at one of the booths. Although Gemma wasn't hungry, Jim was famished, and he ordered some eggs and toast. While downing the first of several coffees, he told Gemma about his accident, and the missing body.

The whole time, she'd stared at him, transfixed, her eyes wide, parted lips framing breathless darkness. When he was done explaining the story, she said in a small voice, "B-but you're okay?"

"Oh, yes. Startled to hell, which isn't very good for a septuagenarian's ticker, but I'm fine. Even my *truck* was fine."

Gemma snickered nervously. "I mean . . . ghosts wouldn't leave a mark."

Jim swallowed. "I'd imagine not. But a living person would."

Grinning, Gemma inclined her head and was about to speak when the waitress came by with Jim's food. "So what do you think he was?" she asked when they were alone again.

"That—is hard to say. But, well, look." He sighed heavily, and even as the aroma of the scrambled eggs made him salivate, he couldn't eat, not yet. "I'm so very sorry. I'm sorry I doubted you."

"And your own eyes."

"And—my own eyes, yes. Which is what I wanted to talk to you about."

He told her about his rediscovered notes, and about Joseph Dunbar. He struggled with telling her about his own embellishments of the story, but as her excited gaze widened, the debate was quickly forgotten.

When he was done, Gemma nodded and looked away. "Joseph Dunbar," she whispered, sitting back in the booth, and she repeated the name.

Finally remembering his cooling food, Jim dug in. Between mouthfuls he said, "I do wonder if he may be the—the man who started all this."

"What do you think happened to him?"

Jim shrugged as he took a bite of his toast. As he pondered a delicate answer, he noticed that one of the two old men at the counter had twisted around and was peering at them. Not wanting the wrong expression to cause animosity, he turned back to Gemma and said, "Perhaps he was hit by a car."

"And then what, though?"

"Hard to say. It's not likely *he* would've gotten up and walked away after."

Gemma smirked. "Unless he did."

Movement caught Jim's gaze, and he saw the two old men were leaving. Now both were looking at the booth. Growing annoyed, Jim glared at them. Gemma must have seen his face, because she peered over her shoulder in time to see the men finally looking away as they reached the door and exited.

"At any rate," Jim said, "I really can't say what happened to him and how—how it relates to what we saw. Something happened to that man, though."

"Now I wish more people knew about Joseph Dunbar! I've been here my whole life, and I've never even heard about him. I wonder if anyone in town even knows about him. This should be an episode of *Unsolved Mysteries!*"

Jim smiled. "Well, I have some news for you. Hopefully, if my agent is still any good at her job, *that* might not be necessary."

Gemma inclined her head, frowning, and then her eyes widened with an excitement that warmed Jim's heart.

Legends are, perhaps, clear evidence of resurrection.

Stories are told, they are created, they live, and they die. But they are never forgotten.

Perhaps somebody writes them down. Perhaps they become whispers repeated over and over, from one person to another. Perhaps they evolve, perhaps they are embellished. But invariably, sooner or later . . . they come round again.

When The Ghosts of Bristol County *was first published by Swamp Oak Press in 1991, I was unaware of how much life the stories therein already held. In my mind, I was simply taking stories that were already known in certain towns and among certain groups of people in various areas in this legend-rich area of southeastern New England and showing them off like exhibits in an archaeological museum. It is a testament to the power of their strange details, and hardly to my own recounting of them, that they have continued to generate interest, curiosity, and repetition, all these many years later.*

The stories contained in this tome are alive, they breathe, and they are self-sustaining. My own words are nothing more than a vessel by which to carry the treasures contained therein. The ghosts that haunt the various locales of Bristol County do so not only in graveyards, on highways, in old farmhouses, or in darkened thickets—they haunt the very fabric of time itself, and find ways of manifesting, again and again, by being pronounced on the lips of the people that call this land home.

It is with exceeding pleasure that now, through the kind and generous efforts of Microbrew Press, to say nothing of the inimitable eye of my career-long editor, Selma Jenkins, and my agent, Betsy Loy, that it is possible to now present this defini-

tive, expanded, and revised edition of The Ghosts of Bristol County *for the twenty-first century. However, none of this would have been possible without the invaluable input of a very special citizen of the town of Baker . . .*

Jim was drumming his thumbs against the spokes of the steering wheel, the grin on his face as wide and lunatic as that of the Highway Phantom.

He'd been anxious to tell Gemma of the good news that had been delivered to him in a thick, padded envelope earlier in the day. But with several months between his last meeting with her, he knew that the news would be best shared in person.

She'd been uncertain on the telephone earlier that afternoon, stating that she had night plans, but she must have sensed the excitement in Jim's voice and agreed to his audience for a short time that evening. He'd wasted no time, and with sun retreating into the cloud-crowned horizon he made his way onto Three-Corner Road.

He glanced down at the passenger seat and chuckled. "Welcome home," he murmured, and turned onto Perkins.

As he approached the intersection, a honk drew his gaze to his rearview. A car was rapidly approaching him, going at least fifty, though the old country roads had signs indicating half that. As the car got closer, it honked again. Jim frowned and pulled onto the shoulder, and watched as a young, tense-looking woman sped by, leaning over her wheel, eyes fixed straight ahead. Shaking his head, he waited for her to be several yards away before he pulled back out onto the road.

Although he peered around instinctively, he saw nothing and nobody in his way on Perkins Road. It didn't matter, really, if anyone did or did not see anything there ever again. The legend of the Highway Phantom was here to stay.

At the intersection, he detected movement near the boarded-up house. He slowed as he passed but was unable to locate its source.

Further ahead, a short woman was walking on the left side of the road, a pale skirt poking out from beneath a denim jacket. Pulling up beside her, he rolled down his window and said, "Hitching a ride, are we?"

Gemma stopped and turned to him, grinning.

He nodded her over and watched as she crossed in front of the truck. With dusk growing deeper around him, he turned on his headlights as she opened the door, and he scooped up what sat on the passenger seat. As she climbed in, he asked, "Where to?"

"Maybe we could back go to the diner in the business district."

"That sounds perfect. But I don't want to keep you, I remember you said you had plans."

"Oh, that's fine. What did you want to talk about?"

"Well, it isn't so much talk as it is show." He held out the printed, bound manuscript.

Gemma frowned at it, then gasped and looked up, eyes wide. "Is—? Is that—?"

"Revised and expanded. Final proofs were sent back to my publisher earlier in the week. They're aiming at a release next spring."

"That's *amazing!* Oh, my God, I can't wait to read it!"

"Well, you might not have to wait." He handed her the manuscript. "This is a copy of the final proofs. I want you to have it."

"Mister . . . Jim, I—" She shook her head, swallowed hard. "Are you sure?"

"I'd all but given up on writing. If it weren't for you." He shrugged. "But here we are. And here it is."

Gemma smiled and twisted herself toward him, raising her arms. As much as the cramped truck permitted, they clumsily hugged. Gemma's cheek was cold where it brushed his neck, and after the hug ended he glanced out his window. "It'll be dark soon. I don't want to keep—"

He fell silent, staring out at the road leading into the woods. Gemma was speaking, but he barely heard her.

". . . straight through the business district," she was saying. "Remember the cafe we met at? Just—"

He silently reached beside him and tapped her arm, and a moment later she gasped.

The Highway Phantom stood at the entrance to the left road.

Jim's jaw worked, but he was incapable of producing a sound.

Gemma said something, but he refused to take his eyes off the roadside figure. Inclining his head, he muttered, "What?"

In response, the passenger door opened, and although he half turned his head, his gaze was fixed on the bearded man in red plaid and coveralls staring back at him, his arms loosely hanging at his sides, his features slack, his eyes unreadable in the twilight.

"I'm filming it *this* time," Gemma whispered.

"G-good," Jim muttered, swallowing hard, his mind racing. On one hand, a new video could be serendipitous publicity for his book. But on the other . . .

"Joseph Dunbar!" Gemma called, and Jim finally snapped his gaze upon her as she walked before his truck, the headlights casting a harsh glow on her as she approached the man, her phone raised, her face pale in its light. *"Joseph Dunbar, I am talking to you!"*

Jim blinked and shook his head. Taking a deep breath, he exited the truck and called out, "All right, all right. Enough!" Gemma turned to him, frowning, and he shook his head and said, "I'm sorry to have to tell you like this, but that is *not* Joseph Dunbar, or even a ghost."

Gemma blinked but didn't say anything.

Jim sighed heavily, lowering his head. "It's—I made it up. I made up the whole story. There may have once been a Joseph Dunbar, but there is no Highway Phantom. I—I made it all up. I'm sorry."

After a long moment, Gemma said matter-of-factly, "I know."

Jim's head snapped up, and he glared at her. "What?"

"I know he's not real, Jim."

The man started approaching them, and Jim glanced at him, then back at Gemma. "I—I don't understand. Why—?"

He fell silent as the man got closer, asphalt grinding softly under his shoes. In the fading daylight he could see a smile broadening his cheeks and spreading the span of his beard.

Jim turned back to Gemma. "You knew. You—" He pointed at her, at the man, and back. "You're in on this."

She smiled and nodded slowly.

"But why? Why do all this?"

"It was for you."

Jim blinked as if water had splashed his face. "Me?"

"Well, yeah! In this day and age, nobody cares about some back-woods town like Baker, *unless*"—she raised a finger—"there's an at-traction. And what a better attraction than a ghost story?"

Jim chuckled, not believing what he was hearing. He shook his head. "So . . . all this time, all these events, was for—me?"

"Well, yeah. Why else would you put your book out again?"

The man came closer, and Jim smirked at him. His big, dark green eyes were bright above his ginger beard, which now parted around a big, yellow-toothed grin. "You certainly gave me quite a scare last year." As the man raised his hands up beside his face, Jim asked, "But please, tell me how you—?"

The man dug his fingertips into his beard and curled them inward, as if scratching deep itches, then he tugged off the beard—along with the rest of his face.

For a long moment Jim stared at the black oval that subsequently appeared, and had time to utter a confused grunt when the oval burst into a blur of tarlike tendrils.

Jim had barely moved one leg back to turn when a multitude of sharp points harpooned his left shoulder and arm, piercing clothes and skin alike. Yelping in pain, he tried to run, but then his right arm was seized by what may not have been a hand. He wrenched his body back and forth, his feet smashing down on the road as more cold, wet points found the back of his neck, digging painfully in like so many oversized needles, and he began to shout and gibber nonsensically.

As even more points began to creep onto his scalp and cheeks, something grabbed him around his waist, more cold points prickling along his abdomen and erupting into pain.

Caught in the maw of pain and terror, Jim was only barely able to see Gemma as she stepped into view before him, smiling. She'd re-moved her glasses and was staring at him with wide, gleeful eyes.

"Thank you for your book, Jim. I mean that, sincerely. I think I know of a great marketing strategy for it, too." Jim shrieked as she raised her hands and flicked her fingers in air-quotes. "'Local folklorist goes missing while researching ghost book.'"

Jim gave a gibbering cry as Gemma moved closer, chuckling as she fanned her hands out in the air before clapping them to her cheeks, shaking her head. "*That'll* sell it, for sure."

Leaning in, she curled her fingers into the flesh of her cheeks, and a black line snaked up the middle of her face, quickly widening into a fissure. "People will come from all over to see where it happened . . ." Her voice dropped an octave, becoming thicker, as if speaking from inside a puddle of syrup between her vertically splitting lips. Jim screamed until he felt his lungs beginning to erupt with pain, but he couldn't tell if the pain came from without or within as the faceless obsidian before him whispered, "*. . . and we'll never be hungry again.*"

Black City Skyline

Instead of talking to me, Detective, you should go downtown for answers. Not that anyone there would know what happened to my roommate, but there is one place you should start your search—the Superman Building.

Providence being such a small city, there aren't a lot of tall buildings here. You know the old gray skyscraper downtown? There is something seriously wrong with that place.

I'm not talking about the spike in traffic and the lack of parking since it was reopened last year. I'm not talking about the building's cracking, stained limestone walls that still haven't been fully restored. I'm not even talking about the extensive security team choking up the front lobby nowadays—which, by the way, is a shameful way to greet visitors. I remember when it used to be fun to walk in there and stare up at the highly decorative ceiling like a twelve-year-old in a museum's dinosaur exhibit.

It's important to keep its history in mind when I tell you the rest of this. Built in 1928, its real name is the Industrial Trust Building. It earned its nickname because it looked similar to a skyscraper in the backgrounds of old Superman comics. It hosted a few banks over the decades, but the last one to move out left the place a complete mess, in need of new wiring, water pipes, and a facelift. Nobody could afford—or wanted to attempt—the restoration job, so it sat vacant and dark for a decade. Lots of people, unfamiliar with its glorious history, considered it an eyesore, and there were various suggestions and even petitions to have it demolished. But most of us only felt sad while seeing the tallest building in Rhode Island, the heart of Providence itself, wasting away like a neglected seashell.

Then a couple of years ago, an accounting firm, Hatton and Burke, landed a deal with the building's owners. They leased out the top floors and paid out of pocket to redo the entire lobby. The owners put half the income toward renovating the next floor below and leased it out to another business a few months later. It went on from there, and as of this year more than half the building is occupied, with the rest under renovation for even more occupants.

That's what all the news reports and online articles talk about, anyway. What they don't mention is the weird stuff that happened since H&B opened those big, metal doors—and the one person who knew the most about that is the same one you're looking for.

Nancy mostly kept to herself. We weren't close, but we talked regularly: usually about how much she hated her old job, and how excited she was when H&B hired her, about five or six months after the building was officially reopened last November.

One afternoon when I got home, she asked if I knew anything about pest control. I must have given her a disgusted look, because she assured me that she wasn't talking about our apartment—rather, she'd been hearing weird sounds in the walls at her job, as if something were in the central air system.

A couple of weeks later I asked if her pest problem had been resolved. She kind of shivered and said she was getting out late one night when she heard a co-worker screaming in the front lobby. Apparently a rat had run through there, big as a puppy, carrying what looked like a crab or something. The security guard on duty freaked and tried to herd it into a vacant office, but the thing ended up running out the front entrance. I'm sure someone downtown must have run into it, but as far as I know it never returned to the building.

This past January, Nancy had slipped on some black ice and badly injured her right ankle. Because of that, she'd been working from home for a couple of weeks. One of those nights, I came home and found her sitting on the couch, mesmerized by a TV news report. Before I could ask what was going on, she silently pointed at the screen, and my jaw dropped open when I looked at it and saw flashing police lights in Kennedy Plaza.

Between the reports that aired and popped up on the Internet, and everything she'd revealed to me from her office's emails and texts from co-workers of hers, what I gathered is that somebody in the newer business in the building, a marketing agency, had fallen terribly ill, but instead of staying home he'd pushed on, until his symptoms had gotten the best of him—and then worse.

Now I don't know how much I buy this, but apparently he'd gotten violently sick, and by the time emergency services had been called in his body had begun to deteriorate, like a Chernobyl victim.

Whatever *did* happen, the building got shut down and all workers who'd been there in the past week were quarantined while the Rhode Island Department of Health and the CDC swept the building for any signs of the mystery disease. No clue what was determined about the poor guy, but fortunately it seemed as if it was an isolated incident. And for a while it was.

A month or so later, as I'm sure you know, there was that big riot in the building that occurred shortly after health officials declared it safe to repopulate. What *was* that about, anyway? I've heard as many rumors that it was a bank heist as I have that it was a religious service. I understand if you can't tell me, and that's fine. Either way, it left a couple of people badly injured and two others dead, and a heap of red tape piled up on H&B.

I don't know if Nancy was always so bold, but as soon as the dust settled and the building was officially reopened she was eager to return. She worked long hours, often coming home so late I'd find her sleeping on the couch. At first I figured it was for a backlog of work, but then she started making the living room her second bedroom. Her laptop, printouts, and increasing piles of books and food containers began to stack up on the coffee table. I had to put my foot down one day when I had a date coming over. Although Nancy apologized and cleaned up, I could tell she was annoyed.

Then, in March, the mystery disease came around.

There were the couple of people who'd died in Kennedy Plaza, followed by the person who'd jumped onto the train tracks, and someone else who'd gotten sick on a bus. And don't forget the "Lincoln Monster" that someone gunned down, who turned out to be a man with serious deformities. Finally came the lockdown and quarantine, the business failures, and all the governor's spiels about bravery and safety, and the rest is history.

I'm personally ready to go back to work the second this insanity ends. I can't keep living from one unemployment check to the next. And I'm not going to lie: although the sudden solitude in this apartment has been jarring, and my anxiety over Nancy's well-being is making me physically ill, I have to say the change in pace was, at first, something of a relief. During the early days of the lockdown, having to spend that much more time around Nancy on the regular began to take its toll on our patience with each other.

You see, over the next couple of months she spent increasing amounts of time in her room after that. I didn't need to ask to know what she was up to: I'd gotten more than a few glimpses at the books and papers on the table. She was researching something.

What that research was about, I couldn't tell you—it was literally all over the place. I saw books on history, folklore, and occultism. There were printed photographs of vintage architecture. She even had several books and printed articles about missing persons reports, ironically, but most of them were about kids from back in the '80s, so I don't think you'll find anything useful or related to her case there.

Whatever it was all about, she was so wrapped up in it that she was late paying the rent a couple of months in a row.

The one time I tried to ask her about the fruits of her labor, she said that it was too much to explain, but she promised me "it'll explain everything."

And then, on the twenty-third last month, a little after three thirty in the afternoon, she headed out and never came back.

All the cops and all the questions came at me in the weeks following her disappearance.

There was no sign she'd logged in for work that day, but not being in the office, there was no footage of her. She might have walked to her destination or she might have taken the bus, because she doesn't own a car. I didn't get any calls, texts, or emails from her. There have been no signs of foul play. It's as if she fell into a hole and took the hole with her.

I've been going through her research, trying to spot anything that might hint at her whereabouts. You might know better than me what's relevant and what's not.

Take this binder, for instance. It's full of reports on the varied and terrifying effects of the mystery disease that still has everyone holed up in their homes or wearing masks outside, including a few interviews with alleged victims. If anything, it might be more helpful to the World Health Organization than you.

Or look at this notebook. It only has a few pages filled out, but it might be useful. The first page has a few news sites and dates listed for, from what I could see, articles about a bonfire that someone had started on a small island in the Seekonk River last fall. After that, there's this weird symbol that she drew. Does it look familiar? Well, look at the list she wrote beneath it. Those are all locations throughout the city, and if the spray-painted tag I've seen on at least two of them are any indication, she was keeping track of where it popped up.

Then there's this stack of books on occultism and fringe science. The Dr. Garrett one is particularly riddled with highlights and sticky notes, but nothing makes any sense to me.

I've made a list of my own here. These are all links to an assortment of articles and various online video channels focused on unexplained phenomena. Please feel free to take it as well.

And don't get me started on *that* pile—those are all articles, books, and even a couple of documentaries about the Superman Building's initial reopening and later restoration.

As I said, Detective Gafford—none of it adds up.

At times I feel as if I'm catching glimpses of a bigger picture, the outline of a larger shape lurking on the horizon, but then it's gone as quickly as a face in the clouds.

I don't know what else to tell you. I don't think I have anything else worth mentioning. I haven't seen or heard from Nancy since the day she vanished.

Although . . .

Okay. I wasn't planning on mentioning this, because I don't think it has anything to do with anything. But then again, with all the disjointed topics Nancy was researching, who's to say it wouldn't fit into the very same big, weird picture?

Last Saturday I went downtown to meet up with someone I've been seeing. It was a warm, humid night, and I was sweating even as I started walking down College Hill. By the time I turned onto Benefit Street, I was practically drenched.

I walked under streetlights and trees, listening to music coming from windows and the rapid tapping sounds of insects. A couple were walking their dogs across the street, and in the distance an emergency siren wailed.

I thought I heard another set of feet crunching on the bricks and concrete behind me, so I instinctively crossed the street. Out of the corner of my eye I spotted a dark figure moving after me, and I walked a little faster. A wet, hollow sound, somewhere between a pant and a yawn, grew louder behind me. The muscles in my shoulders tightened, and I started to run—and the sounds behind me went abruptly silent.

The reason I bring it up is because . . . I don't know. I thought of Nancy when I heard that sound. It wasn't her, but it put me in mind of what she'd say to me when she would come in from a good day at work, when she'd holler my name in a loud, yowling voice. I must have been projecting the thought of somehow running into her out there that night, but when I stopped and spun, whatever it was had vanished.

I looked back and forth along the street but couldn't see where it had gone. I let out a heavy breath—and then I heard a rustling above me that sent me scurrying to the middle of the street. I looked up and saw the branches of a big tree in a nearby churchyard trembling, swaying, and settling with the obscured movement of something that had leapt beyond the leaves and shadows.

An approaching car honked, and I jogged down onto the nearest side street and continued my way to the lights and pedestrians downtown. Then I called for a ride home.

I can't tell you what's going on in this city, Detective. Maybe it's a combination of gentrification, global warming, and crime, with a hefty dose of lockdown anxiety. Maybe it's something else.

All I know is, Nancy's disappearance has something to do with the Superman Building. For a while I was happy the old place was up and running again. But now, whenever I see that old tower in the city skyline at night I get a chill. I sometimes wonder what kinds of secrets have been kept there, deep down inside all those old safe deposit boxes and sealed vaults—and what may have been taken—or released—from them. Nancy might have known.

And perhaps, somewhere, she still does.

Home Staging

Katrina pulled into the driveway at dusk and frowned at the darkened windows of the house before her. She parked before the closed garage and waited a moment before climbing out, half expecting the front door to open and a smiling person to step out, but neither happened.

"Dammit, Ron . . ." She fumbled inside her purse and removed her phone. Her brother was terrible at responding to texts, so she called him. As she listened to the droning rings, she glanced at the house again.

She'd not stood before 337 Humboldt Street in almost a decade. Even after her father had been put into hospice, she didn't have the heart to put it on the market, but after a heavy conversation with Ron and her husband Connor she'd reluctantly signed her childhood home away.

Ron had been kind enough to hold onto the last of her belongings, but when she'd finally driven up to his northwest Massachusetts condo to retrieve them, he'd greeted her with bad news: he'd forgotten a few boxes in the garage, including one containing some of her oldest childhood belongings. He had, however, arranged with the realtor to pick them up the next day—but Katrina managed to convince him to call the realtor back, for she would drive the additional thirty miles north to the old house and pick up the rest of it herself.

As the phone rang, she looked over the house. The flaking and splintered dark brown shingles had been replaced with pale blue planks of artificial siding. The trims on the windows and doors were a bright white. The shrubs that had once unevenly lined the front were gone, but the lawn seemed so much wider and cleaner for it.

Ron's self-started home staging business had proven far more successful than Katrina could have ever anticipated, and his work here was, admittedly, impressive—but she wasn't in the mood to tell him that.

After four rings she sighed. *"Thank you for calling Home Impressions, this is Ron Gallett. I'm out of the office for the time being, but if you'd like to leave a message, I'll be happy to—"*

While she listened, she took a couple of steps toward the front door, peering through its glass panels and the lattice curtain beyond. "Out of the office," she was sure, meant he was on a date.

Finally, the message beep came over the phone.

"Hey, I'm here, but I don't think the new owners are home. Did the realtor actually *tell* you they would be? Just call me back as soon as you can."

She'd no sooner hung up when the phone vibrated, and she peered hopefully at the screen, only to find a message from Connor.

When do you think you'll be home?

His fever had finally broken, but he was still a weakened snot factory. Normally too proud to let an ailment drag him down, he'd had no choice but to stay in Rhode Island. Since the state was still under quarantine for what had at first been an eerie, but lately more annoying, outbreak of an unknown disease, she'd lost nearly half an hour at one of the border checkpoints to get clearance.

She started to reply when she thought she saw movement out of the corner of her eye, but what had appeared to be a face at one of the windows was now a blurry reflection of gray sky and heaven-reaching trees.

Glancing at the time on the screen, she wrote: *May head back soon, so probably 9:30 or so. Don't wait for me for dinner, just order something in if you're hungry.*

The trees whispered with a gentle breeze, and with it came a series of soft taps. The cool September air crept into Katrina's bones, and she bundled up her coat.

Another breeze came, and with it another round of tapping. She turned to the treeline across the way, then realized that the sound was coming from behind her.

She walked up to the door and peered through the glass and saw a set of raised Venetian blinds along its top, rocking in a draft and smacking against the panes. Squinting deeper into the darkened foyer, she could see the door to the garage on her left . . . and across the way, the sliding glass door . . . and the vertical strip of gray light along its edge.

It had been left open.

Maybe . . .

She shook her head and glanced at her phone again. Another breeze came, and the blinds once again tapped at the window, *clack-clack.*

She stepped back from the door.

The sliding glass door could lock, but the screen door outside it couldn't. The foyer was open.

She had a pen and half of a folded sheet of paper in her purse. She could leave a note saying she'd stopped by and picked up her stuff. It would be invasive and creepy, but dammit, the realtor had *told* these people she was coming.

Right?

She glanced at her phone a final time, then shoved it back in her purse and began to walk around the garage, stopping short when she saw the man standing behind it.

"Oh!" she blurted. "I'm sorry."

He was on the grass beside the old sun deck, his back turned to her. His dark blue windbreaker and khaki slacks flapped in the breeze, but he stood as still as a department store mannequin. As another wind came through, she could hear the blinds inside the foyer tapping again.

"Uh, hello. Hi. Sorry, I'm Katrina Gallett. You probably got a call about . . . ?"

The man didn't turn. His dangling arms swayed slightly in the wind.

Katrina raised her voice and moved closer. "Hello? Sorry, hi. I actually used to live here, and I left—"

She fell silent as she came beside him and saw the smooth, solid shapes of his hands, the lack of three-dimensional ears beneath salt and pepper hair. Empty, gray-blue eyes stared with artificial serenity, perfectly complemented by curved lips frozen beneath. He *was* a mannequin.

The ghost of conversation haunted her wordless, still-working lips. She swallowed hard and stepped back from it.

Another breeze came. *Clack . . . clack-clack.*

She huddled her shoulders under her jacket as she glanced at the foyer, then back at the mannequin. After a moment she made her way to the sliding glass door.

Pulling aside the sliding panels of wire mesh and glass, she stepped inside, her feet crunching on the dull gray-brown polyester that had replaced the old white wool carpet. She grabbed the handle of the garage door and was only half-surprised to find it unlocked.

The interior of the garage was almost pitch-black. She extracted her keys from her purse and picked out a tiny flashlight that hung among them. Its cool white beam temporarily blinded her, and she pointed it around. The walls, once threadbare beams and sheets of plywood, festooned with cobwebs and palm-sized arachnids, were now clean and neatly painted. Finding the light switch, she flipped it, and the newly installed fluorescent bulbs overhead burst to life.

The shelves that had always been cluttered with gadgets, boxes, and dust had been cleaned and varnished, empty but for a few unfamiliar tools, seeming to make the space seem so much larger than she remembered.

And on the floor before her stood three cardboard wine boxes, bulging with contents, *DAD* scrawled in black marker on the nearest one.

"Thank *God.*"

She dropped her keys back into her purse and crouched beside it, then tore open its flaps and peered inside. A few yellowed, broken-spined, and dog-eared paperbacks had been shoved inside, and she pursed her lips as she recalled an uncomfortable conversation with Connor about selling her father's library online.

She opened one that had her name written on it but was puzzled to find that it only contained an assortment of pots and pans. Cringing at the thought of her old journals, toys, and other belongings being crushed by the heavier box, she hefted it off and opened the one below, then let out a heavy sigh.

More kitchenware.

Katrina stepped back into the foyer, removing her phone and jabbing her finger onto Ron's contact icon.

Had he even bothered to check her old room for anything that may have belonged to her? She'd left to some of her earliest childhood memories there—and now they were all gone. *Gone!*

Maybe the new owners had picked through them, amused, before tossing them. Maybe they'd sold some of it—after all, Katrina had always kept her dolls in immaculate condition. They'd probably fetched decent prices at antique shops and in online auctions.

She turned to the doorway that led into the kitchen, listening to the third ring end and the fourth begin, but when it reached his voicemail again she hung up. Anything she said would be full of curses and incoherent grumbles, and that would get her nowhere. With a heavy sigh she opened the door and stepped inside, frowning at the darkness before stopping short.

She'd waltzed into the kitchen like she still lived here. It was a habit she'd picked up from many a sullen teenage afternoon—but she had absolutely *no* excuse for it now.

Even so, why were the doors unlocked? Could the owners have left the house open for her, knowing she was coming? True, their neighborhood had always been somewhat safe, but such an action simply didn't ring true.

Someone *had* to be home.

"Hello?"

When no one answered, she spoke louder, announcing herself, but silence was the only response. To satisfy her curiosity, she peered around the dim kitchen.

In the gray ambiance from the window and the open door, the

counter appeared to be the same as she'd remembered, although but the toaster-oven, the stove and its matching microwave, and the shiny metal of the sink were all unfamiliar. She turned to where their old, fading-white fridge had been, now replaced with a big black monolith, and in the doorway beside it, a woman regarded her.

"Oh! Oh my God, I'm sorry, I—"

The woman didn't speak, didn't even move. A prickly realization crawled up Katrina's neck as she timidly raised her hand and extended her fingers, her wrist twitching in a half-formed wave. When the woman didn't react, Katrina instinctively reached for a switch on the wall nearby and flipped on the overhead light.

The mannequin's empty gaze and pouting lips made her look almost bored as she stared at the window over the sink. A wig of long ginger curls tumbled down over a thin sweater, and her jean-clad hips were angled mid-stride, arms positioned at her side, hands pointing daintily.

Katrina bit her lip as she stared at the mannequin, her adrenaline-fueled pulse thumping in her ears.

She pulled the door shut behind her and moved across the kitchen, uncomfortably peering over her shoulder as she passed the mannequin. She made her way into the murky adjoining hall, past the basement door, the darkened bathroom, and the closed door to what was once her father's office.

In the living room a new couch and recliner faced a wide, glass-centered table. She ran her hand along the newly papered wall beneath the stairs where she could see the dark rectangles of photographs. A large flatscreen TV sat in the corner, and a grandfather clock had been placed on the wall across from the stairway.

Once again she announced her presence to silence.

She stopped at the bottom of the stairs and peered up, but they ascended into pitch-darkness. She found a light switch beside the grandfather clock and flicked it. The steps were as sturdy and noisy as always and creaked under her weight as she ascended. The old, loose guardrails, though, had been replaced with expensive, ornately carved cherry.

Wow, Ron. Way to sell it.

She slowly reached for the handle of her childhood bedroom door, inspected the newly installed brass knob. The door had always been squeaky, but now it opened in absolute silence.

The light from the hallway was enough to see her way around. As she pushed the door wider, it scraped softly over a thick Persian carpet. A full-size bed had been placed on the far end of the room, where she'd once had her desk and shelves. A floral-patterned comforter had been draped over it, and green pillows lay against the headboards, probably now a guest room.

Her gaze wandered over the empty walls where once stood her dresser, bookshelf, and bed. She felt the corners of her mouth twitch.

Stepping further into the room, she shuffled around the open door and groped at the wall behind it until she found the switch for the closet lights. Twin rectangle outlines of gold appeared in the darkness before her.

Reaching for the far right of the door, she found that a metal handle had replaced the notch in the wood. She pulled the sliding closet door open—and her heart sank when she saw only old, scuffed floorboards. She held her breath as she poked her head inside, but sure enough, the space was empty. *"Dammit."* She pulled the door shut and turned off the light.

She stopped on the landing and glanced back into her old room a final time, her eyes stinging. She pulled the door shut after her and turned to the stairs, where the female mannequin waited at the bottom, looking straight up at her.

Katrina snatched her hand away from the banister as if it were hot, and slowly backed up against the wall.

The mannequin's stiff arm was positioned so that its jointless fingers rested upon the newel post, its torso angled back so that it appeared to be looking up.

Suppressing a shiver, Katrina weakly called out once again, "Hello?" Then she immediately regretted it: she didn't want to draw any more attention to herself. Right now, all she wanted was to get out.

With a shaky breath she forced one foot forward onto the top step.

She watched her shadow spilling onto each step as she descended. Approaching the bottom, she realized she'd been keeping her gaze aimed down, actively avoiding meeting the flat gaze of the figure before her.

When she got to the last three steps, she squashed herself against the newel post to keep some space from the mannequin. She debated shutting off the stairwell light; but not wishing to be stuck in the dark with the mannequin, and even less so with whoever had put it there, she continued through the dining room. She made her way back into the sane light of the kitchen, where the mannequin from outside now stood.

She gave voice to a sound that was somewhere between a yelp and a half-formed curse, backing up until something hard rammed into her from behind. She shouted and spun, saw it was the refrigerator, and turned back.

The mannequin had been placed before the foyer door, facing her. She stared at it for a long time, perhaps seconds, perhaps a minute or two, but long enough to determine that it wasn't in fact moving with horrible, animated life. She heard a faint rustle and turned to find the woman was now directly beside her.

Katrina didn't even cry out as she instinctively ran for the door to her father's old office. Ramming her bicep against the door, she swung it open, the light from the kitchen revealing a child-mannequin in colorful pajamas staring up at her.

"*Fuck!*"

She spun and ducked through the nearest door and slammed it shut behind her. Whimpering and panting in the cramped space, she realized where she was and felt along the wall before her until she found a light switch. The first-floor bathroom appeared around her, unfamiliar for its new floral wallpaper and the cabinet above the toilet—but it was mercifully, blessedly *empty*.

As an afterthought, she turned and was relieved to find the door handle was a newer replica of the one she'd grown up with, and she pushed the button-lock in its center.

"Jesus." She looked up at the white door, then raised her voice "I'm sorry! I'll leave, I just . . ." She shook her head, her pulse pounding in her ears.

Who the hell was she even *talking* to? Why were they doing this? What did they want? If they wanted her to leave, they were doing a poor job of it: they'd cornered her, leaving her with nowhere else to go, short of breaking a window.

A thump from beyond the door made her yelp, and she stepped away. Its source was indeterminate. She waited for it to be repeated, but total silence met her ears. She was tempted to listen for tiptoeing footsteps, perhaps a collaborative whisper—but *nothing* would make her move closer to the door.

Police, she thought, pulling out her phone. The station, she recalled, was not even five minutes away, and—

And what, exactly, *would* she tell them?

Hi, I broke into my old home, and I'm being stalked by somebody. No, I don't live there anymore, but there's someone here, and they're moving mannequins around and scaring the shit out of me.

She held down a hysterical urge to giggle, then quickly composed herself. Wasn't that how people had mental breakdowns? Connor, who was getting his psychology doctorate, would know.

Connor! She thumbed through her contacts and nearly dialed Connor, then stopped herself. Even if he was feeling healthy enough to come to the rescue, he was almost two hours away—and with the quarantine, who knew if the authorities would even let him leave?

She considered calling Ron, but after her previous attempts to reach him she doubted any sense of urgency would get through to him now.

And then another thought came to her, one that brought a new fear.

What if the *owners* had already called the police—on *her?* Perhaps they'd used their strange collection of mannequins to terrify the strange woman who'd broken into their home, ushering her into a locked room until the cops came.

She squeezed her eyes shut, pondering what other surprises

they may have brought into the house. She imagined they had even more of those horrible mannequins at their disposal—maybe it was some kind of weird fetish. Shivering at the image of shelves crammed with assorted artificial body parts, she called out, "*Please*, look, I'm sorry! I know I barged in. I'm Katrina Gallett. I used to live here."

More of that awful silence came from the other side of the door. It was hard to imagine who may have been listening, much less what they must be thinking of her. All she could envision were the mannequins waiting outside.

"I just came to get some stuff of mine that I accidentally left here, up in my old bedroom. I didn't see them, so . . ." She shrugged to nobody. "I guess you got rid of them, so there's no reason for me to stay. Can you just *please* let me go? I'll *never* come back. I promise."

Silence.

She shot a glance at the window. Perhaps she could knock out the screen and crawl through. The window was roughly chest-level, and although she might knock her breath out, so long as nobody was waiting for her she may be able to get out easily enough.

Then came another thump, followed by a soft creak— unmistakably from the basement door being opened.

What if there *was* someone waiting for her beyond the door? What then? She didn't carry around pepper spray. She glanced at the cabinet above the toilet, full of half-visible objects. Maybe—

A hard series of raps came from the door behind her, and she started back from it. Then again—*clack-clack-clack*.

She shuddered, glancing back at the window, then at the medicine cabinet.

She tiptoed across the room and opened the mirror-fronted panel. Sure enough, nestled between a roll of bandages and a bottle of hand lotion, a pair of solid metal shears promised escape. She pulled them out, then walked to the window, her lips tightening as she realized that even if she were to smash her way through the glass panes, she'd still have to climb up onto the toilet to squeeze herself through the window. And by then, someone could be waiting outside for her.

She glanced back at the door, then noticed the framed picture hanging on the wall beside it. She hadn't noticed it when she'd first barged in. She tiptoed closer and leaned in, squinting, wanting to see who *really* lived here—who was waiting for her on the other side of the door.

Three figures stood in front of a small house in some anonymous rustic neighborhood. A bird was taking flight behind them, and the child in the front had turned his head and was pointing after it. The couple behind him may have been amused by this, but they weren't laughing—they weren't even smiling. They couldn't—because their faces had been manufactured with only one expression.

Katrina continued to stare at the picture even as she shuddered. What did it mean? What *could* it mean?

Another thump from outside jolted her.

She turned back to the door, considered charging out, screaming and swinging the scissors violently—and before she could reconsider . . .

. . . she decided to do exactly that.

Moving to the door, she repositioned the scissors so the joined blades poked out from below her hand like a knife. She flicked off the lights, and the edges of the door glowed faintly. Placing her hand on the doorknob and turning it, she suppressed the click of the disengaging lock. She braced herself, adrenaline shooting through her chest and into her limbs. *One, two—*

She threw the door open and jumped out, lifting the scissors to head level.

The basement door was still open, the lights still on, but nobody waited for her on the stairs. The former office door was open but was now unoccupied. The dining room doorway was empty, and she turned to the kitchen. The mother-mannequin was there.

Katrina raised the scissors. "*Stay back!* I'm leaving. You'll never see me again, so *please let me go!*"

When no reply came, Katrina moved slowly into the kitchen, glancing back at the open doors behind her. Nobody had appeared behind her, so she turned back.

The boy-mannequin was now also in the kitchen, peering out from behind the woman. They were both facing her.

Shivering, Katrina glanced around, grateful that nobody else was in the kitchen or behind her. Then came a faint scraping sound, and she started and shot a glance back.

The mother-mannequin's arm was now raised, pointing directly at the door, and the fabric of its blouse swayed slightly, settling from unseen movement.

Katrina's eyes darted from the door to the mother, then to the boy, and back to the door. Then she sprinted past them, wrenched the door open, and ran through the foyer and outside.

The procession of dusk had reached its end. The lack of streetlights in the neighborhood left the far end of the lawn in darkness, and it was only as a motion-sensor light turned on that she spotted her car waiting for her—and before it, the father-mannequin.

She came to a staggering halt.

His unmoving eyes stared at her.

"Please, *please!* I just want—"

A sensation tugged her attention away from the father to the doorway. The mother was there, staring out. The boy stood behind her, observing the showdown.

Katrina turned back to find the father had turned his side to her, one arm extended, his hand pointing down . . .

She blinked at what she saw, looked up at him, then down again. Two cardboard boxes had been set on the ground before her car.

"Are . . . ?"

The question died on her lips as she stared at the boxes. When she looked up, the father had lowered his arm.

Clutching the scissors tightly, she walked in a slow, wide arc around him, then crouched before the stacked boxes. With her gaze fixed on him, she reached out and gingerly pulled up the folded corners of the top box. A dusty smell rose to her nostrils, and she looked down.

Bill, the blue, plush bunny that had been the same size as her when she'd first gotten him, peeked up with his wide, flat eyes. A stack of journals from her final single-digit years were shoved in beside him. A sparkling tiara, which Dad had gotten her as a joke when she was eleven, sat upon several dolls' heads. And when a tear fell into the box, Katrina lifted a hand to her cheek to wipe away another.

She looked up at the father, who had turned to regard her silently.

She rose, her mouth working silently. As she clenched and unclenched her hands, she realized that she was still holding the scissors. She lifted them, made sure they were closed, and tossed them, handle first, onto the ground before him.

He stared back at her, his eyes full of artificial non-judgment.

She nodded weakly, and bending again, she grabbed the boxes and lifted them, then carried them behind her car. She fumbled in her purse for her keys and used the remote to open the trunk. She squeezed a box inside, then stood, half expecting the father to be standing beside her, holding the box—or the scissors. But he now stood at the front of her car, and behind him, mother and son waited outside the door.

Katrina closed the trunk, then opened a rear door to shove the other box into the backseat.

Closing the door, she turned back to the family.

"I—I'm sorry."

She didn't know what else to say, but they seemed to understand.

She turned back to the father. "Thank you."

They held each other's gaze for another moment, and then she looked away.

She climbed into the car and keyed the ignition. The headlights illuminated the family that now called 337 Humboldt Street their home, and as she slowly reversed down the driveway and turned into the street, she thought she saw the boy raise an arm to wave.

M.O.T.W.

He reached for the boombox and hit the pause button, and the crooning melodies of World Party's "Ship of Fools" fell silent. He listened carefully—then smiled. The screaming was all he'd heard all morning when he wasn't blasting cassette tapes, but now there was, finally, blessed silence.

He waited for a few heartbeats, his index finger extended to press the play button in case the screaming began anew, but seconds turned into a minute, and a minute soon gave way to three. The only sounds he could hear were the drone of cars and the warbles of distant emergency vehicles, the fan purring in the nearby window, and his own ragged, gentle breaths. He crossed the living room and through the door into the front hall.

The building was vacant, and he walked without scrutiny to the stairwell and opened the door to cold, humid, stale air and silence, and descended.

Robbie glanced up when he heard the bell over the door jingle, quickly averting his gaze from the tired-looking man in the mirror across from him to behold the visitor. The figure behind him appeared to have dully glowing yellow eyes that stared expressionlessly at nothing and everything, but as the visitor approached, his face—and his actual eyes—moved into view from beyond the spots of booze and juice and God knew what else was sprayed, splattered, and caked on to the mirror. Robbie smiled flatly and nodded at the approaching patron, then cast his gaze to his right as a wrinkled manila folder was tossed onto the stained brass counter, followed by a pair of long, thin hands and a short, stocky abdomen that half slid, half twisted onto the stool beside him. "Jeremy."

"*Officer* Robbie."

Robbie rolled his eyes and took a big sip from his three-fourths empty glass. He'd been a detective since December, but Jeremy, who'd known him and his ambitions for the badge since they'd first met in East Boston High, always made fun of his advancing rank. "How goes the pencil-pushing?"

"Oh, you know. Pretty sure I have lead poisoning at this point." Jeremy, who had a habit of second-guessing everything, had restarted his career plans at least three times in the past decade, although he'd recently seemed to have settled in at Boston Metro Properties as a property manager.

Robbie snickered, peering down into his glass as Vanessa sauntered over behind the counter. Her mane of curls was pulled up into a side-pony against the sweaty, mid-May heat, and the bracelets piled around her wrist jangled noisily as she tossed a cardboard circle onto the counter. As it spun on its edges like an oversized coin, she asked, "What're you having, hon?"

Jeremy ordered his usual whiskey sour and watched Vanessa's retreating form, then turned to find Robbie's attention was focused upon the droplet-level amber liquid in the bottom of his glass. "Last or first of those for you?"

"Second. No guarantees it's my last, though."

"Talk to me."

Robbie shrugged, glancing up as Bon Jovi came blasting over the radio behind the counter, which somebody cranked up as the talking-guitar warbles began. He lowered his head and scoffed, his own prayers outlived by the overplayed hit from the year before. "Not if I have to shout over this shit!"

Jeremy snickered, rubbing the tips of his thumb and forefinger down the corners of his mouth as Vanessa returned with his drink. He looked up at her, then pointed to Robbie's empty glass, and she nodded and scurried off for a refill. When he turned back to Robbie, he shrugged. "Something to keep you busy until the song's over."

Robbie smirked as Vanessa returned. "I hate you," he muttered after she left, and Jeremy snickered as he raised his glass in a toast.

After the song and several singing patrons concluded, Jeremy raised his brow at the already half-downed bourbon in Robbie's glass. "So let's hear your three-drink story."

Robbie shook his head, downed a slug of bourbon, and opened his mouth for what could have been a loud belch but instead only produced a quick, shallow breath. "Found another kid."

Jeremy tutted. "I'm sorry, man. Dead?"

Robbie glanced up at Jeremy, whose thick brows were knotted over his glasses, his beard-wreathed mouth curled into a frown.

"I wish."

His shoes fell upon the metal steps with a series of echoing clangs and clunks as he descended. The stairwell was growing damp with the advent of summertime sweat in the cool, clammy basement, the beginnings of rust building up on the welding. He paused on the landing, peering down at the dim space and the paler and darker shapes within it, then continued down.

The walls seemed to glow softly in the pale murk cast by the fluorescent bulbs hanging on long chains from the ceiling. A large, lumpy mass of black fabric was piled up in one corner. The stained concrete floor was smooth, but for a few cracks that nested silverfish and rodents and for a perfectly round, four-foot-wide hole cut into its middle.

He walked past the hole, almost ten feet away but as timid on his feet as if balancing on a wire directly over it. On its far side, a filthy, stained mattress had been cast upon the floor, and atop it, face down, legs and bare feet resting on the concrete, lay the supine form of a little boy.

He moved over the boy and crossed his arms over his chest. The kid's shirt was torn and ragged on the back, but the skin beneath was unblemished, as if a phantom whip had only marred the fabric. He held a hand out over him and snapped his fingers, but the kid didn't move. He repeated the sound a couple of times, and when nothing happened he gently pushed his foot into the kid's side. He sighed heavily when the kid remained motionless, then relaxed when he realized the small abdomen was slowly rising and falling.

After a moment he crouched down and gently pushed his right hand under the kid's shoulder and pulled, twisting him over—then gasped and rose to his feet as the limp form dropped back down into the mattress.

He stepped away, turning to one of the concrete walls and tapping his foot for a couple of minutes. He turned back, cursed softly, then made his way back upstairs.

He went back into his apartment, grabbed the phone in the kitchen, and dialed.

"She was one of those girls from the milk-cartons you see everywhere nowadays." Robbie sniffed. *"'Have you seen me?' 'Please call . . .' 'Last seen . . .'"*

Jeremy nodded. "See them every morning over cereal."

Robbie made a sound between a snicker and another sniff at this, and told the story of Hilda Seinwick, age six. She was last seen with her mother down at the Cypress Street Playground about two weeks before. Mrs. Seinwick had turned around for one moment and felt her daughter let go of her hand. She tried to tell her to not do that, only to run into an elderly couple who were standing behind her, confused. No amount of quick thinking and quicker timing was enough to overcome the panic that ensued, nor to bear fruit in a frantic search that soon led to a whole police shutdown of the market to scope the area. Hilda was gone, and that was that.

"What happened to her in the week following could have been any number of things. Yet as for what *did* happen . . ."

When Robbie blinked, staring at a point that only he could see, Jeremy muttered, "Look like you need another sip for this one."

Robbie glared at him but followed the suggestion. He set his jaw, then muttered, "She was covered in bugs."

Jeremy flinched. "Thought you said she wasn't dead, man!"

"She wasn't. A street vendor over on Gloucester and Beacon found her wandering, totally out of it. He thought she was dirty at first—I mean, she *was* dirty, unwashed for an unknown number of days, some signs of battery, nothing sexual fortunately—but that wasn't what made him drop everything and run out to her. It wasn't even the car that skidded to a halt right beside her. It was the damn roaches and other bugs crawling around in her hair and on her person."

The corners of Jeremy's mouth twisted down, and he nodded, glanced uncertainly into his glass, then took a quick sip. "She got stuck in a sewer or something?"

"Or something. See, when a couple of officers showed up to look—one of them was Meghan Reiner, remember her? You were talking her head off at the fundraiser last—?"

"Oh, right!" Jeremy smirked. "She was bodacious."

Robbie blinked slowly at this, saving his criticism of Jeremy's hip lingo for another day. "Anyway, she got over there shortly after the poor girl was found. The vendor had kept an eye on her, even when some punk swiped the tip jar right off his table, because he was trying to clean her off. The bugs, you see, were *all over* her. I mean *all—over.* In her hair, in her skirt, in her shoes . . . probably elsewhere. And they just kept appearing. The poor guy kept trying to brush them off, but they kept coming. It was practically like she was sweating them."

"Maybe she . . ." Jeremy tried to think of something to say, then gave up and shook his head.

"Officers Reiner and Vinnage show up and take her back to the station. Reiner stayed in the back of the car with Hilda to keep her calm—not that she needed to do much. From the moment the vendor found her, the poor girl had been as silent and dead-eyed as a mannequin. But the whole time, those damn bugs kept crawling all over the place. Reiner even said she thought they were coming out of her skin. And even though Reiner has a stomach of iron, even she had her work cut out for her. She swatted or picked a few off and threw them out the open windows, but more and more of them kept appearing. Roaches, like I said, but also spiders, beetles, uh, center—center—"

"Centipedes?"

"Right." He shook his head. "And after they got out at the station, Officer Reiner even swore she saw a rat appear directly under the car, which would be just about perfect if poor Hilda had it crawling around on her person somewhere, right? So they all make it inside, and even after they get into one of the rooms the damn bugs just don't stop."

"Jesus. *Did* they ever stop?"

"Eventually. And suddenly. They got Hilda a blanket and some water, and someone from Children and Youth Services shows up with word that her mom is on the way—and poof, like nothing, bugs are gone, all is well." He shifted, emitting a muffled, breathy belch, and spread his hands apart like he was holding up a rainbow.

"'Poof' like—?"

"Like where the hell were all those bugs coming from? The poor girl was wearing a teal skirt with flowers printed on it. Had one shoe. Hair came down to above her shoulder. There wasn't anywhere she could, you know, *hide* that many bugs, Jeremy." When Jeremy didn't say anything, Robbie shrugged again. "Exactly."

Jeremy remained silent, then took a short, shallow breath and said, "Wasn't there some woman in the seventeen or eighteen hundreds who gave birth to a ton of rabbits?"

Robbie snorted and shook his head. "Beats me. Weird as that was, that was hardly the issue. Where the hell had she *been* in the meantime? I don't know if they've uncovered anything since"—he glanced up at the bar, where a white rectangular clock advertising Miller beer slowly rotated its second hand—"three-thirty-seven, give or take a minute. And even though she hadn't said hardly a word, I'm not too worried about that yet."

"Why's that?"

Robbie examined the remaining third of his glass, then downed it in a single gulp. "Because that wasn't the first case of its kind."

After she arrived, they both went downstairs. She'd been silent since he'd broken the news to her earlier, and he had a feeling she was going to be horrified, confused, even enraged, when she saw the results of the labor—but instead, she quietly tutted as she stared down at the mattress, shaking her head. "Well, shit."

"That's one way to put it."

She crossed her arms over her chest. "But he's alive?"

He nodded. "Still breathing, at least." He glanced at the form on the mattress, then shrugged. "Somehow."

She looked at the kid for a long moment, then turned to him. "Well, this didn't work, so obviously we've got to try again."

He sighed. "How much longer do we have to do this?"

"However long it—"

They both fell silent as a dull *click* filled the air. They both looked to the kid, but he didn't move, aside from the rise and fall of his chest, and then peered around as the sound came again. It wasn't quite like a droplet of water landing into a puddle, or a rat clambering up a pipe. It reminded him more of a katydid stridulating its exoskeletal segments.

After a moment, she muttered, "I hate this place."

"*You* don't have to live above it."

"Well, neither do you."

"Don't even start. Go get the van and I'll bring him up."

She sighed, shaking her head, and made for the stairs.

He went over to the boy and crouched, grabbing his limp arms and legs, and hoisting him over his shoulder with a grunt. As he did so the sound returned, and he twisted on his feet, trying to ignore the face that hung beside his own, and peered down at the pit.

He thought of a hand somewhere at its bottom, twisting its fingers and thumb inward and snapping, producing a sharp echo—of a massive limb in a vast chamber beneath it, flexing and straightening, its arthritic joint producing a terribly loud crack of cavitation. A great, dark mouth yawning beneath the world, its lips narrowing into a pucker as its tongue curled against its roof, thudding back with a tremendous, moist *click*.

Suppressing a shudder, he moved for the stairs and ascended as quickly as he could.

"One night about two months ago, Reggie Hewitt shows up on the Orange Line platform at Boylston and Washington. A few folks hear screaming and find this eight-year-old kid struggling to get out of a big, jagged crack in the wall. Seemed he got his left foot stuck and twisted around inside it, so he's standing on his right foot and flailing his arms around. And his foot wasn't just stuck—it was wedged in so tight it was like someone poured the concrete around his foot, let it dry, then chiseled it partway out. Poor kid was damn near hysterical, but even before authorities came in the passengers managed to pull him loose. A little worse for wear, but he was okay. And of course, he turned out to have been missing for five days prior."

Jeremy's lips became a solid line as he shook his head slowly. "Terrible. Did his family—?"

"Oh, yeah. I think I heard they were moving out into the countryside after that, closer to extended family in Illinois. But that's the only part of the story the public has heard about."

"What's the non-public version?"

"Well, the kid himself seemed to be okay, like I said. People heard him screaming and looked and found him at the hole in the wall, right? Thing is . . . a few people insisted that that hole wasn't there before."

Jeremy frowned, his head slowly tilting toward his right. "What . . . ?"

"That's right. It's like the kid *popped out of* the wall and broke it in the process. And even if the hole *was* there beforehand, how the hell did he get his foot stuck in it? And how did he wind up down there in the first place?"

When Jeremy said nothing, Robbie took another slug of his drink.

"Poor kid had some weird stuff to report from wherever the hell he was, too. Said it was super-dark. From his descriptions it sounds like he was in a basement, but God knows where that could've been. But what was weird was, he said he kept hearing people singing to him."

"Singing?"

"Or chanting. He couldn't recall the words. He just remembered a bunch of times hearing at least two people speaking in long, drawn-out tones, but harmonized, you know? And there was someone else, laughing. Lots of laughing, like someone was enjoying the funniest joke in the world. And at one point, someone started touching—"

"Yeah." Jeremy raised his hand and shook his head. "Okay. I'll exit the conversation here."

"Nothing sexual. Just felt someone putting their hands on his back. Kid was so scared he passed out, but then the next thing he knew he was on the subway, stuck in that wall."

The two looked at each other for a long moment, then turned back to their respective glasses.

After a moment Jeremy signaled to Vanessa. She had her back turned, and he lowered his hand partway, not saying a word as he watched her cleaning the far end of the counter. As soon as she turned, he signaled for her and requested pretzels.

"Ask her out already," Robbie said.

"Nah. I'm not going down that road again." Ever since the former Mrs. Dunning had dropped out of the picture, Jeremy had been, in his own words, "allergic to romance." He cleared his throat. "You said there were others? As in more than one?"

Robbie puffed out his cheeks as he let out a drawn-out stream of bourbon-scented breath. "Last spring. A girl was found floating facedown in the Charles. No signs of trauma to the body . . . well, make that, nothing obvious, no bruising or injuries. But she had long, ropelike things sticking out of her back and shoulders. It was assumed they were somehow implanted on her, by some kind of sick plastic surgeon in the making—but then medical examiners identified them as cartilage and chitin—and what's more, they matched her DNA."

Jeremy's eyes and lips narrowed for a long moment as he digested this. "Wait—like they were *growing* on her?"

Robbie nodded. "Weird enough, right? And you'd think maybe the kid died of her deformities or something. Lots of people with bad enough deformations don't have a very healthy system and don't live as long as others would. Except for one detail: she'd gone missing the week before and had absolutely no medical or familial history of having *anything* like extra appendages on her person."

"Gag me with a spoon!"

"Something's going on, my friend." He downed the last of his bourbon, then opened his mouth around a breathy gurgle. "Think this is going to be a four-drink story." He held his glass up and nodded.

"You think there's a connection between them all?"

"Kids go missing, they turn up again, but kinda weird. One after another. There's been ten cases like this that I know of over four precincts—and I'm getting the feeling that there's bound to be more. You tell me."

They were both silent as Vanessa returned with Robbie's next round, then Jeremy stuck his hand in his pocket to fumble out his wallet. "These are on me."

"No, man, don't," Robbie muttered, but didn't make any other move to stop him.

"Trust me. It's the least I can do for you, having to carry all this around."

He slammed the door shut behind him and leaned against it, gritting his teeth as he gingerly grabbed his wrist, his sore hand trembling. His cheek was stinging, where three parallel streaks of red puffed up from where fingernails had dragged minutes before. And his ears still rang with the feral shrieks that echoed up from the stairwell behind him.

The kid had begun waking up before he'd gotten him inside, but he was weak, and it only took a hand over his mouth to keep him silent long enough to bring him down—but the kid had nearly broken the skin of his hand with a hard bite, and he'd begun wildly thrashing as he was set down on the mattress, managing to flip over and scrape one of his bound hands right along the side of his abductor's face. It didn't take long for the next step to begin, however, and he'd quickly made his way back upstairs.

He looked at his hand and cursed at the scarlet crescent that had risen on it.

The screams then began to transition into piercing screeches, and he moved away, thinking of what he could pick from his cassette collection to cover the racket while he worked on some bills.

"Hello?"

"Jer, it's me."

"No, it's pronounced Jeremy."'

"Nyuck-nyuck-nyuck. Wanna meet up tonight?"

"Twice in one month? To what do I owe the—?" A brief silence. *"Oh, no . . . was there another one?"*

"It's a four-drink night."

"Jesus Christ. Are you okay, man?"

"I don't think I'll ever be okay again."

The foundation of the basement rattled and hummed as trains sped through the bowels of the city around it.

A rat, beholding the space below from a secret vantage along the ceiling structures, squealed and fell as the unsteady, human-made quake dislodged it. It fell to the floor with a startled squeak, righted itself and scurried away from the forms and shadows at the center of the room.

The hole in the floor stretched down past concrete and bedrock alike with a blind disregard for the surface world's definitions of light, transcending the earthly structure in its ages-old burrow into mystery.

The soiled mattress beside the hole creaked and sighed with shifting weight upon its layers of fabric and metal springs.

A soft, breathy moan filled the darkness, accompanied by the whisper of fabric.

Then came a sharp gasp, obscured by a low, throaty chuckle that gave way to brays of hearty laughter—and then the screams began.

"His face was gone."

Jeremy's mouth opened into a perfect O, his eyes as wide as Roger Rabbit's.

"Not like cut off, but—" Robbie twirled his index finger around the shape of his face. "Smooth. Like he put a bowl over his face, but it was made of his skin. And the sick thing is, somehow, he's still alive. Still *breathing.*"

"What the *hell?*"

"Examiners are on it, but . . ." Robbie downed more than half his glass—rye, this time—and coughed as he half set, half slammed it onto the counter. "Doubt they'll have any straight answers. Family is begging them to keep it quiet from the public, but we'll see if *that* lasts."

"Monster of the week, eh?"

Robbie glared at him. "The poor kid isn't a damn *monster*. Don't be a prick."

"What's a monster but just another misunderstood being?" Jeremy shrugged. "I doubt the kid had any say in what happened to him."

Robbie continued to glare at him for a moment, then looked away and muttered, "The only monster in *this* case is whoever the hell is doing it to them."

They were silent for a couple of minutes. Vanessa was out for the night, and a skinny girl with short, spiky, silver-tipped hair was hefting a tray full of empty tumblers out from the back and lowering it onto the far counter.

On the television balanced atop the liquor shelves behind the counter, a report parroted the recent speech from the president, who'd urged Gorbachev to tear down the Berlin Wall. Margaret Thatcher was already laying out the groundwork for her newly won third term. A masked vigilante had been pursued from Providence and along several highways before authorities had lost him in southeastern Massachusetts. Donald Harvey, an Ohio hospital orderly and self-proclaimed "Angel of Death," had been arrested for murdering in excess of thirty patients on his watch.

"Are we sure it's a person doing this, though?" Jeremy offered.

Robbie frowned and glared at him.

"Just saying, what if something *happened* to those kids. Like, not for nothing, but *how* exactly would or even *could* a person begin to—*do* all this to these kids?"

Robbie frowned, and Jeremy held his hand up.

"Hear me out. Chernobyl last year did all *sorts* of weird stuff to people who were near it. Some people practically *melted* from radiation. Wouldn't be surprised if, somehow, this was a similar thing, no?"

"So, what . . . ? These kids were blasted with radiation and wind up all—" Robbie scrunched up his face and shook his head. "Sorry, no. This isn't a damn comic book. People *die* from radiation poisoning."

"Well, didn't that girl in the river die?"

Robbie began to nod, then looked away, lowering his voice. "From drowning. Not from—whatever the hell happened to her."

"*Exactly!*" Jeremy pointed at him. "*That's* what I'm saying. What if it's not radiation but something else? What if these kids are . . . ?" He shook his head. "I don't know, maybe they're getting lost, and wind up somewhere where something is affecting them?"

"'Somewhere'?"

"I don't know. Have you ever heard theories about parallel universes? Pocket universes? That sort of thing? Who's to say that there aren't places in our world, our existence, where our reality blends and blurs and breaks into other ones? And—I don't know, maybe it's like, we can't handle the atmosphere over there?"

Robbie held his gaze for a long time, then looked away. "Sorry to disappoint you, Mr. Sagan, but whatever's going on, it's not the stuff of science fiction. This is more insidious. Hell, I'll go ahead and call it evil. They're *kids*. Never adults, at least none that I've been informed about."

"Well, what's evil but just a human action? My buddy Jesse got stung by a wasp, and he's allergic as hell. Damn near killed him. But the wasp didn't go seeking him out because it was evil. He just happened to be near its nest or maybe he accidentally hit it or who knows what? It wasn't evil—it was just a wasp. Life doesn't pick who it affects or how. It doesn't know what it's doing. It just—does it. And sometimes it feels unfair and cruel, but it is what it is."

"Well, if that's the case, and something . . . 'other-natural,' whatever you want to call it, is affecting them—then why is it only happening to kids? Who've gone missing? *And* then they miraculously turn up? Sorry, but regardless of whatever the hell may be happening to them, that sounds an awful fuck like a person is involved."

Three more missing kids were found in the last full month of summer. Jeremy didn't need to meet with Robbie to know that they were victims of the same strange and terrible circumstances that had befallen the others.

A seven-year-old boy was found walking near Newbury and Fairfield one twilight hour, his face and shirt bloody. After being taken in by authorities, only rumors of his state lingered, with a few witnesses claiming that his arms and legs had terminated in narrow, lumpy, prehensile shapes where hands and feet had been, which had not been the case when his picture had first appeared on milk cartons around the region only a couple of days before.

Two parents were relieved to hear from their apartment building neighbors that their runaway eleven-year-old daughter had showed up, miraculously, after having been missing for twelve days. She claimed she'd been invited into a building by a strange but compassionate man who offered her shelter and food while his wife called the police, only to be led down into a darkened basement, inside which newspapers and TV reports only vaguely hinted at terrible things occurring. And although her reunion with her family was celebrated, if briefly, many took note of the complete loss of hair on her head and eyebrows in the pictures and videos that surfaced after. And like the boy found in the subway earlier in the year, she recalled hearing multiple voices in the dark around her.

The final missing child was found dead in a Chinatown alley. Her death was seen more as a notoriety than a tragedy, as her body seemed to have been slashed and traumatized with the savagery of wild animals, although there wasn't so much as a single fowl or rodent reported anywhere near her at the time of her discovery.

Although a few tabloids and 'zines blamed the crimes on everything from a serial killer to a deranged scientist at work, the differences in the cases were too great for the public to think that there was a singular villain behind the kidnappings.

Jeremy would read about the stories in the paper or occasionally see reports on his television. He'd often follow them up with a glass of water foaming with antacid. He met up once with Robbie in the first week of fall, and although Robbie seemed to have a lot on his mind, they talked about everything but work on that long night full of booze and live music.

Only a few people, besides Jeremy and Robbie, took note of the dark pattern forming among the missing and the rediscovered. Whatever interpretations or agendas they inferred from these statistics, there would be no ultimate analysis, no publicized response, to the strange affectations of the found children. To some of them, the discoveries proved to be more disquieting than the disappearances themselves.

And despite the excess of seven hundred independent dairies working overtime to produce milk cartons showcasing the faces of missing children across the country for the past couple of years, the numbers of those who were actually found as a result were so low that the campaign began to die out.

By the end of the year, more than four hundred thousand children in America had been reported as missing, and most of them were never seen again.

Jeremy lowered his copy of the *Globe*, frowning and looking around.

The recently refurbished brownstone's first floor apartment was, in his definition, perfect. The staging crew had done a good job in restructuring and repainting the old walls. The bathroom's clawfoot tub would be a high selling point, as did the wide bay windows that illuminated the living room. And although he'd not tell prospective tenants about his recent stay in the place, he could honestly promise them that it was a comfortable place in which to live.

After a moment, the rapping of knuckles on wood came again.

Who the hell?

He got up and walked across the room. He'd set up a few amenities throughout the apartment, officially to accent the staging, although his first showing wouldn't be for another couple of weeks. Nobody at Boston Metro Properties knew that he was staying here. In fact, he'd made a point of checking his mail for the past month at his official home in Somerville. And only one other person knew he was going to be here today—and *that* visit was still a couple of hours away.

He walked up to the front door and squinted through the peephole; then his face slackened like a popped balloon. He lowered his head for a moment, clenching his jaw.

When the knocking came again, he took a deep breath, reached up and pulled the chain free from the doorframe, and unlatched the deadbolt. He pulled the door open and smiled weakly. "Officer Robbie," he muttered.

Robbie gave him a long look, then strode in toward him. "Not speaking as a detective, I think we both know why I'm here."

Jeremy pushed the door shut behind him, swallowing hard. He walked across the room to a boombox sitting on a bookcase and switched off the music. "I *think* I know what you're thinking."

"Enlighten me."

"It's probably a four-drink reason."

Robbie held his arm up and twisted his wrist over, peering down at his watch. "At some point tonight, for sure. Probably more."

Robbie sighed heavily, crossing his arms over his chest, and lowering his head. "Jer—*why*? What the hell, man?"

"It's . . . complicated."

"Should I call Dr. Westheimer for this?"

"No!" Jeremy held his hands up, shaking his head quickly. "No. It's nothing like that."

"Well?"

"It's— Well, remember what I mentioned, about pocket universes and . . . ?"

"Spare me the Flatland mumbo-jumbo."

"Well, if you want to know, you'll have to pardon some 'mumbo-jumbo.'"

Robbie's lips pulled tightly across his lower face. "Go on."

"Imagine if there was a way to talk to a god. And not just praying up a million questions into the ether, but to actually *speak* to it directly—and to hear back. What would you ask it? What would you ask *of* it? And if it could do things *for* you . . . what would you do *for* it?"

"I think Indiana Jones has already asked *and* answered these questions a couple of times."

"I'm not talking about Kali or even the popular one. Nothing like that. I'm talking bigger."

"'Bigger'? What the hell does *that* mean? And *what the hell does this have to do with the kids?*"

"They're—" he stammered, and Robbie noticed the sheen that had developed on his forehead. He sighed and looked down. "We didn't *want* to use kids, not at first. But eventually we learned that they have such better capacities for—"

"For what, you sick fuck?"

Jeremy shook his head, cringing, then sighed. "Let's just say capabilities. We wouldn't've been able to do this with—"

"'This' being—?"

"I told you. It's complicated."

"What, kidnapping kids? Torturing them? Doing mad scientist experiments on—?"

"That's not what—" Jeremy raised his hands, and Robbie snapped his fingers and pointed at him.

"Hands down."

"Jesus, Robbie!"

"Jesus has *nothing* to do with what you've been doing to those poor kids."

Jeremy glared at him for a long moment. "You're right about that much. And what's been happening to them—*none* of that was the intent."

"Side effects, eh? Throw out the rejects?"

"We let them go!"

"What a good Samaritan you are." Robbie pressed his fingers very hard against the inner corners of his eyes, then sighed. "Please, make this easy on yourself. Or at least make it easy on me. You owe me that much, after all these years."

Jeremy chewed on his lower lip. "Okay. Follow me." When Robbie tensed, he quickly added, "Pull out your gun, if it'll be *easier* for you."

"Or for you."

Jeremy held his gaze for a long time, then nodded.

Robbie held his hand out, fingers flat, and gestured toward the door. "Lead the way."

Jeremy led Robbie into the front hallway and down a stairwell. Their feet clanged noisily upon the metal stairs. Robbie sniffed, then groaned noisily.

"Pardon the smell," Jeremy muttered. "Need to get that cleaned before we start showings."

"Probably a good idea."

The concrete floor was dimly illuminated by the light from the stairwell behind them. Jeremy knew Robbie was watching him closely as he reached up to a thin, beaded chain dangling from the ceiling, which he tugged with a rattling click. Fluorescent lights flickered on overhead, and Robbie sighed heavily behind him.

The mattress on the floor was cloudy with innumerable stains of sweat, piss, and darker body fluids. Robbie stared at it for so long that for a moment Jeremy was hopeful he somehow hadn't noticed the open hole in the floor beside him. But then his friend turned to the space and walked closer, peering down. He reached over it and snapped his fingers, listening to the cracking echo bounce deeper and deeper, growing fainter and fainter until it vanished, along with any hope Jeremy had left that this would somehow be something they could put behind them.

As the rumble of a passing subway train filled the space, Robbie turned and faced Jeremy, his lips a flat line again. "What the *hell* is wrong with you, man?" he asked in a quiet, even voice.

"It's—"

"'*Complicated.*' I know. But that's not good enough. Even if you're not going to tell me, you're sure as Shinola going to have to explain yourself to someone. So you'd better start getting your story straight."

Jeremy opened his mouth, peered past Robbie, then sighed again.

"Okay. You know what? You're not going to believe anything I have to say. Are you?"

"Sad to say, probably not. I used to believe a lot of things about you, man. But once I started adding up the numbers and figured it all out, it's been harder and harder to believe *anything* anymore."

He went on to explain about those numbers, about the radius of the disappearances—and reappearances. About the composite descriptions of the abductors from a few of the kids. After a while his explanation became a series of echoing warbles to Jeremy as his plans, his hopes, his dreams, his whole world, began to crack and fall apart and get sucked into the void of unknowns beyond.

When Robbie was done, Jeremy croaked, "But—why? Why *you?* Why aren't we surrounded by badges right now?"

Robbie took a deep breath and held it, then muttered, "I guess I just really hoped to hear you say one thing."

"And what's that?"

"How about *'I didn't do it,'* maybe? And yet, here we are."

Jeremy lowered his head and nodded. "Monster of the week."

"Monster of the week." He nodded, then frowned. "Who else?"

"What—?"

"*Who else is involved?* Who are your partners? Several of the kids said they heard at least three separate voices down here."

Jeremy swallowed hard, then looked away. "Nobody you know."

"Good. I don't think I can handle any more surprises about people I thought I knew."

The two remained silent for a long moment.

"So . . . do you want to cuff me now, or—?"

The click that sounded was sharp and loud enough to be a gunshot, and Jeremy twitched with a grunt, his heart skipping a beat as he looked at his friend—who was also startled, peering around. "The hell was that?"

Jeremy peered past him again. "This place is . . . old. Makes weird sounds sometimes. The subways go all around us, as you probably—"

"Jesus!"

Jeremy spun and found Robbie backing up, peering down into the hole, and gingerly stepping around it, then looking up at one wall, where streaks of yellow paint on the bricks formed a wide, serpentine cross. He'd had his own instances of thinking the symbol was something alive, something moving, but he was not about to share such small talk now. Then he looked beyond Robbie, and his eyes widened.

Robbie sighed heavily as he turned to him. "Jeremy Dunning, you're under ar—"

When the laughter burst out behind Robbie, he spun, his right hand seeming to flash with light for a moment before the handcuffs he'd produced were flung into the air as he backed away from the naked, bald man that had appeared behind him.

Jeremy's own hands flew up as he shouted, "*No!* Watch—"

Too late, Robbie's shifting foot planted onto the edge of the pit beside him, and gravity and adrenaline took him away.

Jeremy had no voice as his mouth dilated into a perfect tribute to the hole into which his friend fell. His gaze guided his head as he watched Robbie pitch down into the shadow, shouting nonsense before the black and the silence below swallowed him.

The span of a second passed like an eternity, only to be interrupted by the sharp clatter of metal on stone as the cuffs landed on the floor somewhere nearby. Jolted out of his transfixion, Jeremy looked up, his eyelids widening more and more, retreating from what his eyes beheld before him.

The naked man grinned at him, his own eyes narrowed with a joy, as well as an incandescent orange glow that Jeremy was incapable of comprehending. On his hairless chest a black star of chitinous, spider-like limbs quivered and clawed at the air with the frenzied movements of alien ecstasy.

The basement rumbled and rattled with another passing train.

The spider-chested man chuckled throatily.

And the hole remained perfectly silent.

After a long moment Jeremy's eyes began to sting. He didn't shake his head so much as it began to twitch back and forth. His jaw and cheeks trembling, he huffed a few shaky breaths before stammering, "Wh-what the fuck? What the *fuck* am I supposed to do *now?*"

The man didn't say anything as he stared back at him, jack-o'-lantern eyes glowing.

Jeremy let out a heavy sigh and lowered his head, unable to speak, unable to think. When he looked up again, he was alone.

He looked around, feeling his eyes stinging. When his wandering gaze reached the mattress, he lashed out one foot at its edge, then kicked it again, harder. His feet switched as he began pummeling it, again and again. Something dark was flung into the air from its surface, its bulbous shape and long, stringlike appendages reminding him of a jellyfish, but then it was gone from sight before he could identify it. He stopped, glaring around, then turned away with a frustrated snarl.

He glanced at his watch. His "partner," such as she was, would be here in an hour. *And* she would probably have another candidate in tow.

He sighed, jabbing his fingertips against his eye sockets and rubbing the moisture from them, then turned and headed upstairs.

He had a lot of work to do.

Tripping the Ghost

M ark looked up from the spread of papers on the desk before him when he heard a vehicle pulling up outside. He glanced at the clock—six-thirty on the dot, exactly as Constance had promised.

"Chad," he called into the next room, "she's here." He got up from the desk and stepped out the front door, where he was surprised to find a gray minivan idling in their driveway, and even more so at the bald man climbing out of the driver's seat. The autumn sun had almost completely set, but the man was wearing sunglasses.

What is up *with these people?* "Need any help?"

Instead of a response, the man went around to the back of the van.

Footsteps approached Mark from behind. "Where's Constance?"

"Dunno."

Chad peered over his shoulder. "Who's *that?*"

Mark turned and shaped a word with his lips, but couldn't bring himself to speak as a sick, cold feeling wriggled through his chest.

Maybe Constance hadn't felt the need to be present for the dropoff. Or, worse, maybe this man wasn't even an associate of hers.

Chewing on his lower lip, Mark stepped back inside and reached up to a secret shelf they'd installed above the nearest window and removed a .38 revolver.

"Oh, great." Chad turned and walked further into the room behind them, probably grabbing the shotgun hidden beneath the desk.

Holding the revolver against the back of his thigh, Mark slowly headed outside.

There was a thump from behind the van, and something big and dark moved into view from behind its open rear doors. Tensing, Mark lifted the gun—then lowered it as he saw the man step into view, carrying something big and dark above his right shoulder.

"Did Constance send you?"

The man didn't reply. If he nodded, it was hard to tell, as his head and torso were crooked under his burden's weight. He approached steadily, showing no signs of strain or even discomfort, nor any sounds of labored breathing. Mark could only hear the soft thumps and crunches of his feet on the dead grass and leaves as he stopped directly in front of him.

"Oh, uh—" Mark unconvincingly tried to tuck the gun behind his leg, but if the man had seen it, he didn't seem bothered. "Follow me."

Chad was waiting in the front door, one arm out of view, no doubt holding the shotgun.

Mark shook his head, and Chad closed the door.

Mark led the man around the back of the house. Its backyard was a pool of shadows crowded by a tight ring of trees. They'd not invested much time or money in maintaining the property: even during the day it was dark and foreboding, choked with weeds and shrubs and the occasional yard pest. The lack of care had made for a big price cut on the property, along with the realtor's allegation that the house itself was haunted. It had been the perfect location for their business.

He nodded to the sloped cellar doors. "Right over here."

He glanced sheepishly at the man but couldn't make out much more than his shape in the dark, stooped crookedly beneath the case. Praying he didn't accidentally shoot his foot off, Mark shoved the revolver into his pocket. He reached for the short, heavy chain that had been threaded through the handles on the cellar doors and undid the combination lock there, then pulled the chain out with a noisy jangle. As he did so, a hairline of pale light appeared between the doors and around their edges, and muffled thumps rose from within. The left door thumped, then popped open, swinging up with a rusty squeal, and Chad appeared, silhouetted by the lights from the basement. He stared the man and frowned, then back at Mark, who offered a slight shrug in response. Mark pulled open the other door, and the man stepped forward and carefully descended the concrete stairs.

Mark let out a heavy breath and looked around, following the man down.

Chad was directing the man to a long, empty table. The man wordlessly moved beside it, crouched beside it and half slid, half shrugged the case onto its surface. Under the fluorescent bulbs set along the middle of the ceiling, Mark could see now that the case was made of dark wood, its surface mottled with worn, water- and dirt-stained blemishes. But despite its familiar, blackened metal handles on its sides and its arched upper surface, and size was tellingly small.

It was a child's coffin.

"Uh . . ."

The man straightened and turned to him.

"This— This is it? This is from Constance?"

Mark expected silence in response, and that was exactly what he got. His hand moved alongside the gun as he watched the man reach inside his jacket pocket, but he relaxed when a thick envelope appeared. The man silently held it out, and Mark cautiously took it. "Thanks." It was all he could think to say.

The man didn't smile or nod as he turned and walked back to the stairway.

Mark and Chad exchanged another look, then followed him up the stairs, back along the house, and stopped as the man returned to the minivan. They watched him climb inside and reverse down their driveway, and then he was gone.

"What the hell was *that* all about?" Chad said.

Mark shook his head, puffing his cheeks out as he looked down at the coffin. "I know as much as you do."

"How much is in there?"

His hand clenched around something flat and stiff, and he looked down and saw the envelope he still clutched in his hand.

"That *is* money in there, right?"

Briefly nauseous, he lifted the metal fasteners on the top of the envelope and pulled it open, sighing with a slight chuckle as he saw the sandwiched lines of greenish-gray inside. *"Whoof!* Yeah, it is." He frowned, lifted the envelope closer, and saw a folded white sheet inside.

"How much?"

"Hold on." He pulled the paper out and unfolded it. Chad snatched the envelope from his hand and Mark glared at him, then began to read the typed letter.

"Holy . . ." Chad began leafing through the wad of bills he'd removed from the envelope. "There's gotta be—" He began counting, but Mark didn't look up nor listen as he read the letter.

> *Hello, boys.*
>   *As promised, here is your* resource commandée. *I do think you'll find it perfectly meets the requirements of your methods (Mark, hadn't you said something about "quality and quantity"?) and should adequately provide the desired effects. But of course, please don't hesitate to reach me if there are any problems with it—I would be happy to provide a different resource for your fascinating production.*
>   *Sincerely, Constance*

Mark didn't move, didn't even lower the letter. Instead, his eyes darted up over its edge to glance at the coffin on the table.

"What's up?"

"I'm—not sure if I like the sound of this."

"Why?"

Mark handed him the letter and waited while he read it. When he was done he was frowning, too, and they both turned to the coffin.

"So what's *in* there?" Chad asked.

"Well, we're about to find out." Mark approached a cabinet on the wall nearby and started pulling down gloves, face masks, and tools. They geared up, then set to work opening the coffin. It was unmarked, but it looked a bit like one that they'd unearthed several months before from a Rhode Island grave dating back to the 1870s. If this was even remotely similar, it would be easy enough to open.

As Mark tapped a chisel and hammer along the dirt-lined seam of the coffin's lid, Chad wheeled over a large, re-purposed aquarium tank on a small cart.

A series of ticks and creaks came from the coffin as Mark loosened the lid and, planting his fingers into its edge, gave it a cursory tug, its hinges working with a squealing groan. Even through his mask he thought he could smell the unsealed air that wafted out. He pulled the lid up—then gasped and dropped it back in place with a hollow thud.

"Oh, what in the Christ?" Chad cried, backing up, and Mark found himself doing the same.

"That—that—"

"That's *not* a kid!"

"That's not *human!*" Mark's mask threatened to slip down off the bridge of his nose as he shook his head. "Oh, God . . . did Constance pull a fast one on us or something?"

"A *ten grand* fast one?"

His eyes widened. "Seriously?"

"Yes!" Chad pointed at the coffin. "But *that*—I mean, who the hell would want anything to do with *that?"*

"Okay, okay. Hold on." Mark turned away, taking a deep breath, almost pressing his hand to his head before remembering where it had just been. "So whatever that is, *that's* what she wants us to work with. Assuming it even works." He shook his head, feeling an itch in his shoulder erupt into a full-body shiver.

"Well, do we even have a choice at this point?"

Mark looked back at the coffin, then sighed heavily. "All right, all right. Let's give it a shot. Worse comes to worst—"

I would be happy to provide a different resource . . .

He suppressed another shiver.

Chad stepped forward, tugged the lid up, and threw it against the wall. Mark slowly peered into the coffin and gave its occupant a good long look.

To say that time and the elements had been kind to the body was an understatement. Perhaps, instead, they had taken pity upon the de-formed entity inside the coffin—pity, or fearful avoidance. The jumble of too-too-many twisted appendages reminded Mark of gnarled tree roots and overgrown vines, yet were punctuated with angled joints—they were, unmistakably, *limbs*. The skin was a sickly brownish-gray, spongy, and moist. Each limb ended in uneven appendages. Some were fully formed fingers, and others were little more than a cluster of lumps. Between what may or may not have been a couple of legs, a dark, shrunken mass offered no suggestion of a sex. And its *head* . . .

Mark looked away, knowing full well that that twisted, forever-silenced scream would never leave his mind in even the most restful slumbers. He turned to Chad, but all they could do was stare at each other.

No amount of hesitation could prepare them for what they had to do next. They moved the tank beside the table and reached inside the coffin. Mark wriggled his fingers beneath a few of the more heavily layered groups of limbs, and Chad its tiny shoulders. They counted to three and carefully lifted it out.

The body was surprisingly light, no more than fifty pounds. Mark held his breath to avoid gagging as he felt the squishy give of thing's flesh in his gloved hands. They carefully maneuvered it above the rim of the coffin and over the tank and began lowering it in—

Chad yelped and dropped his end of the body.

Cursing, Mark followed suit, and the body fell into the tank, landing with a sickening cacophony of dull thuds. "What?"

"It fucking moved!"

"*What?*"

"I *swear* to God, man, that *thing* moved a couple of its arms!"

"That was probably *me holding it*, jerk!"

"I *felt* it!"

Mark's jaw worked as he looked at the still thing in the tank. "Whatever. Let's—just get it ready." *And then get some questions ready for Mrs. Constance.*

They brought the tank to the stairwell and began hoisting the cart up on sheets of plywood. Once it was upstairs, Mark slammed the basement door shut. They'd not bothered to do anything with the coffin. They'd made an unspoken agreement to leave *that* for the next day.

Wheeling the cart into the nursery—a converted living room—Mark felt an odd comfort as they passed all the other tanks. So much routine, so much normalcy, so much *sanity* lay inside each one.

They turned the corner and moved to the empty row of tables on the far wall. They stopped at the far end of the tables, then hauled the tank up, grateful to have a quarter of an inch of acrylic between them and its contents as they slid it onto a table.

Mark turned to the refrigerator—then stopped and looked quickly back at the tank.

It didn't move, he told himself, staring the snarl of tangled limbs for a long, breathless moment. *Not earlier, and not now.*

He walked to the other side of the room and opened a small refrigerator. Inside, bottles of water crowded the top shelf, and beneath, rows of small, foil-sealed containers filled the remaining shelves beneath. He took an open bottle and one of the containers back to the tank, then removed a small cork that crowned a hollow pin in the middle of a socket on the top of the tank.

Chad approached with an extension cord. Plugging it in, Mark reached for a switch on the top of the tank cover, and bright lights flicked on. Ignoring what they illuminated, he turned on the vents, then uncapped the water and poured some into a small tube. Upending the foil-topped container, he pushed it onto the pin, hearing it puncture the foil as he screwed the container's mouth into the socket. He waited to make sure that the aeration process began, and when a fine, faint fog of greenish-gray began puffing and swirling into the tank, they walked away.

Nearby, the most recent acquisition had begun to take. An older specimen, it had taken nearly a week to grow, but yesterday the incomplete stack of shins, femurs, and vertebrae had finally sprouted a gray coating. Earlier that morning a few buttons had begun to form. Chad had been especially curious as to what results it would yield. The bones were those of a man whose house had sometimes smelled of the fire that had killed him nearly twenty years before.

The specimens in the next row were much farther along. Skulls, shins, pelvises, and rib cages had begun losing their familiar shapes under blankets of young fruiting bodies. The newest ones were still weeks away from cultivation, but judging from their sheer numbers, they would make for a good batch.

The ones in the last row were at their most advanced stages of necrosynthetic myceliation, the bones literally falling apart under the mere weight of the fruiting bodies that sprouted thick and moist above them. Two of the tanks were nearly empty, the cultivated mushrooms leaving only anonymous piles of wrinkled, shrunken, crumbling remains of old bones.

Mark had been planning to check on a few crops that he'd gathered earlier, but after everything that they'd dealt with tonight, all his energy was spent. He and Chad locked up, then muttered superficial wishes of good nights that both knew they'd not be getting.

Chad couldn't help but grin as he stared into the tank. "Look at you."

The strange body had proved to be unique in more ways than one: only twelve days after they'd prepared it, a gray mold began to form a blanket that mercifully obscured the revolting shapes beneath. The very next day, buttons had begun to form. And now, not even a full week later, the fruiting bodies were growing perfectly.

Chad jotted a few lines down in his notebook. If *this* was any indication of how bountiful the batch was going to be . . .

He licked his lips and looked back in the tank.

Most of the fruiting bodies were still young and small, but a few larger ones were sprouting up from the middle—such as it was—of the disproportionate cadaver, their caps nearly at full width. It was too soon to pick them, he knew—but then again, it was also too soon for them even to be *growing*, and yet here they were.

He started to pull his phone out of his pocket, then put it back. Mark was over in Providence, picking up a fresh batch of spores from his supplier. *He didn't need any more stress.* Chad set his notebook and pen down beside the tank, then fetched a pair of gloves and a small knife from the supply cabinets. He removed the lid of the tank, set it aside, reached in, and grabbed the largest cap and gingerly tugged it.

It was, of course, still firmly rooted in the body, and so he brought the knife in and began slowly cutting around its base, the spongy matter between fungus and flesh splitting moistly around the blade. He gave the mushroom another tug—and frowned when it still refused to separate. *"C'mon . . ."* He pulled with a little more force, and it finally obliged.

He lifted the mushroom out and held it up in the light, but as he examined it his grin withered into a frown.

Liquid, a shade of green so dark it was nearly black, glittered on the base of the mushroom, swelling into a bead that dripped down onto his jeans. Cursing, he held the mushroom away from himself, glanced into the tank—and gasped.

The spot that he'd cut the mushroom from was now a glistening puddle of that same dark liquid.

Groaning in disgust, he set the mushroom down on the table and forcefully shoved the lid of the tank back in place. He tore his gloves off and tossed them aside, cursing again as he realized he still had to pick up the mushroom.

He grabbed his pen and notebook, jotted down a few quick lines, then delicately carried the mushroom into the kitchen. While he fired up the oven, he cut off a few slices and threw them onto a baking sheet, which he then shoved into the oven.

When their distinctly acrid odor hit his nostrils, he took them out, grabbed a bag of stale bread, and removed a slice, placing the cooling, dried mushrooms onto it. He took some more notes, then dumped the soft tan coins onto the bread, folded it over, and took a tentative bite. *"Eurrrmph,"* he groaned, forcing himself to chew and swallow the rancid sandwich.

He poured himself a glass of water from the sink and started to down it when he heard a soft thump behind him. He lowered the glass and listened, but it didn't repeat.

He suppressed a shiver, remembering their first weeks in the house. They'd seen no specters, nor heard any disembodied wails or the clanking of phantom chains, but there *had* seemed to be a draft bringing cool air into rooms during those long hot summer days. Of course, all that had come to an end when they'd found the overgrown grave in the backyard, but—

There, again.

It hadn't come from the front door, nor the back. Its origin was hard to determine, and he doubted it was an effect of the mush-rooms—the trip hadn't even started yet. Chad uncomfortably found himself thinking of the strange body again, of how its arms had *twitched* as he and Mark had lifted it out of its coffin. He'd known what he'd seen that night, what he'd *felt* . . .

He went back to the nursery and straight to the tank, his breath held until he saw the body was still there, exactly as he'd left it earlier.

Letting out his breath, he shook his head, then gasped. Little black spots had begun to appear in his vision.

Grinning, he ran back into the kitchen, fetched his notebook and pen, and went down into the basement, where an armchair and a lamp stood in a corner for exactly this purpose. Flipping open his notebook to a blank page, he poised his pen over the paper. As the black spots began to multiply and swell, crowding his vision, he thought he heard another thump, much louder now. But when the black spots coalesced, he could only stare straight into the opening window of darkness they revealed, and what waited beyond.

Mark's finger tapped harder and faster against the back of his phone, and he disconnected. Chad wasn't picking up, so their conversation would have to wait until he got back. Even so, he had a lot to get off his chest, and the sooner he could vent the better.

He'd gotten alarming news back in Providence. Apparently, the city's latest industrial work posed a threat to the location—and its unique growing conditions—in which the mushrooms were grown. To make matters worse, his supplier had revealed that his price rates were going to go up—substantially. Mark had considered telling Constance, thinking perhaps she could talk to his supplier and make a more afford-able trade—but he immediately dismissed the thought. If that bizarre body she'd commissioned them with was any indication of her idea of business, then this was the *last* he wanted to deal with her.

Crossing into Massachusetts, he turned off the highway and down several long, winding roads. He pulled into their driveway and hauled out the tub of freshly picked mushrooms.

He wrinkled his nose at the immediately familiar, acrid, burnt-smelling odor on the air. "*Dude*, really?"

He walked into the kitchen to find, as expected, a half-sliced mushroom lying on the counter beside an empty pan, and his patience evaporated.

"Chad, come *on!*"

He moved into the nursery and straight to the tank on the far side of the room, then gasped. The fine grayish mold ringed the bottom of the tank, pockmarked by a few half-formed buttons—but the middle of the tank was an expanse of stained, moist glass in the rough size and shape of the bizarre body that no longer occupied it.

His wide eyes wandered to the top of the tank, and he frowned when he saw that the lid appeared to be very much in place. Around the tank he saw a pair of discarded latex gloves and a filthy knife. "*Chad!*" he shouted, and looking around, he saw the basement door was ajar.

He descended the stairs, ready to yell at him, to ask him what the hell he'd been thinking, to demand where he'd moved the body. All those thoughts vanished, however, when the burnt smell was replaced with a thicker, more coppery one.

And then he saw the red puddle spread across the floor. Blood, so much blood, everywhere. In the middle of it was something small, dark, and rectangular. Chad's journal.

Mark's jaw worked uselessly, trying and failing to form words that he already knew nobody else would be able to hear.

He was so transfixed by the sight that he almost didn't notice the figure slumped on the chair. His eyes widened when they met Chad's—or as much as was left of them in the red ruin spread upon the chair—and then he finally found his voice.

Mark stood in the front doorway and stared at his twin reflections in the huge, round, black lenses of Constance's sunglasses. As with the first time he'd met her, they'd stayed on, even though the sun had long ago set. She was dressed in a neat gray business outfit, her skirt and jacket clean and well-kept, jewelry glittering at the base of her neck and her wrists.

He'd spent the long wait for her arrival debating exactly what he was going to tell her. More than once he'd suspected her of somehow being behind what had happened, although he knew this was unlikely. There were a million other ways she could have stolen the body without having to harm a hair on either of their heads.

He waited for her to scowl, to yell, to coolly threaten him. Instead, she cocked her head, eyebrows disappearing behind her black shades. "Let me see."

He turned and led her inside, listening to the clicks and snaps of her high heels on the floorboards behind him. He took her through the nursery, not stopping to show her the empty tank—not yet—and brought her straight downstairs to what was left of his friend.

"Oh, *my*." She walked closer to the armchair, stopping and crouching down directly before the uneven ring of red gobs and puddles.

He kept his gaze fixed on the other side of the room, cringing as he noticed the nearby puddle of puke he'd left upon discovering the massacre.

"This *is* quite bad," she muttered, and when he looked, he saw her hand moving beside her face, fingers lifting away from her shades. She stood slowly, one heel tapping on the concrete as she straightened and turned to look back at him. "You don't know what happened?"

"No."

"Do you have any kind of indoor security cameras?"

He shook his head, looking away, glassy-eyed.

He could hear Constance murmuring something about tunnels, and turned to find her glancing around at the basement floor. After a moment she slowly looked back to the glistening, red flower spread out on the chair.

Mark felt a chill in the back of his neck even before she turned back to him, and he started shaking his head.

Constance continued to stare at the bloody chair. "Perhaps—"

"No," he growled.

"—*he* could show us," she said, her thin lips curling into a smile.

She spoke to him as if he'd agreed to her proposal, as if he were even considering it—but all he could do was silently stare at the nearest area of unbloodied floor and listen. When she was done talking he silently walked upstairs, and she followed.

In the nursery he showed her the empty tank. *"Fascinating,"* she muttered, and Mark turned to find her staring at it. "It came from a former parish in Barbados." Mark tented his hands over his nose and lower face and closed his eyes as she went on to explain something about coffins that had moved every time the mausoleum was opened, then he interrupted her with a sharp sigh.

"Stop." He lowered his hands and found her staring silently at him. "Enough. We're done."

He waited for an inevitable retort, an aloof but menacing promise that he couldn't back out of their deal—but much to his surprise she simply said, "I understand." His twin reflections peered back out at him from her round black lenses as she stared at him for a moment, then she sighed heavily. "I'm very sorry about your friend."

His lips tightened.

After a long moment she turned and made her way to the door. When her car started up he forced himself back into the basement.

He spent the rest of the night throwing six years of raised beers, bad movies, girlfriend stories, and a steady business partnership into several black garbage bags, which he then buried in the woods behind the house.

Over the next several days Chad's phone buzzed and chimed with increasing frequency. At first Mark ignored it, but as more and more texts, calls, emails, and other messages came through he knew it would only be a matter of time before the authorities would pay him a visit.

He also spent hours every day trying to clean Chad's notebook, but soon resigned himself to the fact that it was permanently stained. It didn't contain much that he hadn't already seen— mainly notes on different bodies and the locations haunted by their spirits, the growth and quality of their mushrooms, and descriptions of the subsequent trips.

And then there had been the last entry.

Darkness, a huge, black sky, he'd written. *No stars, but there's a moon, too big & close.*

Dead land, gray rock stretching to every horizon. No wind but echoing hol-lowness.

Something standing in the middle, staring up at the moon. Head like a skull.

It's screaming, but I can't hear it. There's nobody, nothing else, absolutely nobody.

No—I'M screaming, screaming, and screaming again and again, but no-body can hear me. It's the great silence, the ultim

There was only a single crooked line from the pen after that, which stretched to the edge of the page.

On more than one occasion Mark was tempted to ask Constance more about the coffin and its damned contents.

He also frequently thought back on what she'd suggested.

And then, one night, after waking from a vivid terror of his friend standing beside his bed, screaming, he grabbed a shovel and trekked back into the woods.

Mark set his jaw as he stared down at the cooling, amber slices of mushroom. "Sorry, buddy."

They'd sometimes made sick jokes about this, but most of them revolved around the image of them as a couple of crotchety old men. They'd never *really* considered this, even as a remote possibility.

With the same numb, automatic mind that had guided him on the night he'd cleaned up Chad's eviscerated body—the same one that had controlled his hands while digging the grave, and again when he was digging it back up, and when he placed the decomposing remains into one of the tanks—he scooped up the slices in his hand and shoved them into his mouth. He didn't bother to grab a slice of bread—nothing in the world could cover the flavor of what he was eating.

He sat down at the kitchen table and crossed his arms, ignoring the disgust that threatened to gag him. He waited for the black spots to open into the final sights of his dead friend. He coughed once, twice, opened his eyes—

Chad was in the basement.

He shook his head. Now *that* had been a crazy trip, *he thought.*

He looked back over his notes, making sure he'd jotted down everything—

That strange thumping sound again.

He began to rise from the chair, but his head spun and his stomach lurched. Dropping back down, he let out a shaky breath.

The thump came again, and with it a high, keening cry.

Chad looked around, frowning, the sound seeming to come from everywhere and nowhere, all at once—above, below, inside, out. What the hell was *it?*

He pressed his thumb and forefinger against his eyes, rubbing out some of the lingering headache from the trip, and when he opened them he saw the body from upstairs hovering directly before him.

It was still covered in mold and mushrooms, but its many arms and legs had spread, were twisting and swaying, because something was holding *it.*

Chad looked up and gasped. He understood then—understood everything *as he saw its full shape, all its many arms—fully formed, as they should be, not the short, stubby hybrid appendages of the poor, failed offspring that had somehow been cruelly wrested from a despairing mother and into the horror of light that was this world.*

He looked down at his notebook as the mother's arms reached for him—

—and Mark began to scream.

Projector

1

Headlights appeared from a nearby corner, and Ava's lips curled to whisper *Hurry up*. Then came a sharp, metallic click, and she turned to watch the man's arm twist and lift away from the door, the padlock clutched in his gloved hand. The door groaned softly as he slid it open, and he slipped past it with the grace of a dancer. She followed, and the only light in the darkened interior narrowed and vanished as he pulled the door shut behind them.

As she removed a flashlight from her pocket, he whispered, *"Wait."*

She did as instructed and peered around, her eyes wide in the darkness. The air was cool and dry but smelled musty.

A moment later he said, "All right."

She pressed the button on the flashlight, catching the man's boots standing on a worn, stained carpet. She raised the beam to watch his gloved hands slipping a small leather case into his dark jacket. In the ambiance, his light brown eyes lifted to hers and his lips tightened. He'd called himself Winston, but she had a feeling that wasn't his real name.

She gasped. "Wait—the lock. Did you put it back?"

"How am I going to do that from inside?"

"But the door is unlocked! Someone could—"

"Who's coming here at *this* hour?"

She shrugged and swept her flashlight's beam around.

Large, empty picture frames lined the walls. A few hung wide open, their metal frames and dusty glass fronts now only displaying cobwebs and flecks of dirt. A counter filled the middle of the space, glass fronts opaque with accumulated dust, its far end closed in with a pair of sagging swinging doors. Ava walked closer, shining her flashlight at one of two large metal-framed cubes that sat on either side of the counter. She cast the beam through its grimy glass walls, her jaw tightening as she spotted the metal cooking pot hanging from its top, moldy flecks of popcorn littering its bottom.

When she'd seen the news about the Kingdom Theater two years before, she'd been sitting in a drive-thru with her boyfriend at the time, thumbing through her phone when a headline caught her eye— *LOCAL LANDMARK THEATER CLOSING.* She'd been so shocked and transfixed by the news that she'd dropped the soda her boyfriend had been handing her. Although the news upset many people, she had not anticipated how much the loss of the theater would affect her.

"Your show, kid."

She blinked and wiped her knuckle on the corner of her eye. "Can you please give me a minute?"

"You all right?"

"Yeah." She turned, sniffing, and stared at the two doors at the back of the theater. She didn't believe in ghosts, but could imagine a tall man emerging from one of the doors, the yellow light from the concession stand flashing in the lenses of his glasses, a big, toothy, infectious grin appearing in the middle of his bearded face—

A soft rustle came from behind her. She turned to see what Winston was doing and yelped aloud as something big and dark appeared from beneath one of the concession stand's swinging doors and scuttle across the floor. It jumped up to a low, jagged hole in a nearby wall, wriggled and scraped, then disappeared.

"Awesome," Winston muttered nearby.

"Not surprised. My dad used to work here, back in the day. Had to deal with a lot of rodents."

"I'm sure they'd love it now."

Ava suppressed a shudder as she thought of all the fabric from the theater seats that could be used for nests. "I'm okay with skipping the auditoriums for now. It's probably not in there anyway." She pointed to a door at the other end of the lobby. "That's the stairway to the projection room. Let's go."

The stairs were concrete and metal, but still produced noisy creaks and groans underfoot. In the ceiling overhead, dark holes yawned like starving mouths waiting for light bulbs to give them new life. Ava instinctively ran her hand along the old wooden guardrail, which wiggled and rattled unsteadily. They reached the landing and rounded the corner into the projection room.

She frowned, casting her flashlight beam about the room, then sighed. "I thought so."

The space was empty. Twin squares of solid darkness were cut into one wall, but no equipment sat on the shelves beneath them. In one corner a pale gray, waist-high cabinet stood open, its crooked doors spread wide like hands offering an apology.

Ava cursed under her breath. "This is a bust."

"Hey, now. It was a good guess it'd be here. You couldn't have known. These things happen. Take it from me."

"I know, but . . ." *I need the money,* she wanted to say, but held her tongue. Winston didn't need to know anything about her. Hell, she knew nothing about *him,* besides what she'd been told by their employers—that he was good with locks, and that he would get her in and out.

But then, what if he *did* know about her? What if their employers had told him about her?

She'd first been approached by one of them at a bus stop a few months ago. A woman wearing leather gloves had sat down beside her and started talking. She'd somehow known about Ava's years visiting and working with her father in the theater, her father's death, and her subsequent anxiety-meds abuse. She'd known about the ongoing years of Ava's unemployment struggles—for which she'd had a most enticing offer. And she'd apparently also known that, no matter how uncomfortable the conversation was making her, Ava would comply.

"'But'?"

"Let's go back downstairs."

As Winston scoured the lobby, Ava explored the concession stand. She pulled open the counters' sliding doors, peering inside but seeing only dust, droppings, and scraps of garbage. The registers were long gone, likely sold or auctioned off with any other working equipment. She got on her knees and shone her flashlight inside the several small shelves below the front counter, only to find dust and neglect.

"Huh," Winston muttered.

Ava got to her feet and glanced around to see him leaning against a section of wall between two empty poster frames, the side of his face pressed close to the drywall. "What is it?"

He raised his hand and rapped his knuckle against the wall. "This is hollow."

Ava cocked her head, frowning, and stepped out from behind the concession stand. "But I don't remember a door there or anything. That wall was always just . . . a wall."

"Do the auditoriums run along the side here?"

"No, they're at the back, and go straight that way." She flattened her hand and traced a line through the air.

"Bathrooms? Closets? Anything?"

She shook her head. "All in the back, next to the auditoriums."

"Hm." Winston stepped back and examined the length of the wall. "Wait a minute. Do you have your phone?"

She pressed her hand to her back pocket, frowning. "Yeah, why?"

"Do me a favor and look up a picture of the front of the theater. Thought of something."

She pulled out her phone and did as instructed, flipping through a few screens until she found a street-view photograph of the building on an anonymous sunny day. "Okay," she said, and Winston moved beside her and leaned in. Nodding, he reached up and pointed to the right side of the screen, beside the entrance.

"See this? This is the wall." He lifted his hand and pointed toward the front of the lobby. "Notice something inconsistent about it?"

She glanced up at the entrance, then back at the image on the phone. Something *was* off about it, yes, but she couldn't—

"Why is the space next to the door so wide on the outside, yet there's a wall along the inside?"

Ava's eyes widened, and she looked up. "It's—too narrow inside."

"*Because* . . . I think there's another space on the other side of this." He lightly hammered his fist against the wall, and something rustled below them.

Both flashlights pointed down at once, and Ava yelped as a rat— probably the same one as earlier—dropped out from behind the fabric facade and scrabbled across the floor, its squeaks sounding annoyed.

She let out a shaky sigh and put her phone away. "So how do we get in there?"

"You know this place better than I do."

Ava chewed her lower lip and glanced around. Back in the day, with proper lighting, colorful posters, and people and kids milling around, she had only ever been aware of the very same doors and spaces that she could see now. She and Dad had lived close enough to the theater that she would sometimes visit after school. He worked as the night manager, and she'd gotten to see her share of free movies. He was often able to share a few containers of popcorn and soda on the sly. Occasionally she'd assisted him while he set up the snack machines for the next day, helping haul out bags of uncooked corn kernels from one of the storage rooms—

Her gaze fixed on a door at the back, and she began walking toward it. Two naked strips of adhesive marked it at eye-level, a meaningless, uneven pair of Roman numerals. On the floor before it lay a fallen plastic sign, its back marked with the stripped counterparts to the abandoned adhesive strips. Ava crouched before it and turned it over. In the middle of the maroon plastic, white letters spelled EMPLOYEES ONLY. She stood and turned, lifting a hand toward the locked door. "Can you . . . ?"

Winston silently came over and reached inside his jacket. Instead of his leather toolkit, he produced what looked like a small silver gun, but instead of a barrel, what looked like a long, thin, black nail pointed off its top. He walked by, and she watched as he raised the object before the door handle and eased the nail into the lock's opening. There was a muffled, metallic snap, and when he grabbed the handle and tugged, a rectangle of solid darkness yawned open before them.

"Ladies first," Winston said, stepping aside.

2

The former storage room was as threadbare as Ava was worried it would be. The sagging shelves were littered with incidental configurations of dust, cobwebs, stains, flakes of plaster and paint, and flecks of dull pink insulation. A few dead flies and cockroaches lay amongst the detritus, their upraised legs forever displaying their final, lonely moments.

"I'm sorry."

Winston rapped his knuckle on something. "For what?"

"This *is* a total bust. I don't even know why they hired me."

"Well, first, you don't have to apologize to me. *You* didn't hire me. Secondly, your knowledge is valuable. They said you know this place better than anyone alive—right?"

Ava cringed, nodding.

"And thirdly, there's this."

She turned and found him crouching before a metal shelf that had once been full of sacks of corn kernels, cups and lids in plastic bags, and boxes of straws. He reached between a couple of the lower shelves, and there came another snap from his pick-gun. His arm jiggled, and he rose to his feet and turned to her, barely able to contain a grin. "This shelf is fixed to the wall."

"Okay . . . ?"

He placed his hand on the upper right frame. "There are only two reasons a shelf gets fixed to a wall. Either to keep it steady, or—" He tugged, and the entire unit came away from the wall with a loud, heavy crack and groan. Ava instinctively ducked back, then gasped as it began to swing outward. Winston moved aside as he tugged the shelf away from the wall on hidden, squeaking hinges—and the hidden doorway behind it yawned open. He didn't have a chance to ask her to do the honors: she all but ran past him, her flashlight trained ahead.

As she stepped through the doorway, something invisible touched her face. She jumped back with a grunt, shaking her head and wiping her face into the crook of her elbow. *"Ugh!"*

"What?"

"Spiderweb," she muttered, and although she rubbed her face with her sleeve until she was sure her features were red, she still could feel the gossamer touch on her skin. "Bleh." She spat, shook her head, then her gaze spotted something before her, and she slowly lowered her arm, her eyes widening.

"What's that *smell?*" Winston asked, then fell silent as his flashlight beam joined hers.

What appeared to be a tree had grown in the middle of the room. At least two feet wide, it stretched from floor to ceiling. Its dull gray, lumpy bark was riddled with bulging, smooth, light-brown domes. Multitudes of branches stretched up and spread across the ceiling. And on the floor a thick tangle of curling, overlapping tendrils spread, the strange, spongy wood seeming to be growing straight up from the floorboards.

"Hey." Winston pointed at its lower half.

She squinted, as though peering through a fog, at the indicated area. Peeking out from along the trunk came the vertical, gray glint of metal. She moved closer to Winston for a better look, and frowned when he saw a corner of flat, angular surfaces poking out from the yellow, glistening matter. "Is that a . . . table?"

"Looks like it."

"Did—did this *thing* grow around it, or—?"

A soft scrape made Ava's heart leap into her throat, and she jumped and twisted back. Her and Winston's flashlight beams met on the floor in time to see the dull gray fur and the long, naked tail of the rodent that had followed them into the room. It scurried behind the tree-thing and vanished, aside from the scrabble and click of its claws on the floorboards.

Winston turned back to her. "I've seen some weird shit before, but *that* takes the cake. My number one rule? Don't ask questions." He hooked a thumb over his shoulder. "And since *that's* not what we're here for, let's keep looking, okay?"

Before she could respond, he stepped away.

Ava swallowed hard and looked back at the tree-thing, her pulse freezing when she thought she detected movement among its branches, but the only thing that crept and scuttled between them was her own gaze.

"Hey, now . . . come look at this."

Ava followed Winston's voice, keeping as much space between herself and the tree-thing as possible. Her flashlight beam traveled over uncovered pads of insulation, naked beams, and uneven nails. The floorboards were crooked and upraised in places where the tree-thing's roots bulged. And on a tangle of them a metal case lay ajar, its narrow clamshell shape unmistakable.

It was an empty film canister.

"No . . ." Ava balled her fist. *"No!"*

Winston turned to her, a grin evaporating from his face. "What?"

"It's empty. Someone's been in here already!"

"Doubt it. Not for a long time. That door was pretty hard to open." He looked down, then chuckled. "And besides, look at that."

Her jaw tight, Ava stepped toward him, her gaze following his extended arm and finger, then gasped.

A sagging cardboard box sat on the floor, its sides bulging from moisture and neglect. Two of its flaps were flipped up and out, exposing rows of thin, metallic shapes beneath.

Scrambling closer and crouching beside it, Ava grabbed the flaps and tugged them up and back, and gasped when she saw the row of canisters that filled it. She snatched one out, found the latch on it, and tugged it open, grinning as she saw the spooled reel of celluloid inside.

"Is it . . . ?" Winston asked behind her.

Ava blinked, then shook her head. She closed the canister and turned it over, her eyes adjusting to the glare of the flashlight beam on the metal—and the white strip of tape on one side of it, upon which thick black letters spelled out *M. Booth.* She lowered it into the box, then pulled out a neighboring canister, similarly labeled *J. Rex.* Another read *M. Gaumond.* Two of them were labeled *F. Donohue,* with *I* and *II* added. Another was simply labeled *Francisco.*

"How many are there?"

"Ten." She looked up. "We're bringing all of them."

"Our bags'll be pretty full."

"Yeah, well—" She stood, then started, certain that someone had moved into the room beside her, but her flashlight only revealed a dark gray curtain hanging on the wall beside her. The fabric was wrinkled and mildewed, hanging loosely from metal rings looped over a black rod. It was another doorway.

"Hold on." She walked over and flung the sagging curtain open, then gasped.

"What is it?"

She didn't answer as she cast her flashlight beam into the space beyond. Jaw agape, she stepped slowly inside.

Three arched wooden chairs stood in a neat row ahead of her, their shared armrests poking out from between the upraised seats. Red upholstery lined their backs. Another set of chairs sat in front of them, followed by another—five rows in all. Faded, scuffed wood, stained with water and darker, less easily discerned leaks, creaked and groaned underfoot. The ceiling and walls were painted with ugly splotches of red and black. And at the far end of the room her flashlight beam caught the pale expanse of a small screen installed upon the middle of the wall.

It was an auditorium.

Winston's boots shuffled to a stop behind her. "Huh. Weird. Why's it so small?"

"Why is it *hidden?*" Ava reached out to the closest chair, running her gloved fingertips along its wooden back.

"How old is this theater?"

She pressed her hand to the top of the chair, squeezing the upper edge of the squishy cushion. "I remember my dad saying it was built in the twenties."

"Prohibition era. Maybe it was a speakeasy or something back then, and they later converted it into a theater."

Ava released her grip on the cushion, feeling the fabric spread and swell beneath her fingers. "But again, *why* is it hid—?" She yelped and snatched her hand away, training her flashlight before her in time to see a finger-length clump of dust and far, far too many moving appendages as it crawled along the top curve of the fabric, then up and over the wooden back, where it disappeared.

Behind her Winston muttered something, and she turned, relieved to find him standing before one of the walls, silhouetted by his flashlight beam. She stepped quickly away from the chairs and moved beside him. "What is it?" She leaned in, then pulled back, flinching, and shining her own flashlight beam around along the wall. She now noticed the plywood walls were not, in fact, painted—they were covered with layers upon layers of red and brown tendrils, twisted and curled and knotted between, over, and around one another, a ruddy, knotted nightmare.

"Looks like vines," Winston said.

"Or fungus." Ava hugged her arm round herself.

"All right, I think I've—" Winston fell silent and spun, shining his flashlight across the room.

Feeling the skin on her neck tighten, Ava silently turned and tried to see what he was looking at.

After a long moment he murmured, "Thought I heard something."

Ava's eyes widened as a lumpy shape rose from one of the rearmost seats, two bright pinpricks flashing in its small head. With a choked cry she turned her flashlight upon it. It was a rat, probably the one that had followed them inside.

Then a bright flash of light filled the room, and the rat screeched.

"*Ho—*" Winston shouted, and for a second, Ava could see every seat, every red wall, and then the light was gone as instantly as it came, and in the remaining circle of her flashlight's comparatively dim beam she watched as the rat dropped out of sight and vanished. He spun to her, eyes wide. "Did you see that?"

"The rat?"

"No, the screen! It lit up!"

"What?" She spun and pointed her flashlight at the front of the auditorium.

The screen was about fifteen feet wide and ten high. Rusty stains stretched in uneven concentric triangles down its right side, and its upper left corner was peeling and tattered. The fabric had faded to a shade of dull yellow—but the only light that appeared on it came from her flashlight.

"It was just for a second, and . . ." He trailed off, and she turned to find him facing the back of the room, squinting as he looked around. After a moment he took a heavy breath, then nodded and turned back to her. "It's your call if you want to poke around some more, but as far as *I'm* concerned, we've found what we were looking for. And if the film's not in that box, well, at least we can say we tried, right?"

Ava nodded, then glanced back through the door and started when she thought she saw the upper branches of the tree-thing moving. After staring at them for a long moment to make sure they weren't, she stammered, "R-right."

"Then let's get the hell out of here, shall we?"

They exited the theater and split up.

Winston took a long way back to the car, taking a few extra blocks to make sure that he wasn't being followed. That had, of course, been his plan all along, but he'd not expected to come out with two satchels full of film—because if Ava had the one reel that they had come there for, and she got caught . . .

He snapped himself into the present and made his way to the back of the pizza place where he'd parked and was relieved to find Ava waiting for him a few yards from the car.

"About t—" she said, but he raised a hand to silence her as he unlocked it and climbed inside. Once she was in, he started up the car and began to cruise for the highway. "We're going the wrong way."

"No, we're not."

"But Cumberland's back . . . ." She sighed, and from the corner of his eye he saw her cross her arms over her chest.

He took an exit back into Providence and began to cut through the East Side.

After a few minutes she reached down between her feet, where she'd set her own bag of films. He was about to suggest she put it back when she pulled a canister out and removed its lid. She leaned over, dug her phone out, the screen's pale light filling the dim car.

"Shouldn't you wear gloves for that?" he asked.

"I'm holding it by the edges," she said, lifting out the spool of film inside. "Besides, this isn't a crime scene."

He opened his mouth, then shut it and shook his head.

The phone's glow moved by his face, and he heard the rustle of celluloid. As he made his way toward another highway entrance, Ava gasped.

He didn't look.

"There's . . ." she tried, and there came a soft whir as she pulled out another section of film. "Okay, this is weird. There's a . . . forest, looks like, and there's a guy standing next to some trees. But there's—" She gasped, and he glanced over to see her raising and lowering her hand, squinting into the film by the light of her phone. "There's something coming up next to him. It's like a big deer or—wait, no." She switched the film to her other hand, pulled out another length, and lifted it a little faster.

He turned onto the highway and was grateful for several minutes of silence as Ava looked over more of the film.

When she was done, she lowered it with a heavy sigh and began winding it back onto the spool. She put it back into the canister, then asked, "Do you watch monster movies?"

He'd not seen any since he was little. "No."

"I wonder if that's what this is. There were *two* of them, not one.

They were like—giant, round, buglike things. And they both floated up on either side of this guy, and he turned around and raised his hand to them, and . . ." She shook her head. "What *was* that thing, back in the theater? What does this all *mean?*"

"I'm perfectly fine going through the rest of my life *not* knowing."

As Ava put the film back into the satchel and produced another, he puffed out his cheeks and sighed.

Should've stayed on the highway.

3

The job done, they exited the building and stepped outside. On the front porch, Ava spun on her heel and faced him, her mouth open but silent.

He raised a quizzical eyebrow as her jaw worked. "Spit it out."

"I want to go back."

He said nothing.

"It's . . ." She sighed and shook her head. "I have too many questions. I need to know more."

He chose his next words carefully. "I thought they hired you because you knew the place really well."

"I do. I mean, I *did*." She looked away. "I visited my dad there all the time, growing up. He showed me *The Lion King* there the night before it came out. But now, it's like . . . I don't even know what to think. He never said anything about another room, much less—"

"Can you ask him about it?"

"He's dead," she said, almost matter-of-factly.

"Oh. I—I'm sorry."

"*That's* why I need to get back in there. And why I need *you* to—"

"Hold on." He raised his hands. "Slow down a minute there, kid. I *am* a contractor. I have fees."

"All right, well, how much?"

When he told her, her eyes widened and she fell silent.

He let her ponder this while he glanced around the property. The droning chirps and snaps of nocturnal insects filled the air. The shadow of the looming Victorian behind him was foggy with the pale wash of the front porch's light, but its looming edges stretched along the driveway, toward the woods that ringed the property, where he thought he saw shapes, black amidst the black, skulking and creeping beneath the trees.

"I told you what was on that first film."

He turned back to her, his lips pursed.

"The second one I looked at had a woman sitting on a floor, hugging a mannequin and crying. Another one showed a girl, a *little girl,* screaming behind a couple of big black claws that were, like . . ." She held her hands up, so their backs faced Winston, and she looked at them in turns. "It's like they were hers, but—"

"Yeah, I—" He held up a hand. "Okay. Point being?"

"What the hell were those films?" she hissed. "Are they movies? And if not, then . . . what *are* they? What the hell was that—thing? And why was that room *locked,* even?" After a moment, she spat, *"And how didn't my dad know about it?"*

Winston shrugged helplessly.

Her gaze stayed fixed on his for a silent moment, and then she reached beneath her jacket, fumbled behind her back, and held out a manila envelope, thick with her payment inside.

He gave the envelope a long look, unsure of what to say. He had a feeling that she wasn't ready to throw away that much money.

"Please. This is extremely important to me. I *need*—" Her voice quavered, and she broke off, swallowed, then said more quietly, "I need you to get me back in there. Please."

He stared at the envelope, clutched in her long, thin fingers. In the porch light he could see the telltale flecks of dead skin and quick-bitten cuticles. After a moment he looked up into her dark blue eyes and nodded.

4

Ava had been upset to hear that they were going to wait a week before returning to the theater, but he'd made the severity of his discretion abundantly clear when he'd threatened that she would never see him again if she persisted. But despite her impatience, she'd acceded.

She met with him outside the theater, accompanied by the smell of marijuana. "Sure you're up for this?"

"I'm here, aren't I?"

He nodded, his eyebrows lifting and dropping for a moment, then turned and set to work on the lock.

Unlike last week, there had been no passing cars to rush their entry this time. They went inside and crossed the lobby in silence, save the scrape and thump of their shoes on the worn carpet.

They entered the storage room, and she stood aside as he reached inside the shelves and picked the lock. He gripped the shelf and stepped back, pulling it open after him—then stopped when he heard a muffled *pop*.

"Did you hear that?"

"It came from the—" She gasped and pointed, her arm glowing in the light of her upraised flashlight. He stepped around the door, following her gaze, and his jaw dropped open.

The tree-thing was no longer dark gray: its surface had lightened to the sickly, mucoid yellow of a spoiling banana. And the domes that spotted the trunk were no longer dark brown, but rather bright scarlet, glistening and pulsing wetly in the shared beams of the flashlights, looking like giant droplets of blood.

She moved past him for the door, and although he was in no hurry to join her, he didn't like the thought of her—of *anyone*—going near that thing. He forced himself to move after her but came to a stop in the doorway as she walked into the room and began to circle the tree-thing, staring at it with wide eyes. "It's like it's . . ." Her whisper trailed off into silence.

He registered motion above her and looked up in time to watch one of the domes near the top of the tree-thing twitch, quiver, and swell. *"Get back!"* he barked, and she backpedaled to the wall as the orb burst like an oversize pimple with a sickeningly wet *pop,* the same sound as before. A spray of clear fluid glinting in their flashlight beams before falling to the floorboards.

Ava groaned loudly. "Jesus!"

"Did any get on you?"

"No, I—"

Another wet pop filled the air, and he shone his flashlight at the tree-thing but couldn't see where the sound had come from. He shook his head. "All right, kid, I'm sorry, but this is too much. You wanted me to get you in, I did. So—"

"No!" she snapped, walking over to him, her eyes a mix of confused fear and anger. *"No.* You can't just leave me stuck in here! I need you to—"

"I'll wait for you," he said, and hooked a thumb over his shoulder. "I'll stay out in the lobby while you—" He cringed as the tree-thing made another disgustingly loud, wet pop. "Look, just come get me when you're done, but in"—he pulled back his sleeve and glanced at his watch—"fifteen minutes *I'm* done."

"And *then* what? You'll lock me up in here?"

He hadn't expected her to call his bluff so quickly. Pursing his lips, he shrugged, hoping the lack of confirmation was enough to convince her.

Ava's eyes narrowed, and she shook her head. Without another word she turned and walked past the tree-thing and into the auditorium.

He took a heavy breath, then stepped moved back through the storage room.

In the lobby he impatiently glanced around the empty space. Times like this, he wished he carried a more contemporary mobile phone, as the old flip-phone in his pocket was a work-only burner.

His eyes followed the murky beam of the flashlight as he cast it across the filthy carpet. His upper lip curled as he spotted a cockroach as long as his thumb on the floor nearby.

Turning, he saw a black rectangle beside him—one of the auditoriums. He wandered inside and stared at the twin rows of seats as he walked between them. He wasn't from the area originally, but he could easily imagine the theater when it was still open. If the Rhode Island Historical Society could have declared the location historical, the required money and efforts to restore it to its former glory might not have been a problem. But in recent years, having seen more and more of the city's old and historic buildings being leveled to make way for anonymous, shiny facilities, complexes, and parking garages, Winston knew that this old theater was very likely gone for good.

He glanced at his watch. Six minutes to go.

He made his way back into the lobby and into the storage room. He stopped in the doorway before the tree-thing and cringed as one of its boils burst again.

"Got about five—" he called, then fell silent when he heard a low murmur.

He cocked his head, listening. It was a voice.

"What?" he called.

Ava continued speaking, oblivious to him.

He moved into the room, keeping well away from the tree-thing, then nearly jumped out of his skin when his foot kicked something with a loud, metallic scrape. He shone his flashlight down and saw one half of the empty film canister.

Ava spoke a little louder, and he turned and realized she was in the hidden auditorium.

He walked through the doorway, getting annoyed as he anticipated coming in to see her talking on her phone—then stopped short.

The old upholstered chairs before him were glowing.

No—not glowing. They were caught in a bright light.

He turned to the front of the auditorium and gasped when he saw the illuminated screen. She must have gotten the private auditorium's projector working.

He squinted into the screen's light, his gaze starting to register colors, shades, and motion. After a moment he realized he was seeing a familiar, street-level view of houses, shops, and other buildings under a gray sky. A woman and a boy were walking on a sidewalk, cars passing by on the street. No sound accompanied the image.

Ava said something, and he tore his gaze from the screen, finally spotting her. She was sitting in one of the chairs toward the front, her head tilted back as she stared up at the screen.

"Five minutes," he called, but she ignored him, still muttering to herself. Sighing, he turned and shone his flashlight between the nearest seats and started.

A dead rat lay on the floor, its milky eyes wide, its jaw frozen open. Its body was obscured by a snarl of thick, red filaments, probably its own guts from an unseen predator's savagery.

He leaned down, frowning, as his eyes studied the scarlet chaos heaped around the rat—and felt the skin tighten along his spine as he realized that they were identical to the vines that covered the walls. He shone his flashlight closer to the floor and was sickened to see the vines trail out from beneath the base of the chair, creeping up the metal frames and dangling limply off its upraised cushion to cling, weblike, around the rodent's body.

Cringing, he looked back up at the screen, then frowned when he recognized the tall, wide building that now filled the shot.

It was the Kingdom Theater, back in its heyday. Its two-sided marquee displayed the films that were currently showing, but the forward-facing shot warped the words into an obscure series of blocks and lines. A girl, probably eleven or twelve years old, walked toward the entrance, and the shot changed.

The girl was inside the lobby, which was clean and bright. Posters for various movies lined the walls. The counter was full of candy bars, soda cups, and popcorn bags. The popcorn oven was half full. The girl walked past the counter and toward the back.

Ava murmured something from her chair.

"What?"

When she didn't answer, he pursed his lips and walked closer. As he neared her row, he heard her ask quietly, "When are you coming home?"

"What are you talking about?" When she didn't respond, he shook his head. "Look, I know this is all very nostalgic for you and everything, but we really can't be here like this." He glanced at the back of the auditorium. "Here, let's get the film, and you can take it home and—" He fell silent, frowning, and shone his flashlight to the back wall. After a moment he stepped away from the chairs and walked slowly toward the back, staring up.

He'd never been a big moviegoer, and had been even less so in recent years, but he knew how a theater worked and where the projections came from. Yet the entire back wall of this bizarre auditorium did not have a window to the projector room, or any other kind of hole high up in the wall. It was flat and featureless but for those strange red vines that covered it.

"Hey, this is weird." He turned back to her, frowning. "There's no . . ."

Then he saw what was on the screen.

It was the storage room, back when its shelves full of containers of corn kernels, plastic bags full of cups, and boxes of snacks. The girl was standing in the middle of the room, her eyes wide, her jaw agape as she stared at the metal shelf, containing various cleaning supplies, which stood crookedly apart from the wall, its hidden door open. Her mouth worked silently, and she moved past the shelf.

The tree-thing was smaller in those days, its branches only beginning to touch the ceiling, its skirt of roots upon the floor narrower in width. It was bright yellow, but the red orbs on its sides looked the same. The girl cowered away from it, flat against the wall, her face wrinkled in horror, as she stared at it, then quickly turned her head toward the door to the hidden auditorium.

"*Dad,*" Ava called, her voice low but keening. and Winston blinked, looked down, and shook his head.

"All right, time's up," he said, walking back down the aisle, until he reached Ava's row. "Go get the film. We're outta—" He paused when he saw her.

Ava's body shook with sobs as she muttered. The corners of her mouth were curled down, her cheeks glistening with trails of tears . . . and above them, her eyes glowed with bright, pale light.

She raised her voice and whimpered, "What *is* this place?"

"Hey!" he barked. "Hey, kid!" He clapped his hands beside her, but she didn't even blink. The ambiance from the screen dimmed, and he risked a look over his shoulder—and froze, eyes widening.

The girl was standing inside the darkened auditorium, next to the last row of chairs. She was shaking her head, her own wide eyes transfixed by the glowing screen. She shook her head and spoke—and as her mouth began to work, Winston was startled to hear Ava's voice beside him, speaking in perfect time. "What *is* this? *What are you watching?*"

The shot changed. The screen appeared within itself, the glow of its own projection outlining the rows of chairs. The screen within the screen grew larger as the shot zoomed in toward it, and then its own visuals filled the frame.

A robed figure stands before a metal door, face obscured by a wide, deep hood, a yellow symbol woven upon the dark gray fabric of its chest. The shot slowly turns, revealing another robed figure standing beside the first, and another, and another. At least fifteen of them stand in a circle inside of a wide, dark room, illuminated by rings and rows of candles set along the concrete walls, upon which were painted big yellow shapes, like the one on their chests. On the floor before them stretches a large black circle—a round, deep pit, going straight down. The figures raise their arms—

Now it was the view of the theater from the back. The rows of seats were outlined by the light of the screen—and so were the head and shoulders of a person sitting in one of them. Then it switched back to the screen within the screen.

A naked person kneels before the pit, leaning forward, spreading its arms out, and in the pit the darkness lightens and shifts with movement—

The theater again, as another figure appeared beneath the screen, walking down the aisle. Tall and thin, his face became clear, even in the darkness, a bearded man wearing glasses.

"No!" Ava cried. "I'm sorry, Dad! I just wanted to—"

The bearded man obscured the screen as he walked closer. He said something, and Ava squealed as a shape appeared beside his head—his upraised hand, in the split second before it came sweeping down, a black blur that filled the shot, making Winston blink, wincing.

Ava cried out, sobbing. "*Please*, Dad! I'm *sorry*, I—" She yelped again, louder.

The naked figure's head snaps upright, and it backs away from the hole—

"Hey, kid!" Winston shuffled into the row beside her, reached for her—and started.

Her hands were in motion, fingers groping and clawing at the air on either side of her knees. But even as she cried out again, her arms bucked and thrashed atop the chair's armrests, unable to lift—for they were ringed and tied down with red vines.

He shoved his hand inside his pants pocket. He produced a blade, and it twinkled in the screen's light as he knelt beside her. He found where the vines crept up to her left arm and began cutting one of them. It was tough, and he had to saw the blade back and forth until it snapped loose—and Ava began to scream.

He cut another, and another. She screamed louder, and he began cursing, again and again, until her arm swung up and around, hitting his shoulder a few times. He shot a glance over his shoulder as he reached for her other arm. The screen had become a bright blur of indiscernible shapes. As he returned to his task, she screamed louder and louder. She began bucking and thrashing about in the seat, and as the last of the vines snapped loose she let out a final, choked cry. He looked up in time to see her head pitch forward, her glowing eyes closing—and the auditorium fell into darkness.

"Hold on, kid, hold on . . ." Winston grunted, half carrying, half dragging Ava's unconscious form through the auditorium's doorway.

After freeing her from the chair he'd given her face a couple of firm pats, but she didn't stir. Fortunately, she was breathing, but he couldn't think of anything to do other than get her out of there.

As he entered the room with the tree-thing, his mind crowded with one idea after another, but every one of them sounded as if they would land him in a world of trouble that he'd spent years working hard to avoid. He debated contacting their employers, but he had no idea if they'd be of any use, much less how quickly they might be able to help.

They began to pass tree-thing, her feet scraping and thumping over its roots—and he heard something rustle faintly. His pulse froze in his veins and he twisted back, unsteadily pointing his flashlight behind him, but saw nothing. He let out a quick breath, then saw something move beside him and shone his flashlight beam down.

At first he thought it was part of the tree-thing, one of its branches or roots reaching out to grab him—but then he recognized the flat, narrow shape, twin rows of holes in each side. The reel of film continued to spill out from one of the burst boils of the tree, glistening damply as it stretched down to heap upon the floor at his feet.

Ava's breath continued sluggishly but steadily beside his face. He glanced at her face, then back down at the film on the floor, and his lips tightened.

5

"—cky that they found you."

Ava blinked and shook her head. "What?"

The woman smiled and shook her head, her thick, light brown curls bobbing about. "I said, you're lucky that whoever it was found you."

Ava took a shaky breath. The inside of her skull was pulsing with a dull pain larger than it felt it could hold, and her eyes were dry and sore, their lids crusty. *Worst hangover ever,* she thought, until her memory came crashing into her head with another painful lurch.

She'd been passing in and out of consciousness all morning. The doctor had come by a little while ago. She'd said that Ava was found about a block from the hospital, on the front lawn of a nearby apartment building. The only reason a resident had noticed her was because of a fire down the block—

Ava blinked, looked up. "Wait—a fire?"

"Yeah, an old movie theater near there." The doctor shook her head. "Really sad. I used to go there when I was younger."

Ava felt tears sting her eyes, but she shook her head. "Wait . . . sorry. Time's all messed up. How—how long was I . . . ?"

The doctor winced a little as she said, "You've been here for a little over two—"

Another black wave came through her consciousness, then the room returned and Ava said, "Sorry, two what?" She glanced around, confused.

The doctor was gone.

Letting out a heavy breath, she glanced at the table to her left, then froze.

Upon it sat a lamp, a fake potted plant, a plastic water bottle . . . and a metal film canister.

Ava reached over, then hissed as pain shot up through her left arm. She instinctively tried to cradle it, but her right arm flared in pain as well. She lowered them both onto her lap, panting, and noticed that both were wrapped in thick gauze. From somewhere nearby a soft electronic beep she'd not noticed before increased its tempo.

She took a few heavy breaths, steeled herself, and reached over and grabbed the canister, wincing in pain. The beeping increased as she set it down on her lap. Slowing the movements of her arms, she lifted the lid off and stared down at the film inside. There was no spool, and the film was a narrow, uneven spiral inside. She picked up one end and held it unsteadily to the light above, and saw a familiar bearded face inside the frames, its open mouth silently shouting.

She felt pressure around her sore eyes, and it gradually turned into the sting of tears as memories—*all* the terrible memories—returned.

She dropped the end of the film back into the canister, her lips quivering as they pulled back over clenched teeth—and then she stopped when her gaze fell on something else. She carefully pulled the entire reel of film out of the canister and saw the thick manila envelope that had been hidden beneath.

Ava dropped the film back into the canister as her hands lifted to her face, and she covered her eyes as the tears began to flow.

Crossback

The week Lou moved in with Rayna, summer was far into its retreat into fall. The slowly cooling temperatures had begun to rescind the privilege of wearing T-shirts and shorts, and Rayna was shoving a bag of summer clothes into an open cardboard box in a closet when she saw the edge of a metal box straddling the edge of the cheap wood of the top shelf.

She stepped back and looked up at the box. It was about the size of a typewriter, and heavy, too. She cringed at the thought of it tumbling upon someone's head, and pushed it back on the shelf, closer to the wall. It seemed to stay put, and so she let go and turned away when a tugging sensation on her wrist brought her attention back to it a split second before it followed her lowering hand toward her face. She yelped at the approaching projectile, and her other hand darted up and caught the heavy box.

Lou's voice drifted in from elsewhere. "Hon? You okay?"

Hefting the lockbox before her, glaring at it as if it were a misbehaving pet, she noticed now what had brought it down after her hand: her bracelet, a charm-studded double-hoop that Lou had given her for her birthday the previous month, was clinging to its front edge. She pulled her arm slowly away, noting how the bracelet stuck to it until it could resist her muscles no longer, and snapped off from the worn metal surface. As an experiment she moved her wrist closer to the lockbox again, and sure enough, her bracelet jumped forward and grabbed an invisible hold to the metal with a metallic snap. *Magnet,* she thought as she flipped up its silver latch and opened it—then immediately flinched as a faint but rank odor hit her nostrils. She coughed, then forgot all about the smell as she stared at the contents of the lockbox.

A snarl of wires, dully shining metal discs and bands, and blocks of other, even more unrecognizable electronics that filled the box could have been no different to her from the innards of her first car's dashboard, mid-dissection during its many tune-ups. Circuits ended and began, forming patterns in the wire—a stark contrast to the absolute nonsense of what sat in the middle.

A little smaller than her fist, the brick-colored, glossy object looked at first like a strange, sculpted pastry. Then she began to recognize the overlaying rings as chitinous layers, forming the unmistakable arched shape of a thorax and abdomen, and she flinched and held the lockbox away. The oversized insect's head and legs were embedded into the surrounding circuit board, secured with silver blobs of solder.

Still flinching, she moved out from the foyer and into the den, setting the box onto the coffee table's waist-high surface and lifting the curious electronic collection out from it. The wires were piled upon one another, and she lifted them slowly out one by one, careful not to tangle them as she draped them over the edges of the box like tissue paper from a gift. She reached in and pulled the strange insect-crowned circuit board out of its middle. The box got lifted up with its contents' magnetic properties, and she had to hold it down as she pulled the rest of the device free and held it aloft in the scrutiny of the afternoon sun.

The circuitry hung from her hand like the limp arms of a dead octopus, and she gently poked at the dangling wires, noting how they were grouped into—indeed—eight arms radiating out from its center, each one ending in small metallic beads and round, flat pads of thick rubber. Unlit LEDs glistened like berries along garlands of vines. The longest wire ended in a gray, flat box, slightly larger than a matchbook, one side of which was flat and shiny.

She looked slowly up. Lou had disappeared into his studio a few minutes earlier, but as he generally took a while before he could settle down and focus on a sketch or illustration enough to need to be left alone, she knew an interruption would be okay in the meantime. "Lou?"

"Yeah?"

"What *is* this?"

A brief pause. "What is what?"

"This . . ." Rayna moved through the den and towards the studio's door. "This . . . *thing?*"

She held the device out in the air before her as she stepped through the doorway, so it would be the first thing Lou would see when he twisted around upon his old, squeaky diner chair.

"Uh . . ." he croaked in the moment before she entered the studio and stopped to find him facing her.

Her face mirrored the look on Lou's as she stared at him, and as he in turn stared at the device in her hand. His beard only served to frame his lips as they puckered into a silent O, his eyes wide behind his thick-rimmed glasses.

"Lou?"

He twitched, then looked quickly up at her. "Care—" he muttered, and raised his hands before him, a charcoal pencil still clutched in his right. "Careful with that."

She felt abruptly uneasy. Glancing down at the device, she suddenly had the urge to drop it—to toss it aside.

"L-lou?" Her voice was a choked whisper.

"Don't worry." Some of the tension had leaked out of his features, but he still looked uneasy as he added, "It's not a bomb."

"That's not comforting."

"It's not a bomb," he repeated. "It's not meant to cause pain."

"Then what is it?"

"Just hand it to me, carefully. It's—delicate."

She brought it over, her hands almost shaking, and watched as he gently took it from her. He looked at it, touching and moving its loose components with all the delicate familiarity and care she'd hoped he would someday show for their children.

"I'm sorry." His words were almost as strange as the device he now held, and when he looked up she was shocked to see his eyes had a faint red tinge to them, as if he'd taken drugs—a proclivity he never indulged in—or about to cry.

"Why? Lou . . . *what* is that thing?"

"I don't think I can explain it," Lou said, and the corner of his lips tugged, like a grin forming and dying all at once. "You just need to find out for yourself."

"Lou." She raised her hand slowly. "Remember how I said there are few things in this world that scare me? And how one of those things is feeling I'm not getting the whole story from someone I trust. Well, right now, that's *exactly*—"

"I promise, I'll explain."

"Lou, what—?"

"Do me a favor. Put it on." He lifted the device out before him.

"Are you kidding me?"

"I promise, it's not going to hurt you."

"*Still* not comforting. Why can't you just tell me what—?"

Lou pursed his lips, then turned the device around in his hands, craned his neck down, and raised the masses of wires above his head. He unceremoniously crowned himself with it, then began to press its beads and pads to parts of his scalp. She began to realize that its size and shape was intended for cranial application

Lou's eyes, unable to see the tasks he was conducting, darted back and forth, and once or twice met Rayna's, but the unspoken questions in her gaze went unanswered. His jaw twisted to the side as he worked at the wires, trying to put them in place. After a moment he grinned and lowered his hands. On his head, the device was like a bizarre hair-styling instrument. For a moment Rayna was tempted to laugh, but the mystery occluded her sense of humor.

He reached behind his head and brought his hand forward. In it he held the tiny gray box on the longest set of wires—some kind of controller. Although he didn't appear to do anything to it, its polished side unexpectedly lit up with soft blue light. He lifted it before his face, his features awash in the light, his glasses reflecting back twin illuminated squares. He thumbed the tiny unit, then gasped, his body shuddering. He dropped the control and pitched forward in his chair.

Rayna shot forward. "Lou!"

This wasn't the first time he'd had an episode like this. He'd mentioned in their earliest dating days that he was occasionally prone to seizures, which hadn't been nearly enough to prepare her for the first couple of instances she'd witnessed it. Even so, he'd only had a few since then, and he always seemed to come out of them feeling refreshed—and sure enough, he threw up his hand, took a deep breath, and lifted his head, straightening slowly and flinching as he muttered, "Geoff DiNapoli."

Rayna paled. "What did you say?"

"A senior when you were a sophomore, up at your college in Vermont. You always regretted meeting him. He—" He winced and shook his head, the wires and device jiggling around his cranium like a loose wig. "He *groomed* you all the way until he graduated, and got you to drop out and move in with him down here."

Rayna's jaw clenched so hard as Lou spoke that she thought she was going to crack a molar. She'd spent over two years trying to leave that undesirable chapter of her life behind when she'd met Lou during a summer daytrip in Boston, where he'd been living at the time. The distance had been difficult enough for her as it was, but they'd made it work for a few months, until the spike in travel restrictions that had been instituted following Rhode Island's statewide lockdown, which was now in its sixth month. Moving in with each other had been a choice that was as terrifying as it was exciting, but she'd known in her heart the whole time that it had been for the best.

Yet in that whole time she'd only hinted at a bad relationship in her past, and had never told any of the uncomfortable specifics with Lou.

Her voice was a choked whisper as she said, *"How do you know about him?"*

"It's like I've told you before," Lou continued, reaching up with unsteady hands to remove the ends of the wires from his temples, then lifting the whole device off and lowering it to his lap. "You're always too down on yourself. You take too much blame. But I guess I can see why now. Geoff was a classic narcissist, *and* unfortunately, your first serious relationship. Bad combo." He shrugged, looking sad and angry as he shook his head, then looked up at her. "But I know you're better than that."

"What—the hell are you . . . ?"

"And even though *he* was the one who got all removed from the relationship, he had no shame in manipulating you into thinking it was all *your*—"

"Stop it," Rayna snapped, and then surprised even herself when she shouted, *"Shut up for a second!"*

Lou stared at her, calm and unfazed by her outburst.

"What are you doing? And what *is* that thing? And how do you know about all that? I never told you that story!"

"Sorry." He took a deep breath. "I'm sorry. What do you want to know?"

"I want to know what that thing is, and how you know so much about stuff I've never even *told* you!"

Lou's lips worked for a moment, then he smirked and shook his head. "Actually, I think I've always known how the story ended, even though I didn't always know how it began. It had a happy ending— you met me." He lowered his head, thought for a moment, then said, "I don't really *want* to talk to you in paradoxes or riddles, but it's kind of hard not to." He held up the device. "You've seen what happened when I put this on. Somehow I wound up knowing about something you never told me, right? So why don't you put this on, ask me about something I never told you, and—"

Rayna scoffed. "Like *hell* I will!"

"After everything that we've experienced together, and everything we trust with each other, I'm just asking you to trust me on this." He held up the device. "Put this on, and then ask me anything. Just make sure it's something I haven't told you about." When Rayna remained silent, he shrugged. "It can be about anything. Something totally innocuous. Just as long as it's something you never knew about me." He snapped his fingers and pointed, a smile breaking the tension on his face. "Ask me about the dead bird my friend Mike found."

"Lou . . ."

"*Please*, Rain."

She now saw something in his face, something that might have been there the whole time—a pleading look of *yearning*, one she'd known all too well in the past. She didn't know what the hell was going on or why she should participate in *anything* that he was suggesting— but whatever his reasons, he genuinely wanted her to experience them for herself.

She took a shallow breath. "You said that device won't hurt."

He nodded. "It might tingle a bit, and it's a little disorienting when—when it works, but it isn't painful. I promise."

She closed her eyes, took a deep breath, and let it out in a tired sigh. "Oh, why the *hell* am I doing this?" She moved forward and reached for the device.

"Because you love me."

She looked at him for a long moment, then silently took the device from him.

He began to tell a story of when he was twelve and attending summer school. As he did so, he stood up, reaching to help her place the device on her head, but she stepped away, not wanting him to touch her. He respectfully acquiesced, but between parts of his story— in which his friend Mike had found a big dead bird, probably a crow, inside the base of one of the building's furnaces, and how they'd obnoxiously kicked it around and eventually clipped it by its wings to a nearby flagpole and raised it to half-mast—he instructed her on positioning the device on her head and attaching the sensors to her skin. The sensors were warm and loose where they touched her. There was, as promised, a tingling sensation, but in her state of baffled wonder she figured that could have just been her nerves.

Any other day, she would have shaken her head at his story and said, *Boys are weird,* but she remained silent.

He told her to pick up the tiny gray box, which was some sort of controller.

"Lou . . . please. Why can't you just *tell* me?"

"I will in a minute. I promise."

She took a deep breath and held it as she pushed her thumb onto the button.

She was temporarily blinded by the light that filled her eyes, surprisingly bright from such a tiny screen. She squinted, trying to concentrate on the digits that had appeared in the electronic shimmer, but the afterimage was so powerful that for a moment she couldn't even see. She blinked several times, waiting for her eyes to adjust, and a shudder bolted through her body. She gasped and stepped back, turning to leave the studio—

But she wasn't in the studio anymore.

She was in the foyer, in front of the open closet. Instinctively she looked up, and wasn't entirely surprised to see that the lockbox was on the top shelf, precariously balanced on its edge.

"What the *fuck?*"

Lou called from the studio, his voice as comfortable and cool as when this crazy ordeal had first started. "Hon? You okay?"

"It's a time machine, isn't it?"

Lou, sitting atop his stool, leapt to his feet and spun to face her, wide-eyed. *"What?"*

"It's a time machine."

"How—?" he blurted, then blinked, trying a different tact. "What are you—?"

"You told me to put it on, and then you told me about being in your summer school, and how you and your friend Mike found that dead bird in the chimney, and—"

His body twitched and swayed with a shiver. "I . . . did?"

"Yes." She shook her head. "You said it was something you've never told me before."

Lou's gaze darted away, then back to Rayna's face. "What else did I tell you?"

"You promised me you'd explain."

Lou sighed, lowered his head and nodded. "What do you want to know?"

"Well . . ." Rayna snickered as the next thought bubbled to the surface, at how insane it was—how insane *everything* was. "*Is* this a time machine? Or am I possibly having a psychotic breakdown?"

"I don't date psychotic women, so . . . it's a time machine."

She caught herself before she had a chance to let loose a laugh that would have made her pursue the question even further. "Well? What can you tell me about it? Where does it come from?" She thought about it a moment, then asked, "*When* is it from?"

"Honestly?" He looked up at her, and his eyes were open windows to a world of sincerity as he said, "I'm not sure."

"And why do you even have it?"

His mouth twitched with the possibility of a smile, but it was dead on arrival. "It's—kind of a long story."

"I have time." She cringed at her choice of words. Lou, however, didn't seem to notice.

"So you used it." It wasn't a question, but she nodded. "I guess I wanted you to know what it does before I explained anything." He gritted his teeth and hammered his fist through the air, but it had no surface upon which to impact, and he wobbled atop the stool. "Stupid, *stupid.*"

"Excuse me?"

"Not you. Me. I can't believe I'd just *send* you back like . . ." His eyes widened. "When did I do this? When did *you*—?"

"About five minutes ago." She closed her eyes. "I mean, I've only been *here*, now, for about five minutes, so maybe two minutes before *that*."

Lou's eyes widened slightly. "Did I tell you how to use it?"

"No, he—I mean, you . . . Jesus *Christ!*" She was getting a headache. She took a shaky breath. "You used it, and you revealed you knew about Geoff and—"

He frowned. "Geoff?"

Thank God.

She waved a dismissive hand. "Irrelevant. I guess I must have told you about him before—I mean, *after* . . ." Rayna closed her eyes and pressed her fingertips to her temples, which still tingled where the sensors had touched her. "*Fuck.*"

"I think I follow." He looked away. "I wanted to show you how the tech works, so I asked you to tell me a story I'd never heard, waited until it was over, then crossed back and recited it back to you."

"*And* scared the shit out of me."

"I'm sorry." He looked up at her, took a deep breath, and let it out slowly. They faced one another in silence for a long, heavy minute.

"You didn't answer my question," Rayna said.

"What did you ask me?" He chuckled weakly. "*When* did you ask me?"

"Just now. Just a minute ago. Here. Why do you have this?"

He took a deep breath, his lips tightening until his beard seemed to devour them, then spoke slowly. "Someday all sorts of things will be possible. You think the latest smartphones and watches are a big deal now?" He smirked. "Just wait."

Rayna felt a chill as he said this. "So . . . what, you somehow jumped into the future, found this thing, and jumped back with it?"

"No. It doesn't work that way."

"Did a time-traveler jump back and give it to you?"

"No. It's not like *Doctor*—"

"Then why the hell do you have a time machine, Lou?" she nearly shouted, then closed her eyes, feeling tears building behind them. She inhaled sharply, let the breath rejuvenate her senses, and opened her eyes. "Why would you *keep* that from me?"

"Simply put, I didn't want to scare you off. It's crazy, this tech. Most people don't understand it. It only crosses back. It can't take you to a future. If there *is* tech that can do that, I haven't found it yet."

"How did you get it, then? How long have you had it? When did you get it?" Her eyes widened slowly as realization, as large and repulsive as the oversized insect in the device, scuttled across the floor of her senses, and she asked in a very tiny voice, "How old are you? Really?"

The man she would have thought of as thirty-one only a short while ago held up his hands. "Don't freak out."

"*How old?*"

"I'm thirty-eight. I—I'm sorry I lied about the other seven years."

The sting in her eyes grew more intense. "So you've been lying to me about your age, this whole time."

"No, Rain! I mean—yes, I'm not thirty-one, I'm thirty-eight, but everything I've told you is true. My father worked at Stuyvesant, my sister is gay, my favorite ice cream topping is Froot Loops, uh . . ." he shook his head, hitting a mental wall. "It's all true!"

"It's not the *whole* truth, obviously."

He sighed and lowered his head. "No. Not all of it. I didn't want to scare you off."

"Well, you've sure lost *that* battle."

"Look, Rain, I'll tell you everything. Isn't that all you've ever want-ed from me? Total trust, total honesty?"

Her lip curled slightly as she said, "All I *wanted*, yeah."

"Please—" He raised his hands, his eyes widening, getting red be-hind his glasses. "Please. Wait."

"I'm still here, aren't I?"

"Yes, you are, and so am I."

"But if you were holding this right now," she held the lockbox up before her, *"would* you be? Would you still be here if I'd told you I knew about it?"

"Of course I would!"

"You know I don't have any reason to believe that."

"Well, what else do you want to know?"

Rayna looked away, then closed her eyes and pressed her fingertips to the bridge of her nose. "I need to sit down."

They went into the living room. Lou remained mercifully silent as Rayna mulled everything over. The lockbox sat upon the coffee table between them.

"So it only goes backwards?"

"Yes."

"And you jumped back seven years?"

"Ultimately, yes."

"'Ultimately'?"

"I was born in 1982," Lou said, "and then last year I—well, I found the tech. I started crossing back, first a couple of months, then a few years. Then . . ." He shrugged.

"How long? I mean, how many times?"

"Honestly? I've started to lose count. Ten, twelve times maybe."

She shivered. "But—*why?*" She looked up at him. "Why would you *do* that?"

"Have you ever been in a situation and wondered if things could've been different? You know, *Woulda-coulda-shoulda-didn't?* Or ever thought to yourself, 'If I could do it all again, I would'? Well . . ." He snickered, then shrugged. "I did."

She shivered again.

"Anybody who's ever had even the slightest bit of an imagination has wondered about *possibilities,* about how their future could've gone if things had been even slightly different. I've been able to determine some things about myself—certain outcomes that simply *didn't* have to be. I've tried a lot of things out, and I know more of what I want out of life."

"What *do* you want?"

"What I've come to decide is, I want to figure this out." He pointed at the lockbox. "I want to figure out how it works, what its design is like, where all the parts came from, originally, and—"

"You want to make another one."

He stared at her for a moment, licked his lips, then nodded slowly. "It only goes back seven years. I think it has to do with, you know, how cell regeneration works. I think it needs a sort of 'constant' in the user's body to jump back on, like an anchor to recognize where it's sending you. But it doesn't make the crossback *with* you. It just sends your consciousness, your soul." He shook his head. "Something, I don't know what. I'm not sure of any of this, you realize. It didn't come with a manual."

"*Why,* though? *Why* would you want something like this?"

"I want to be able to fix things, to just go back and . . . make sure things just go the way they *really* should be."

She held her hand up, buying herself some time to think of the proper words for her thoughts. "How—*how* can you know that? 'The way things should be'?"

"I've seen the big picture." He narrowed his eyes. "Well, *some* of it. I can tell you about a lot of things that happened—that *might* happen. Technology, space discoveries . . ." His features darkened. "Elections. Diseases." He shook his head, then scoffed. "If you think *this* quarantine is bad—"

"I don't *care* about any of that! I want to know where *you and I* fit into that big picture!"

"Well, I can tell you this much: it's been really lonely for me, doing this."

"So why couldn't you just *tell* me? Why wait for me to find it?" She thought back on the look on his face when she had first arrived from the jump—the "crossback," as he kept calling it. He looked so shocked, so embarrassed. "Why does it feel like I caught you doing something wrong?"

He puffed out his chest and waved a hand in the air. "'Hi, nice to meet you, Rain! You're very pretty. Let's go out sometime. By the way, I'm from a different future. Want to time-travel with me?'" He snorted. "'Hey, where you going? Come back . . .' Imagine if I told you that? You've probably moved back in with your parents in Massachusetts, and I'd have to start over to make sure I didn't scare you off again."

She thought for a moment. "Did you?"

He took a deep breath, then said in a low voice, "Life can be like *Groundhog Day*. You *can* go back and fix things."

She glared at him. "Did you? *Did* you 'go back and fix things?' And what would you have to 'fix,' anyway? What could've been so imperfect in your life that you had to jump back in time ten or twelve times? Did you screw up, or something? Did I leave you? Did it any of it even *involve* me?"

All that had been so perfect for them, all the pleasures and fun and romance that they'd had . . . what did any of it mean, now, literally *now*?

"Rain—"

"Did any of your 'possibilities' even involve *me?"*

"Yes! Ultimately, they did."

"'Ultimately'?" She set her jaw. "'Ultimately'?"

They stared at each other for a long moment, and then she grabbed the lockbox and pulled it onto her lap.

"Wh-what are you doing?" Lou asked.

"What I should've done a while ago." She flicked open the latch and tugging the lid open. Her bracelet clung to the side of the box where the magnetic part of the device was, and she tore her arm away as she reached inside and pulled the tangled affair out.

"Rain, don't! It might be the only one in this timeline!"

She stopped for a moment, looking down at the device as she ran her fingertips over the grey controller, then back up at Lou.

"Rayna, please. Don't do this. Don't destroy it."

"I'm not." She wasn't entirely sure of what she was doing as the screen lit up. A series of numbers appeared, followed by a grid of various symbols and in-screen controls below them. She looked up at Lou, who was now on his feet. She stood and stepped cautiously backward.

"Rayna, don't." He raised his hands. "Please. I—I can make another one. We can go together! We can *live* together—*forever!* We can be *immortal* if we want!"

"That's not what *I* want." She held up the device. "You'll still have this, right? So maybe you can go back in time to before you ever met me and explore your *possibilities* with someone else."

She planted it atop her head, but Lou didn't make a move to stop her as she pressed the various sensors and transmitters to different parts of her scalp, to the best of her memory.

"Rain—"

"Goodbye, Lou," she said, and pushed the button.

"Hon? You okay?"

Rayna started to cry as she gazed up at the lockbox on the shelf. "I'm fine!" she called back, hoping her voice didn't quaver too much. Lou said nothing.

She had to figure out how the device worked before she used it again. It was a daunting task, full of unknown risks and, well, possibilities.

Then she slowly began to smile.

She had all the time in the world to figure it out.

The Night and All Its Visitors

Sergeant Cooper switched off her flashlight and grunted softly as she rose to her knees. "What do you think?"

Burton shook his head. "I'm no animal expert, so I think I'll leave it at that."

At approximately four-thirty that morning, a Connecticut trucker had been driving along Route 44 in southeastern Massachusetts, heading to a shopping center in Raynham. As he'd crossed the Baker town line onto Three-Corner Road, he'd looked down to sip his soda when a big brown shape appeared on the side of the road, not ten feet from his truck. He hadn't even had time to think: the truck had smashed the thing off the road and sent it tumbling onto the shoulder. He'd jumped out, cursing, then stopped in horror when he saw what he'd hit, and called it in.

Cooper and Burton had to calm the trucker down as he grew increasingly apoplectic about making his delivery time. After getting his info, they sent him on his way, then pulled on gloves and dragged the thing to the side of the road for a better look.

Cooper had approached it cautiously, flinching and holding her breath in anticipation, but as she got closer she realized that no cloud of rotting miasma awaited her. She was no animal expert either, but she recognized the thick plates and scales of the carcass as exoskeletal. Crustacean? Insect? Regardless of what it was, it was nearly five feet long and at least four at its widest—it was hard to tell, because half of it had been smashed by the truck. It was a bulbous thing, its bulging, scaly thorax curled slightly behind its legs, several of which were either gone or broken off, probably littering the road and ground nearby or stuck in the grooves of the truck's tires. Between its legs a cavity yawned, smashed or burst open from the impact. And if it had had a head, it was gone with the rest of the broken carapace.

"What the hell *is* it?" Burton asked.

Cooper sighed. *And why the hell couldn't it have been in* any *other town?*

She called the animal hospital. Half an hour later a pickup truck arrived, and two workers emerged. Cooper and Burton helped them load the thing into the bed of the truck—it had to weigh over two hundred pounds—and its broken exoskeleton and protruding legs made lifting it a precarious task. They followed the truck back to the hospital, watching the half-visible limbs swaying and bouncing in the breeze and occasional bump in the road. They exchanged a wary glance at each other but didn't say a word the whole ride.

"Looks like a giant flea." Dr. Edmonds's voice was muffled from where she crouched beside the exam table.

"*Please* don't say that," Burton muttered.

Cooper looked at him and he flinched. "Dealt with a minor infestation my dog brought in last month."

"Of course"—Dr. Edmonds's masked face rose up on the other side of the dead thing—"that's definitely *not* what this is."

"Any clue what it might be, then?"

Dr. Edmonds walked around the end of the table, pointing at the broken fan of jointed legs. "Definitely arthropodal. Its structure is reminiscent of insects, but its size—I don't know. That might suggest something more crustaceous, though generally, larger specimens tend to have smaller carapaces and longer appendages, not . . ." She fanned her hands apart beside the bulky form and shook her head. "Not like this."

"At any rate," Cooper said, "are we getting rid of this thing or what?"

"It's—not typical, but I'm sure pickup shouldn't be a problem. It's not the heaviest specimen they've dealt with."

"Tell me about it." Cooper turned to her deputy. "Last year someone hit a very large deer." She lifted her arms into the air. "Its antlers alone were *this*—"

Their radios squawked, and Cooper answered.

A crackle and a hiss, and a dispatcher's voice came over the line. *"Possible six-oh-two-el spotted at Ridgewood Farm, South County Road."*

She sighed and spoke into her radio. "Copy that. I'll get—" She fell silent as movement caught her eye. Burton had raised his hand to stop her, shaking his head. *"I'll go,"* he whispered, *"if that's okay."* She nodded and filled the dispatcher in. When the acknowledgment came through, she shrugged, frowning.

"If it's no biggie, I'd rather go check out the trespasser. I'm all set with bugs."

Cooper grinned. "Sure."

After he left, Dr. Edmonds hummed from the exam table. "Odd."

"Overall, odd? Or is something else odd about it?"

"A—little of both. Look at this."

Cooper walked around the far side of the table and crossed her arms over her chest. Dr. Edmonds pointed a latex-gloved finger at the hole in the thing's smashed-open thorax.

"See this? Note how the top edges are cracked and splintered. Signs of the impact of the truck, no doubt. Like the splintering and other damage on antlers and other appendages, right?"

"Sure." She doubted she sounded it.

"Now look down here, along the lower edge and bottom, on the abdominal end. See how it's got this sort of 'W'-shaped curve here? And how the bases of the rearmost set of legs meet beneath it? This part of the cavity isn't broken. It's *shaped* that way."

Cooper nodded, then shrugged. "All right, I'll bite. What are you saying?"

"I'm saying, there seems to be a part either missing or . . . that simply wasn't there. It's an *opening*. And judging from the shape at its lower apex here, and the length and curve of the edges over here, I'd say it would be about eighteen inches wide and over two feet long."

Cooper frowned.

"What's more, it's thick. The edges here indicate that the exoskeleton appears to be ... over two inches of solid matter. This thing is made to take a beating. The truck took care of that, granted, but it was a big-rig, yes?"

"Eighteen-wheeler."

"And no sign of any other debris? No innards, no fluids or other materials?"

"Not that we saw. There was only this thing and the broken parts of it on the road."

"Then take a closer look. Notice something else about it?"

Cooper sighed and leaned in, flinching behind her mask. The cavity was dark, and she had a feeling something would drop onto her head or hand if she were to venture any further, but she held her breath and leaned in further, until her head was fully inside the dark, sound-muffling space. "It's—empty." She had almost said *spacious,* and fleet-ingly imagined squeezing her five-foot-four frame inside the thing before shuddering and straightening up.

"Like a shell."

Cooper crossed her arms over her chest. "You mean, like—a shed skin? Is there a bigger critter running around now, Doc?"

Dr. Edmonds inclined her head and shrugged. "Not necessarily. Some of these joints contain tissue and other matter. But the inside is completely clean, with no remaining matter clinging to the exoskele-ton's interior at all. And as you said, it wasn't burst all over the high-way. It's not like a popped tick. And it isn't a molted skin, either. It's more like it was *hollowed out.*"

"What do you mean? How? By what?"

"Couldn't say, without being able to identify it."

Cooper glanced away, recalling a similar conversation she'd had, once. An idea flitted through her mind, but she vanquished it before it could develop.

"Well, your call. Do you want to keep it and examine it?"

"I'll take my photos and samples, but I'd just as soon get this thing properly disposed of."

"Think pickup can handle it?"

"I don't see why not."

She bit her lower lip. "Think I should get . . . another opinion about it?"

Dr. Edmonds shrugged. "That's up to you."

Cooper sighed and took out her phone, nodding. "Have it ready to drop off for pickup at eight."

"Will do, Sergeant."

Later, Cooper and Burton met up again by the highway, not half a mile from the morning's discovery. "Any interesting news from the trespassing front?" Cooper asked, exiting her cruiser.

Still inside his own, Burton snickered and shook his head. "Yes and no. It was Mrs. Medeiros."

"Oh, Jeez. What did she see *this* time?"

Burton climbed out of the car. "For once, *not* the usual. She said she saw a naked woman running through the woods. I looked around her property but couldn't find anything out of the ordinary. Told her to give us a call if she saw her again."

Cooper groaned. "Going forward, I'd suggest simply telling her 'We'll give you a call if we get any leads,' and leave it at that. Now she's liable to call in anytime she sees—well, *anything*."

"Shit."

"Don't worry about it. She was really bad a few years ago. *That* was a lot of fun. Got calls every single night from her." Cooper stared into the shadows between the trees, almost expecting them to share her exasperated look, but they did not react.

"Do I want to hear what you learned about the . . . thing?"

"Probably not, given your disposition."

In the early evening, Cooper followed the animal hospital's truck. They took the old road that curved along a mile stretch of the town line. At one point they passed Matt Horton, one of the two farm heads in town. He was carrying an empty duffel bag and nodded at Cooper as she drove by.

Nearing the quarry, she turned her gaze to the bed of the truck and once again watched the bounce and sway of the thing's upturned legs. She'd gone to the animal hospital, hoping to turn over a mystery, only to find beneath it a pile of wriggling, squirming questions. Sure, Dr. Edmonds had taken her samples and photos, but Cooper was certain that she wouldn't learn anything, not under a microscope, nor with any amount of research.

There was only one person that Cooper knew of who might—*might*—be able to shed some light on the mystery, but she wasn't about to seek out that kind of help. Not with all the risks and red tape it would bring.

At the quarry Cooper unlocked the low metal barrier gate, frowning at the graffiti that had distorted the NO TRESPASSING sign. Beyond it, several headless, eviscerated chickens had been thrown unceremoniously onto the ground. No doubt raccoons had gotten into Horton's coop again.

Cooper stepped aside as the truck backed up into the space. The same two workers from earlier exited and silently hauled out the carcass. She guided them to a wide, flat rock that had been placed at the quarry's edge and waited while they set the thing down on it. As she did so, she glanced into the woods, tightening her lips as her gaze fixed on an old, filthy construction helmet that sat amongst the underbrush.

The workers all but ran back to their truck, and Cooper strolled after them, pulling the gate shut behind her. Turning back to the woods, she glanced up at the sky, which had already shifted from blue to a dull gray. Then she headed back into town.

She saw Mr. Vaughan standing at the end of his driveway, shaking a plastic bag. Several hunks of freezer-burnt steaks were piled up on the asphalt before him, dark brown with yellowish edges. He looked up at her cruiser as she approached, then nodded as she tapped her wristwatch.

Two kids were throwing balled-up wads of hamburger meat onto the street. As soon as they spotted her approaching, they turned and ran. She sighed and shook her head as she drove by. In the business district she passed Burton, who nodded and sped up, anxious to get home.

In the dying daylight the last few cars coming into town were parked and quickly vacated.

Doors slammed shut, and faces began to peer through windows.

As soon as she got home and locked up for the night, Cooper switched on her television. A superhero show was playing, but she didn't stay to watch. She only wanted some background noise as she set about making dinner.

Outside, the shadows grew and shifted. A breeze rustled the trees. No birds, bats, or crickets chirped, no katydids clicked. The town held its breath, silently waiting for dawn, and for the night and all its visitors to retreat into secret.

Cooper crossed her arms over her chest. "I had a feeling this was going to happen."

Shortly after dawn she and Burton had driven out to the quarry and had slowly climbed out of their cars, staring at the massive, broken creature that had been left, seemingly untouched, on the rock beyond the gate.

"But why didn't they take it?" Burton asked.

"Beats me. They got everything else." She noticed the chickens were gone. "Maybe it was too big."

"But didn't you say they took a deer once?"

She pursed her lips. "They did."

"So what does this mean?"

"I'm not sure. But I think I'm going to have to call out of town about this."

"Who? Like . . ." He ran his fingers down the sides of his mouth. "Who would even—?"

Their radios squawked, and dispatch reported a car that had been left parked in front of a driveway overnight. "I can check it out, if you want to make that call."

"Nah, I'll come along." Cooper began walking to her car. *I'll happily take a slice of normal.*

During the long, hot, and slow day that followed, Cooper put off and put off the call. The sun crept toward the west, and although curfew wasn't for several more hours, she knew that the sooner this mess was cleaned up the better, and she finally bit the bullet.

After the expected awkwardness and confusion in the subsequent conversation, she made arrangements for the arrival.

After touching base with Dr. Edmonds and Burton, she sat in her cruiser outside the quarry, wishing for the millionth time that she hadn't quit smoking.

A gray van crawled up the road behind her and stopped. She felt a plummeting sensation in her chest as she saw a pale face in the passenger's side of the windshield. Cooper exited her cruiser in time to see the driver's door open. A balding, tired-looking man in heavy shades climbed out. She nodded to him, but he didn't acknowledge her as he moved toward the back of the van. She watched him for a moment, and then turned back as the passenger door opened.

Sydney still managed to take Cooper's breath away, all these years later. Her features were somehow sharper, more defined, and although her hair was several inches shorter, it still shimmered like a black halo in the warm breeze. Cooper felt the corners of her mouth twitch with the urge to smile, but as Sydney approached, unsmiling, she set her jaw.

"Hi," Sydney said.

"Hi." Cooper sniffed, feeling as if they were standing on opposite cliffs over a gulf of tension. She nodded toward the van. "That your employer?"

"More like a coworker."

There was a metallic thump, and one of the van's rear doors swung open.

Sydney reached up and tucked a strand of hair behind her ear. She was wearing brown leather gloves. "Where is it?"

Cooper silently walked toward the gate. She could hear Sydney's shoes crunch on the asphalt behind her.

"Holy shit." Sydney moved past Cooper and stopped before the gate. Her gloved hands pressed onto the metal, and Cooper watched her shoulders rise and fall as she stared at the quarry beyond.

"One of your . . . career specialties?"

Sydney's head turned, but she didn't look back. "No, but . . . *This* shouldn't *be here.*"

Cooper remained silent.

After a long moment Sydney turned and asked for everything that was known about it. Cooper began to fill her in, but halfway into the story Sydney's features hardened. "Wait—it dropped *yesterday?*"

"No telling how long it was there, but yes. The truck driver found it yesterday morning."

"Why didn't you call me then?"

"We brought it to the vet's office to examine it." She didn't mention the failed pickup.

"Oh, yeah?" Sydney's eyebrows lifted and her lip curled. "Learn anything interesting there?"

"Nothing that tells us anything about it. That's why I called you."

Sydney silently turned and moved past the gate. She stepped toward the thing, crouched beside it, and leaned in close, lowering her head and peering around. After a moment she pulled an old-fashioned flip-phone from her pocket, pushed a button, and rose to her feet.

Sighing, Cooper set her hands on her hips and turned to the van and started when she found the man standing directly beside her. "Jesus!" she hissed, stepping back, but the man didn't move nor say a word. He stared expressionlessly through his dark shades after Sydney, who had moved around the other side of the thing, speaking into the phone, and shaking her head. After a moment she closed the phone with a snap and put it away.

Cooper was about to ask about the call but fell silent when she saw Sydney remove a glove and reach toward the thing. She watched in silence as her long, pale fingers fanned out, the tips pressing delicately to the exoskeleton's surface. "*Oh, fu—*" The curse became a choked grunt. She threw her head back, her hair fanning out temporarily as she seemed to look up at the sky.

"Syd?" Cooper moved closer, tensing. She'd seen her do this routine before, but it had never been this intense. "What do you—?"

Sydney's whole body shivered, then her upper torso wrenched backward into a painful-looking yoga stretch before she violently pitched forward, tucking her arms and legs beneath her, tightening into a fetal position on the ground before the thing.

Cooper darted forward, watching Sydney's body spasm, then become still. She crouched and grabbed her shoulders to pull her onto her side. Sydney's limbs clung tightly to her torso, her face buried between her knees, her body rocking back and forth like a human-size football.

Cooper grabbed her radio and began spitting an emergency code into it when a muffled voice—Sydney's—stopped her.

"No . . . be fine . . ." she stammered through clenched teeth.

Cooper shook her head. "Not this time. Look at you. You're going to the hosp—"

Sydney's head twitched and jerked unsteadily as it lifted. Her face was pale, her mouth a wide grimace as she whispered, "No . . . hospital."

Cooper set her jaw and looked up at the carcass, then at the man. He said nothing.

Following weakly blurted instructions from Sydney, the man loaded the carcass through the van's rear doors, unassisted and seemingly without effort. Cooper carefully put Sydney into her cruiser, and they led the van back to her place. She ushered the two of them indoors and locked up for the night, now less than an hour away.

She half led, half carried Sydney to her couch and laid her down, then pulled a quilt up over her. The man stood beside her and watched, his black lenses like the eyes of an owl.

Cooper went into her kitchen and poured herself a glass of Scotch.

She'd often warned Sydney that her "talent" might well cause more trouble than it would tricks. Being able to read things by touch had made for some neat exploits, to be sure. It had also made for amazing sex. The conversations about using it in future careers had painted a fascinating picture.

And then Cooper had met Ruth, and the picture was torn apart.

Cooper downed her Scotch in one swig, then went back into the living room.

Sydney was still asleep, and the man may as well have been a statue. Cooper walked past them, to a window, and glanced outside.

The night had emerged from the tree line. The shadows pulsed and squirmed beyond the murky pools of radiance from the neighboring houses. She leaned in closer when a figure moved beneath one of the streetlights further down the road, but she couldn't make out anything definite.

"What's going on?"

She turned and saw Sydney sitting up, groggy and squinting. She noticed then that Sydney's left hand was still bare, and realized that she'd forgotten the glove back at the quarry.

"You should rest."

"What time is it?"

"Eight thirty-three."

"*Shit!* My boss is gonna—"

"Your boss is going to have to understand that you're not coming back tonight. You're not in Rhode Island, but we also have a curfew, and for good reason. I can easily put you and your—friend up for the night."

"No thanks, Ellie. We have a delivery to make."

"Sydney, *not tonight.* I mean it." Cooper swallowed hard as she debated telling Sydney outright—and then she had a better idea. She walked over to the couch and held out her hand.

Sydney glared at it, then looked up at her with a frown, her eyes narrowed, but she slowly reached up and took the offered hand. Although Cooper didn't share Sydney's talent, she nonetheless felt something electric when their skin touched for the first time in nearly a decade.

Sydney's eyes closed and she gasped.

Cooper could only imagine what Sydney was seeing—and what she'd think of it. What did she think of the accident out at the quarry, a year and a half after she'd left town? What did she think of what happened at night? Of the compromise? The curfew?

Sydney's hand squeezed around Cooper's, then released. She let out a slow, shaky breath before opening her eyes. "What the hell happened to Baker?"

"It's still the same town. We just"—she shrugged—"have some new rules."

Sydney blinked slowly. "Ellie. Seriously."

"Well, what would *you* have done? We gave everyone a chance to get out, but most people were willing to stay put, under the circumstances. They're happy. They're safe."

"Are *you* happy?"

She snorted. "'Course I am! I'm healthy, I'm working. I get all I need."

"You work in law enforcement and you're *still* not a very good liar."

She glared at her, then sighed heavily. "Not around you." She nodded at Sydney's hands. "Even when you're not touching me."

Sydney held up her hands and turned them over, curling her fingers, the single glove's leather making soft creaks and whimpers. "I've worn these since we broke up."

"Afraid you're going to learn something about someone you don't want to know again?"

Sydney glared at her. "At first, yes. But they help me concentrate."

"Oh, yeah? What did you see when you touched it?" When she didn't reply, Cooper asked, "And what the hell *are* you doing nowadays, Syd? Or do I even want to know?"

"You probably don't."

Cooper sighed heavily.

After a moment Sydney looked up at her. Although she was frowning, her gaze was no longer hard. "Why are you still here, Ellie? I would've thought you'd have moved in with Ruth, or at least have gotten out of Baker while we were still young and stupid."

"Because it's—" Cooper fell silent as she spotted more movement outside, shadows spilling across shadows.

She heard movement in the living room behind her. A moment later Sydney joined her at the window and peered through the glass. Cooper swallowed hard as she glanced at Sydney, waiting for an inevitable reaction, but none came, and she turned her gaze back to the road.

Massive and black, the shape was the length of a car and nearly as wide. Its front end hit the ground and its middle rose as it swung its rear half closer, a gargantuan, nightmare parody of an inchworm. Two humanoid figures materialized out of the nearby gloom and walked toward it, gorgon heads rippling with writhing appendages. They stopped around a small pile of offerings that had been left at the end of a neighbor's driveway and waited. The black thing approached them and obscured the view of what happened next.

"Because it's home."